An
Acceptable
Time

OTHER NOVELS IN THE TIME QUINTET

Many Waters

A Swiftly Tilting Planet

A Wind in the Door

A Wrinkle in Time

An Acceptable Time

MADELEINE L'ENGLE

SQUARE
FISH

FARRAR, STRAUS AND GIROUX

**SQUARE
FISH**

Square Fish

An Imprint of Holtzbrinck Publishers

Library of Congress Cataloging-in-Publication Data

L'Engle, Madeleine.

An acceptable time.

p. cm.

Summary: Polly's visit to her grandparents in Connecticut becomes an
extraordinary experience as she encounters old friends and mysterious
strangers and finds herself traveling back in time to play a crucial role
in a prehistoric confrontation.

ISBN-13: 978-0-312-36858-6

ISBN-10: 0-312-36858-5

[1. Space and time—Fiction.   2. Time travel—Fiction.   3. Druids
and druidism—Fiction.]   I. Title.

PZ7.L5385 Ac 1989

[E]—dc20   89-84882

Originally published by Farrar, Straus and Giroux

Book design by Jennifer Browne

First Square Fish Edition: May 2007

10 9 8 7 6 5 4 3 2 1

For

Dana, Bér & Eddie

———

Ron, Annie & Jake

Chapter One

She walked through an orchard, fallen apples red and cidery on the ground, crossed a stone wall, and wandered on into a small wood. The path was carpeted with leaves, red, orange, gold, giving off a rich, earthy smell. Polly scuffed along, pushing the toes of her running shoes through the lavish brightness. It was her first New England autumn and she was exhilarated by the colors drifting from the trees, dappling her hair with reflected amber and bronze. The sun shone with a golden haze through a muted blue sky. Leaves whispered to the ground. The air was crisp, but not cold. She hummed with contentment.

The trees were young, most no more than half a century old, with trunks still slender, completely unlike the great Spanish-moss-hung water and live oaks she had left less than a week before. Apples from a wild seedling had dropped onto the path. She picked one up, russet and a bit misshapen. But the fruit was crisp and juicy and she wandered on, eating, and spitting out the seeds.

Now the path led her toward a forest of much older trees, towering maples, spruce, and pine. Reaching above them all was an ancient oak, with large, serrated leaves of a deep bronze color, many still clinging tenaciously to the branches. It was very different from the Southern oaks she was used to, and she had not recognized it as one until she learned her mother and uncles had always called it the "Grandfather Oak."

"When we first moved here," her grandmother had explained, "most of the oaks were gone, killed by some disease. But this one survived, and now our land is full of young oaklings, all evidently disease-resistant, thanks to the Grandfather Oak."

Now she looked at the oak and was startled to see a young man standing in its shadows. He was looking at her with lucid blue eyes which seemed to hold the light of the day. He wore some kind of white garment, and one hand was on the head of a tan dog with large, pricked-up ears, outlined in black. The young man raised his hand in greeting, then turned and walked quickly into the forest. When she reached the great tree, he had disappeared from sight. She had thought he might speak to her, and she was curious.

The wind had risen and played through the pines, sounding almost like the rolling of the breakers on the beach at Benne Seed Island, off the coast of South Carolina, where her parents still were, and which she had left so short a time ago. She turned up the collar of the red anorak she had taken from the generous supply that hung on pegs outside her grandparents' kitchen door. It was her favorite because it fitted her well and was warm and comfortable, and she liked it because the pockets were full of all kinds of things: a small but very bright flashlight; a pair of scissors; a notepad in a leather binder, with a purple felt pen; an assortment of paper clips, safety pins, rubber bands; a pair of dark glasses; a dog biscuit (for what dog?).

She sat on a great flat glacial rock, known as the star-watching rock, and looked up at white clouds scudding across the sky. She sat up straighter as she heard music, a high, rather shrill piping of a folk melody. What was it? Who was making music out here in the middle of nowhere? She got up and walked, following the sound, past the Grandfather Oak, in the same direction as the young man with the dog.

She went past the oak and there, sitting on a stone wall, was another young man, this one with lustrous black hair, and skin too white, playing a penny whistle.

"Zachary!" She was totally startled. "Zachary Gray! What are you doing here?"

He took the whistle from his mouth and shoved it into a pocket in his leather jacket. Rose from the wall and came toward her, arms outstretched. "Well met by sunlight, Miss Polly O'Keefe. Zachary Gray at your service."

She pulled away from his embrace. "But I thought you were at UCLA!"

"Hey." He put his arm around her waist and hugged her. "Aren't you glad to see me?"

"Of course I'm glad to see you. But how did you get here? Not just New England, but here, at my grandparents'—"

He led her back to the wall. The stones still held warmth from the autumn sun. "I called your folks in South Carolina, and they informed me you were staying with your grandparents, so I drove over to say hello, and they—your grandparents—told me you'd gone for a walk, and if I came out here I'd probably find you." His voice was relaxed; he seemed perfectly at home.

"You drove here from UCLA?"

He laughed. "I'm taking an internship semester at a law firm in Hartford, specializing in insurance claims." His arm about her waist tightened. He bent toward her, touching his lips to hers.

She drew away. "Zach. No."

"I thought we were friends."

"We are. Friends."

"I thought you found me attractive."

"I do. But—not yet. Not now. You know that."

"Okay, Pol. But I can't afford to wait too long." Suddenly his eyes looked bleak. His lips tightened. Then, deliberately, he gave her one of his most charming smiles. "At least you're glad to see me."

"Very glad." Yes. Delighted, in fact, but totally surprised. She was flattered that he'd gone to the trouble to seek her out. She had met him in Athens the previous summer, where she had spent a few days before going to Cyprus to be a gofer at a conference on literature and literacy. It had been an incredibly rich experience, full of joy and pain, and in Athens Zachary had been charming to her, showing her a city he already knew well, and driving her around the surrounding countryside. But when he had said good-bye to her in the airport after the conference had ended, she had never expected to hear from him again.

"I can't believe it!" She smiled at him.

"Can't believe what, Red?"

"Don't call me Red," she replied automatically. "That you're here."

"Look at me. Touch me. It's me, Zach. And what are you doing here?"

"Going for a walk."

"I mean, staying with your grandparents."

"I'm studying with them. For a few months, at any rate. They're terrific."

"I gather they're famous scientists or something."

"Well, Grand's a Nobel Prize laureate. She's into little

things—sub-subatomic particles. And Granddad's an astrophysicist and knows more about the space/time continuum than almost anybody except Einstein or Hawking."

"You always were a brain," he said. "You understand all that stuff?"

She laughed. "Only a very little." She was absurdly glad to see him. Her grandparents were, as she had said, terrific, but she hadn't seen anyone her own age and hadn't expected to.

"So why are you doing this instead of going to school at home?" he asked.

"I need lots more science than I could get at Cowpertown High, and getting to and from the mainland from Benne Seed was a real hassle."

"That's not the only reason."

"Isn't it enough?" It would have to be enough for Zachary, at least for now. She looked away from him, across the star-watching rock, to an autumn sky just turning toward dusk. The long rays of the sun touched the clouds with rose and gold, and the vivid colors of the leaves deepened. A dark shadow of purple moved across the low hills.

Zachary followed her gaze. "I love these mountains. So different from California mountains."

Polly nodded. "These are old mountains, ancient, worn

down by rain and wind and time itself. Perspective-making."

"Do you need perspective?"

"Don't we all?" A leaf drifted down and settled on Polly's hair.

Zachary reached out long, pale fingers and took it off. "It's the same color as your hair. Beautiful."

Polly sighed. "I'm just beginning to be reconciled to my hair. Given a choice, I wouldn't have chosen orange."

"It's not orange." Zachary let the leaf fall to the ground. "It's the color of autumn."

—Nice, she thought.—How nice he can be. "This is the first time I've seen autumn foliage. I've always lived in warm climates. This is—I don't have any words. I thought nothing could beat the ocean, and nothing does, but this—"

"It has its own glory," Zachary said. "Pop's living in Sausalito now, and the view from his house can over-whelm, all that incredible expanse of Pacific. But this, as you say, gives perspective and peace.

"Your grandparents," he continued, "offered tea and cinnamon toast if I could find you and bring you back."

"Sure." She jumped down from the wall. As they passed the Grandfather Oak, she asked, "Hey, who was that blue-eyed guy I saw here a few minutes ago?"

He looked at her. "I thought he was someone who

worked for your grandparents, a caretaker or gardener or something like that."

She shook her head.

"You mean they take care of this whole place themselves?"

"Yes. Well, a neighboring farmer hays the fields, but he's older, and this man was young, and he didn't look like a farmer to me."

Zachary laughed. "What do you think a farmer looks like? I grant you, this guy had a kind of nobility."

"Did you talk to him?"

"No, and that was, as I think about it, a little weird. He looked at me, and I looked at him, and I was going to say something, but he gave me this look, as though he was totally surprised to see me, I mean totally, and then he turned and walked into the woods. He had this big-eared dog with him, and they just took off. Not running. But when I looked, I didn't see them." He shrugged. "As I said, I thought he must be a caretaker or whatever, and a lot of those types are sort of surly. Do you suppose he was a poacher? Do you have pheasants or quail?"

"Both. And our land is very visibly posted. It's not big enough to be called a game preserve—most of the old farms around here were a hundred acres or less. But my grandparents like to keep it safe for the wildlife."

"Forget him," Zachary said. "I came out here looking for you and I've found you."

"I'm glad. Really glad." She smiled at him, her most brilliant smile. "Ready to go?"

"Sure. I think your grandparents are expecting us."

"Okay. We'll just go back across the star-watching rock."

"Star-watching rock?"

She stepped onto the large flat glacial rock. Patches of moss grew in the crevices. Mica sparkled in the long rays of the descending sun. "It's always been called that. It's a wonderful place to lie and watch the stars. It's my mother's favorite rock, from when she was a child."

They crossed the rock and walked along the path that led in the direction of the house. Zachary walked slowly, she noticed, breathing almost as though he had been running. She shortened her pace to match his. Under one of the wild apple trees scattered across the land the ground was slippery with wrinkled brown apples, and there was a pungent, cidery smell. Inadvertently she moved ahead of Zachary and came to a low stone wall that marked the boundary of the big field north of the house. On the wall a large black snake was curled in the last of the sunlight. "Hey!" Polly laughed in pleasure. "It's Louise the Larger!"

Zachary stopped, frozen in his tracks. "What are you talking about? That's a snake! Get away!"

"Oh, she won't hurt us. It's only Louise. She's just a harmless black snake," Polly assured Zachary. "When my uncles, Sandy and Dennys, were kids—you met Sandy in Athens—"

"He didn't approve of me." Zachary stepped back farther from the wall and the snake.

"It wasn't *you*," Polly said. "It was your father's conglomerates. Anyhow, there was a snake who lived in this wall, and my uncles called her Louise the Larger."

"I don't know much about snakes." Zachary retreated yet another step. "They terrify me. But then isn't this snake incredibly old?"

"Oh, she's probably not the same one. Grand and I saw her sunning herself the other day, and she's exactly like the old Louise the Larger, and Grand said there hasn't been a black snake like Louise the Larger since my uncles left home."

"It's a crazy name." Zachary still did not approach, but stayed leaning against a young oak by the side of the path, as though catching his breath.

—It's a family joke, Polly thought. Zachary knew nothing about her family except that it was a large one, and she knew nothing about him except that his mother was dead and his father was rich beyond her comprehension. Louise later. "Ready?"

His voice was unsteady. "I'm not walking past that snake."

"She won't hurt you," Polly cajoled. "Honestly. She's

completely harmless. And my grandmother said she was delighted to see her."

"I'm not moving." There was a tremor in Zachary's voice.

"It's really okay." Polly was coaxing. "And where you have snakes you don't have rats, and rats carry bubonic plague, and—" She stopped as the snake uncoiled, slowly, luxuriously, and slithered down into the stone wall. Zachary watched, hands dug deep into the pockets of his leather jacket, until the last inch of tail vanished. "She's gone," Polly urged. "Come on."

"She won't come out again?"

"She's gone to bed for the night." Polly sounded her most authoritative, although she knew little of the habits of black snakes. The more tropical snakes on Benne Seed Island were largely poisonous and to be avoided. She trusted her grandmother's assurance that Louise was benign, and so she crossed the wall and then held out her hand to Zachary, who took it and followed tentatively.

"It's *okay*." Polly tugged at his hand. "Let's go."

They started across the field to what Polly already thought of as home, her grandparents' house. It was an old white farmhouse which rambled pleasantly from the various wings that had been added throughout the centuries. Like most houses built over two hundred years ago in that windy part of the world, where winters were bitter and long, it faced south, where there was protection from the prevailing northwest winds. Off the pantry, which led from the kitchen to the garage, was a wing that held Polly's grandmother's lab. Originally, when the house had been part of a working dairy farm, it had been used as a pantry in which butter was churned, eggs candled.

To the east was the new wing, added after Polly's mother and uncles had left home. It held an enclosed swimming pool, not very large, but big enough for swimming laps, which had been strongly recommended for her grandfather's arthritis. Polly, like most children brought up on islands, was a swimmer, and she had established, in only a few days, her own pattern of a swim before dinner in the evening, sensing that her grandparents liked to be alone in the early morning for their pre-breakfast swim. In any case, the pool was large enough for two to swim in comfortably, but not three.

The downstairs rooms of the old house had been opened up, so that there was a comfortable L-shaped living room, and a big, rambly area that was kitchen/sitting room/dining room. Polly and Zachary approached the house from the north, climbing up onto the tiered terrace, which still held the summer furniture. "I've got to help Granddad get that into the cellar for the winter," she said. "It's too cold now for sitting outdoors for meals."

She led Zachary toward the kitchen and the pleasant aromas of cooking and an applewood fire. Four people were sitting around the oval table cluttered with tea cups and a plate of cinnamon toast. Her grandmother saw them and stood up. "Oh, good. You did find each other. Come on in. Tea's ready. Zachary, I'd like you to meet my old friend Dr. Louise Colubra, and her brother, Bishop Nason Colubra."

The bishop stood up to shake hands with Zachary. He wore narrow jeans and a striped rugby shirt and his thinness made him seem even taller than he was. He reminded Polly of a heron. He had strong, long hands and wore his one treasured possession, a large gold ring set with a beautiful topaz, in elegant contrast to his casual country clothes. "Retired," he said, "and come to live with my little sister."

Little indeed, in contrast to her brother. Dr. Louise was a small-boned woman, and if the bishop made Polly think of a heron, Dr. Louise was like a brown thrush in her tweed skirt and cardigan. She, too, shook hands with Zachary. "When Kate Murry calls me her old friend, I wonder what the 'old' refers to."

"Friendship, of course," Polly's grandmother said.

"Dr. Louise!" Polly took her place at the table, indicating to Zachary that he should sit beside her. "We saw your namesake!"

"Not the original Louise the Larger, surely?" The doctor took a plate of fragrant cinnamon toast and put it in front of Zachary.

"I'm sorry." Zachary stared at the doctor. "What's your name?"

"Louise Colubra."

"I get it!" Zachary sounded triumphant. "Colubra is Latin for snake!"

"That's right." Polly looked at him admiringly. Zachary had already shown himself to have surprising stores of knowledge. She remembered him telling her, for instance, that Greek architecture was limited because the Greeks had not discovered the arch. She went to the kitchen dresser to get mugs for herself and Zachary. "My uncles named the snake after Dr. Louise."

"But why Louise the *Larger*?"

The bishop smiled. "Louise is hardly large, and I gather the snake is—larger, at least, for a black snake, than Louise is for a human being."

Polly put the mugs on the table. "It's lots easier to explain Louise the Larger with Dr. Louise here, than back at the stone wall."

A kettle was humming on the wood stove, its lid rising and falling. Polly's grandfather lifted it with a potholder and poured water into the teapot. "Tea's pretty strong by now. I'd better thin it down." He put the kettle back on the stove, then poured tea for Polly and Zachary.

The bishop leaned across the table and helped himself to cinnamon toast. "The reason for our unceremonious visit," he said, swallowing, "is that I've found another one." He pointed to an object which sat like a loaf of bread by Polly's grandfather's mug.

"It looks like a stone," Polly said.

"And so it is," the bishop agreed. "Like any stone from any stone wall. But it isn't. Look."

Polly thought she saw lines on the stone, but they had probably been scratched as the old walls settled, or frost-heaved in winter.

But Zachary traced the stones with delicate fingers. "Hey, is this Ogam writing?"

The bishop beamed at him in delight and surprise. "It is, young man, it is! How do you know about it?"

"One of my bosses in Hartford is interested in these stones. And I've been going so stir-crazy in that stuffy office that I've let him rattle on to me. It's better than medical malpractice suits"—Dr. Louise stiffened—"and it is interesting, to think maybe people were here from Britain, here on the North American continent, as long ago as—oh, three thousand years."

"And you flunked out of all those fancy prep schools," Polly said wonderingly.

He smiled, took a sip of tea. "When something interests me, I retain it." He held out his cup and Polly refilled it.

She put the teapot down and tentatively touched the stone. "Is this a petroglyph?"

The bishop helped himself to more cinnamon toast. "Um-hm."

"And that's Og—"

"Ogam writing."

"What does it say?"

"If I'm translating it correctly, something about Venus, and peaceful harvests and mild government. What do you think, young man?"

Zachary shook his head. "This is the first Ogam stone I've actually seen. My boss has some photographs, but he's mostly interested in theory—Celts, and maybe druids, actually living with, and probably marrying, the natives."

Polly looked more closely. Very faintly she could see a couple of horizontal lines, with markings above and below them. "Some farmer used this for his stone wall and never even noticed?"

Her grandmother put another plate of cinnamon toast on the table and removed the empty one. The fragrance joined with that of the wood fire in the open fireplace.

"Two hundred years ago farmers had all they could do to eke out a living. And how many farmers today have time to examine the stones that get heaved up in the spring?" her grandfather asked.

"Still our biggest crop," Dr. Louise interjected.

Polly's grandfather pushed his glasses up his nose in a typical gesture. "And if they did see markings on the stones and realized they weren't random, they wouldn't have had the faintest idea what the markings were about."

His wife laughed. "Did you?"

He returned the laugh. "Touché. If it hadn't been for Nase I'd have continued in ignorant bliss."

Dr. Louise smiled at him. "Your work does tend to keep your head in the stars."

"Actually, Louise, astrophysicists get precious little time for stargazing."

"Where did you find this rock, Nase?" Mrs. Murry sat at the table and poured herself some tea.

"In that old stone wall you have to cross to get to the star-watching rock."

"Louise the Larger's wall!" Polly exclaimed, thinking that it was natural that the bishop should know about the star-watching rock; it had been a special place for the entire Murry family, not only her mother.

The bishop continued, "The early settlers were so busy clearing their fields, it was no wonder they didn't notice stones with Ogam markings."

"Ogam is an alphabet," Zachary explained to Polly. "A Celtic alphabet, with fifteen consonants and some vowels, with a few other signs for diphthongs, or double letters like ng."

"Ogam, however," the bishop added, "was primarily an oral, rather than a written, language. Would your boss like to see this stone?"

"He'd drop his teeth." Zachary grinned. "But I'm not going to tell him. He'd just come and take over. No way." He looked at his watch, stood up. "Listen, this has been terrific, and I've enjoyed meeting everybody, but I didn't realize what time it was, and I've got a dinner date back in Hartford, but I'd like to drive over again soon if I may."

"Of course." Mrs. Murry rose. "Anytime. The only people Polly has seen since she's been here are the four of us antiques."

"You're not—" Polly started to protest.

But her grandmother continued, "There aren't many young people around, and we've worried about that."

"Do come, any weekend," Mr. Murry urged.

"Yes, do," Polly agreed.

"I don't really have to wait for the weekend," Zachary said. "I have Thursday afternoons off." He looked at Polly and she smiled at him. "Okay if I drive over then? It's not too much over an hour. I could be here by two."

"Of course. We'll expect you then."

They Murry grandparents and Polly accompanied Zachary out of the kitchen, past Mrs. Murry's lab, and through the garage. Zachary's small red sports car was parked next to a bright blue pickup truck.

Mr. Murry indicated it. "Nase's pride and joy. He drives like a madman. It's very pleasant to have met you, Zachary, and we look forward to seeing you on Thursday."

Zachary shook hands with the Murrys, kissed Polly lightly.

"What a nice young man," Mrs. Murry said, as they went back into the house.

And in the kitchen the bishop echoed her. "What a delightful young man."

"How amazing," Mr. Murry said, "that he knows about the Ogam stones."

"Oh, there've been a couple of articles about them in the Hartford papers," Dr. Louise said. "But he does seem a charming and bright young man. Very pale, though. Looks as if he spends too much time indoors. How do you know him, Polly?"

Polly squatted in front of the fire. "I met him last summer in Athens, before I went to the conference in Cyprus."

"What's his background?"

"He's from California, and his father's into all kinds of multinational big business. When Zachary bums around Europe he doesn't backpack, he stays in the best hotels. But I think he's kind of lonely."

"He's taking time off from college?"

"Yes. He's in college a little late. He didn't do well in

school because if he's not interested, he doesn't bother." A half-grown kitten pushed out of the cellar, stalked across the room, and jumped into Polly's lap, causing her to sit back on her heels. "So where've you been, Hadron?" Polly scratched the striped head.

Dr. Louise raised her eyebrows. "A natural name for a subatomic physicist's cat."

The bishop said, mildly, "I thought it was a variant of Hadrian."

"Or we were mispronouncing it?" Mrs. Murry suggested.

He sighed. "I suppose it's a name for a subatomic particle or something like that?"

Dr. Louise asked, "Kate, why don't you and Alex get another dog?"

"Ananda lived to be sixteen. We haven't been that long without a dog."

"This house doesn't seem right without a dog."

"That's what Sandy and Dennys keep telling us." Mr. Murry turned from the stove and began drawing the curtains across the wide kitchen windows. "We've never gone out looking for dogs. They just seem to appear periodically."

Polly sighed comfortably and shifted position. She loved her grandparents and the Colubras because they affirmed her, made her believe in infinite possibilities. At home on Benne Seed Island, Polly was the eldest of a large family. Here she was the only one, with all the privileges of an only child. She looked up as her grandfather hefted the Ogam stone and set it down on the kitchen dresser.

"Three thousand years," he said. "Not much in galactic terms, but a great deal of time in human terms. Time long gone, as we limited creatures look at it. But when you're up in a space shuttle, ordinary concepts of time and space vanish. We still have much to learn about time. We'll never leave the solar system as long as we keep on thinking of time as a river flowing from one direction into the sea." He patted the stone.

"You've found other Ogam stones?" Polly asked.

"I haven't. Nase has. Nase, Polly might well be able to help out with the translations. She has a positive genius for languages."

Polly flushed. "Oh, Granddad, I just—"

"You speak Portuguese, Spanish, Italian, and French, don't you?"

"Well, yes, but—"

"And didn't you study some Chinese?"

Now she laughed. "One day, maybe. I do love languages. Last summer I picked up a little Greek."

Mrs. Murry lit the two kerosene lamps which flanked the pot of geraniums on the table. "Polly's being modest. According to those who know—her parents, her uncles—her ability with languages is amazing." Then, to

Polly's relief, she changed the subject. "Louise, Nase, you will stay for dinner, won't you?"

The doctor shook her head. "I think we'd better be heading for home. Nase drives like a bat out of hell at night."

"Now, really, Louise—"

Mrs. Murry said, "I have a large mess of chicken and vegetables simmering over the Bunsen burner in the lab. We'll be eating it for a week if you don't help us out."

"It does seem an imposition—you're always feeding us—"

The bishop offered, "We'll do the dishes tonight, and give Polly and Alex a vacation."

"It's a bargain," Mr. Murry said.

Dr. Louise held out her hands. "I give in. Alex. Kate." She indicated the Ogam stone. "You really take all this seriously?"

Mr. Murry replied, "Oddly enough, I do, Celts, druids, and all. Kate is still dubious, but—"

"But we've been forced to take even stranger things seriously." Mrs. Murry headed for the door. "I'm off to get the casserole and finish it in the kitchen."

Polly shivered. "It's freezing in the lab. Grand was showing me how to use a gas chromatography this morning but icicles trickled off the end of my nose and she sent me in. Uncle Sandy calls me a swamp blossom."

Dr. Louise smiled. "Your grandmother's machinery is all for show. Her real work is up in her head."

"I couldn't get along without the Bunsen burner. Why don't you go for a swim, Polly? You know the pool's the warmest place in the house."

It was Polly's regular swimming time. She agreed readily. She loved to swim in the dark, by the light of the stars and a young moon. Swimming time, thinking time.

"See you in a bit." She stood up, shaking a reluctant Hadron out of her lap.

Up the back stairs. The first day, when her grandparents had taken her upstairs, she had not been sure where they were going to put her. Her mother's favorite place was the attic, with a big brass bed under the eaves, where her parents slept on their infrequent visits. On the second floor was her grandparents' room, with a grand four-poster bed. Across the hall was Sandy and Dennys, her uncles' room, with their old bunk beds, because on the rare occasions when the larger family was able to get together, all beds were needed. There was a room which might have been another bedroom but which was her grandfather's study, with bookshelves and a scarred rolltop desk, and a pull-out couch for overflow. Then there was her uncle Charles Wallace's room—her mother's youngest brother.

Polly had had a rather blank feeling that there was no room in her grandparents' house that was hers. Despite the fact that she had six brothers and sisters, she was used to having her own room with her own things. Each of the O'Keefe children did, though the rooms were little bigger than cubicles, for their parents believed that particularly in a large family a certain amount of personal space was essential.

As they climbed the stairs her grandmother said, "We've spruced up Charles Wallace's room. It isn't big, but I think you might like it."

Charles Wallace's room had been more than spruced up. It looked to Polly as though her grandparents had known she was coming, though the decision had been made abruptly only three days before she was put on the plane. When action was necessary, her parents did not procrastinate.

But the room, as she stepped over the threshold, seemed to invite her in. There was a wide window which looked onto the vegetable garden, then on past a big mowed field to the woods, and then the softly hunched shoulders of the mountains. It was a peaceful view, not spectacular, but gentle to live with, and wide and deep enough to give perspective. The other window looked east, across the apple orchard to more woods. The wallpaper was old-fashioned, soft blue with a sprinkling of daisies almost like stars, with an occasional bright butterfly, and the window curtains matched, though there were more butterflies than in the wallpaper.

Under the window of the east wall were bookshelves filled with books, and a rocking chair. The books were an eclectic collection, several volumes of myths and fairy tales, some Greek and Roman history, an assortment of novels, from Henry Fielding's *Tom Jones* to Matthew Maddox's *The Horn of Joy*, and on up to contemporary novels. Polly pulled out a book on constellations, with lines drawn between the stars to show the signs of the zodiac. Someone had to have a vivid imagination, she thought, to see a Great and Little Bear, or Sagittarius with his bow and arrow. There was going to be plenty to read, and she was grateful for that.

The floor was made of wide cherrywood boards, and there were small hooked rugs on either side of the big white-pine bed, which had a patchwork quilt in blues and yellows. What Polly liked most was that although the room was pretty it wasn't pretty-pretty. Charles, she thought, would have liked it.

She had turned to her grandmother. "Oh, it's lovely! When did you do all this?"

"Last summer."

Last summer her grandparents had had no idea that

Polly would be coming to live with them. Nevertheless, she felt that the room was uniquely hers. "I love it! Oh, Grand, I love it!"

She had called her parents, described the room. Her grandparents had left her to talk in privacy, and she said, "I love Grand and Granddad. You should see Granddad out on his red tractor. He's not intimidating at all."

There was laughter at that. "Did you expect him to be?"

"Well—I mean, he knows so much about astrophysics and space travel, and he gets consulted by presidents and important people. But he's easy to talk to—well, he's my grandfather and I think he's terrific."

"I gather it's mutual."

"And Grand isn't intimidating, either."

Her parents (she could visualize them, her mother lying on her stomach across the bed, her father perched on a stool in the lab, surrounded by tanks of starfish and octopus) both laughed.

Polly was slightly defensive. "We do call her Grand and that sounds pretty imposing."

"That's only because you couldn't say Grandmother when you started to talk."

"Well, and she did win a Nobel Prize."

Her father said, reasonably, "She's pretty terrific, Polly. But she'd much rather have you love her than be impressed at her accomplishments."

Polly nodded at the telephone. "I do love her. But remember, I've never really had a chance to know Grand and Granddad. We lived in Portugal for so long, and Benne Seed Island might have been just as far away. A few visits now and then hasn't been enough. I've been in awe of them."

"They're good people," her father said. "Talented, maybe a touch of genius. But human. They were good to me, incredibly good, when I was young."

"It's time you got to know them," her mother added. "Be happy, Polly."

She was. Happy as a small child. Not that she wanted to regress, to lose any of the things she had learned from experience, but with her grandparents she could relax, completely free to be herself.

She grabbed her bathing suit from the bathroom and went along to her room. Downstairs she could hear people moving about, and then someone put on music, Schubert's "Trout" Quintet, and the charming music floated up to her.

She left her jeans and sweatshirt in a small heap on the floor, slipped into her bathing suit and a terry-cloth robe, and went downstairs and out to the pool. She hung her robe on the towel tree, waited for her eyes to adjust to the dim light, then slid into the water and began swimming laps. She swam tidily, displacing little water, back and forth, back and forth. She flipped onto her back, looking up at the skylights, and welcoming first one star, then another. Turned from her back to her side, swimming dreamily. A faint sound made her slow down, a small scratching. She floated, listening. It came from one of the windows which lined the north wall from the floor up to the slant of the roof.

She could not see anything. The scratching turned into a gentle tapping. She pulled herself up onto the side of the pool, went to the window. There was a drop of about five feet from the window to the ground. In the last light, she could just see a girl standing on tiptoe looking up at her, a girl about her own age, with black hair braided into a long rope which was flung over her shoulder. At her neck was a band of silver with a stone, like a teardrop, in the center.

"Hi," Polly called through the dark glass.

The girl smiled and reached up to knock again. Polly slid the window open. "May I come in?" the girl asked.

Polly tugged at the screen till it, too, opened.

The girl sprang up and caught the sill, pulling herself into the room, followed by a gust of wind. Polly shut the screen and the window. The girl appeared to be about Polly's age, and she was exotically beautiful, with honey-colored skin and eyes so dark the pupils could barely be distinguished.

"Forgive me," the girl said formally, "for coming like

this. Karralys saw you this afternoon." She spoke with a slight accent which Polly could not distinguish.

"Karralys?"

"Yes. At the oak tree, with his dog."

"Why didn't he say hello?" Polly asked.

The girl shook her head. "It is not often given to see the other circles of time. But then Karralys and I talked, and thought I should come here to the place of power. It seemed to us that you must have been sent to us in this strange and difficult—" She broke off as a door slammed somewhere in the house. She put her hand to her mouth. Whispered, "I must go. Please—" She seemed so frightened that Polly opened the window for her.

"Who are you?"

But the girl jumped down, landing lightly, and was off across the field toward the woods, running as swiftly as a wild animal.

Chapter Two

The whole incident made no sense whatsoever. Polly put on her robe and headed for the kitchen, looking for explanations, but saw no one. Probably everybody was out in the lab, where it was definitely too chilly for a swamp blossom in a wet bathing suit and a damp terry-cloth robe.

Her parents had worried that she might be lonely with no people her own age around, and in one day she had seen three, the blue-eyed young man by the oak—though he was probably several years older than she; Zachary; and now this unknown girl.

Upstairs in her room, the stripy cat was lying curled in the center of the bed, one of his favorite places. She picked him up and held him and he purred, pleased with her damp warmth.

"Who on earth was that girl?" she demanded. "And what was she talking about?" She squeezed the cat too tightly and he jumped from her arms and stalked out of the room, brown-and-amber tail erect.

She dressed and went downstairs. The bishop was in the kitchen, sitting in one of the shabby but comfortable chairs by the fireplace. She joined him.

"What's the matter?" he asked.

"I'm just puzzled. While I was swimming there was a knock on one of the windows, and I got out of the pool to look, and there was this girl, about my age, with a long black braid and sort of exotic eyes, and I let her in, and she—well, she made absolutely no sense at all."

"Go on." The bishop was alert, totally focused on her words.

"This afternoon by the Grandfather Oak—you know the tree I mean?"

"Yes."

"I saw a young man and a dog. The girl said the man with the dog had seen me, and then something about circles of time, and then she heard a noise and got frightened and ran away. Who do you suppose she was?"

The bishop looked at Polly without answering, simply staring at her with a strange, almost shocked look on his face.

"Bishop?"

"Well, my dear—" He cleared his throat. "Yes. It is indeed strange. Strange indeed."

"Should I tell my grandparents?"

He hesitated. Cleared his throat. "Probably."

She nodded. She trusted him. He hadn't had a cushy job as bishop. Her grandparents had told her that he'd been in the Amazon for years, taught seminary in China, had a price on his head in Peru. When he was with so-called primitive people he listened to them, rather than imposing his own views. He honored others.

She was so concerned with her own story that she was not aware that what she had told him had upset him.

"Polly," he said, "tell me about the young man with the dog." His voice trembled slightly.

"He was standing by the Grandfather Oak. He had these intensely blue eyes."

"What was the dog like?"

"Just a big dog with large ears. Not any particular breed. I didn't see them for more than a few seconds."

"And the girl. Can you describe her?"

"Well—not much more than I just did. Long black braid, and dark eyes. She was beautiful and strange."

"Yes," the bishop said. "Oh, yes." His voice was soft and troubled.

Now she saw that something had disturbed him. "Do you know who she is?"

"Perhaps. How can I be sure?" He paused, then spoke briskly. "Yes, it's strange, strange indeed. Your grandfather is right to discourage trespassers." His eyes were suddenly veiled.

Mr. Murry came in from the pantry, heard the bishop's last words. "Right, Nase. I'm quite happy to have deer and foxes leaping over the stone walls, but not snoopers. We've had to put a horrendously expensive warning system in the lab. Louise is correct, most of Kate's equipment hasn't been used in decades. But the computers are another story." He headed for the wood stove, turned to Polly. "The lab has been broken into twice. Once a useless microscope was taken, and once your grandmother lost a week's work because someone—probably local kids, rather than anyone who knew anything about her work—played around with the computer." He opened the small oven of the wood stove and the odor of freshly baked bread filled the kitchen. "Bread is something Kate can't make on the Bunsen burner, so this is my contribution, as well as therapy. Kneading bread is wonderful for rheumatic fingers."

Mrs. Murry and Dr. Louise followed him into the kitchen. Mrs. Murry lit candles in addition to the oil lamps, and turned out the lights. Dr. Louise put a large casserole of Mrs. Murry's chicken concoction on the table, and Mr. Murry took a bowl of autumn vegetables from the stove, broccoli, cauliflower, sprouts, onions, carrots, leeks. The bishop sniffed appreciatively.

Mrs. Murry said, "The twins used to have a vast vegetable garden. Ours isn't nearly as impressive, but Alex does amazingly well."

"For an old man, you mean," Mr. Murry said.

"Except for your arthritis," Dr. Louise said, "you're in remarkably good shape. I wish some of my patients ten or more years younger than you did as well."

After they were seated, and the meal blessed and served, Polly looked at the bishop. His eyes met hers briefly. Then he glanced away, and his expression was withdrawn. But she thought he had barely perceptibly nodded at her. She said, "I've seen a couple of odd people today."

"Who?" her grandfather asked.

"You're not talking about Zachary!" Dr. Louise laughed.

She shook her head and described both the young man with the dog, and the girl. "Zachary thought he was a caretaker, maybe."

The bishop choked slightly, got up, and poured himself some water. Recovering himself, he asked, "You say that Zachary saw this young man?"

"Sure. He was right there. But he didn't talk to either of us."

"I hope he wasn't a hunter," Mr. Murry said. "Our land is very visibly posted."

"He didn't have a gun. I'm positive. Is it hunting season here or something?"

"It's never hunting season on our land," her grandfather said. "Did you speak to him? Ask him what he was doing?"

"I didn't get a chance. I just saw him looking at me, and when I got to the tree he was gone."

"What about the girl?" Mrs. Murry probed.

Polly looked at the bishop. His eyes were once again veiled, his expression noncommittal. Polly repeated her description of the girl. "I really don't think they were poachers or vandals or anything bad. They were just mysterious."

Her grandfather's voice was unexpectedly harsh. "I don't want any more mysteries."

The bishop was staring at the Ogam stone sitting on the kitchen dresser, along with assorted mugs, bowls, a gravy boat, a hammer, a roll of stamps.

Mrs. Murry's voice was light. "Perhaps they'll be friends for Polly?"

"The girl's about my age, I think," Polly said. "She had gorgeous soft leather clothes that would cost a fortune in a boutique, and she wore a sort of silver collar with a beautiful stone."

Mrs. Murry laughed. "Your mother said you were finally showing some interest in clothes. I'm glad to note evidence of it."

Polly was slightly defensive. "There hasn't been any reason for me to wear anything but jeans."

"Silver collar." The bishop spoke as though to himself. "A torque—" He was busily helping himself to vegetables.

Mrs. Murry had heard. "A torque?" She turned to Polly. "Nason has a book on early metalwork with beautiful photographs. The early druids may have lived among Stone Age people, but there were metalworkers at least passing through Britain, and the druids were already sophisticated astronomers. They, and the tribal leaders, wore intricately designed torques."

"The wheel of fashion keeps coming full circle," Dr. Louise said. "And how much have we learned since the Stone Age as far as living peaceably is concerned?"

Mr. Murry regarded his wife. "There's a picture of a superb silver torque in Nason's book that I wish I could get for you, Kate. It would eminently suit you."

Polly looked at her grandmother's sensible country clothes and tried to visualize her in a beautiful torque. It was not impossible. She had been told that her grandmother was a beauty, and as she looked at the older woman's fine bones, the short, well-cut silver hair, the graceful curve of the slender neck, the fine eyes surrounded by lines made from smiles and pain and generous living, she thought that her grandmother was still beautiful, and she was glad that her grandfather's response was to want to get his wife a torque.

Mrs. Murry had taken a blueberry pie from the freezer for dessert, and brought it bubbling from the oven. "I didn't make it," she explained. "There's a blueberry festival at the church every summer, and I always buy half a dozen unbaked pies to have on hand." She cut into it, and purple juice streamed out with summer fragrance. "Polly, I can't tell you how pleased I am that your Zachary turned up. It must have been hard for you to leave your friends."

Polly accepted a slice of pie. "Island kids tend to be isolated. My friends are sort of scattered."

"I've been lucky to have Louise living only a few miles away. We've been friends ever since college."

Yes, her grandmother was lucky to have Dr. Louise, Polly thought. She had never had a real female friend her own age. She thought fleetingly of the girl at the pool.

Polly and the bishop did the dishes together, and the others went to sit by the fire in the living room, urged on by Mrs. Murry, who said they all spent too much time in the kitchen.

"So, island girl," the bishop said, "is all well here?"

"Very well, thank you, Bishop." She wanted to ask him more about the man with the dog and the girl at the pool, but it was clear to her that the bishop was guiding the conversation away from them. She took a rinsed plate from him and put it in the dishwasher.

"My sister has taught me to wash everything with soap, even if it's going in the dishwasher. Be careful. The plates are slippery."

"Okay."

"Your young man—"

"Zachary. Zachary Gray."

"He didn't look well."

"He's always pale. Last summer in Greece when everybody was tan, Zachary's skin was white. Of course, I don't think he goes out in the sun much. He isn't the athletic type."

"How was last summer?" The bishop wrung out a sponge.

Polly was putting silverware in the dishwasher basket. "It was a wonderful experience. I loved Athens, and the conference on Cyprus was worth a year at school. Max—Maximiliana Horne—arranged it all. And she died just before I got home."

He nodded. "Your grandparents told me. You're still grieving."

She dried the knives, which were old silver ones with the handles glued on and could not be put in the dishwasher. "It was harder at home, where everything reminded me of Max. Did you know her?"

The bishop let soapy water out of the sink. "Your Uncle Sandy told me about her. They were great friends."

"Yes. Sandy introduced me to her." Unexpectedly her throat tightened.

The bishop led the way to one of the shabby chairs by the kitchen fireplace, rather than joining the others in the living room. Polly followed him, and as she sat down Hadron appeared and jumped into her lap, purring.

"Bishop, about the young man and the girl—"

But at that moment Dr. Louise came into the kitchen, yawning. "Dishes all done?"

"And with soap," the bishop assured her.

"Time for us to be getting on home."

Polly and her grandparents went outside to wave the Colubras off, and the stars were brilliant amid small wisps of cloud. The moon was tangled in the branches of a large Norway maple.

The bishop climbed into the driver's seat of the blue pickup truck and they took off with a squeal of tires.

Polly's grandmother turned to go back into the house. "We're going for a quick swim. I'll come and say good night in a while." It had already become a comfortable habit that after Polly was in bed her grandmother would come in and they would talk for a few minutes.

She took a hurried bath—the bathroom was frigid—and slipped into a flannel nightgown, then into bed, pulling the quilt about her. She read a few pages of the book her grandfather had given her on white holes, cosmic gushers, the opposite of black holes. Her grandparents were certainly seeing to her education. But perhaps it was no wonder that her grandfather had not noticed stones in his walls that had strange markings.

When her grandmother came in, she put the book down on the nightstand, and Mrs. Murry sat on the side of the bed. "Lovely evening. It's good that Nase is living with Louise. Your grandfather and I feel as though we've known him forever. He was a fine bishop. He's tender and compassionate and he knows how to listen."

Polly pushed up higher against the pillows. "Yes, I feel I could tell him anything and he wouldn't be shocked."

"And he'd never betray a confidence."

"Grand." Polly sat up straight. "Something's been bothering me."

"What, my dear?"

"I sort of just got dumped on you, didn't I?"

"Oh, Polly, your grandfather and I have enough sense of self-protection so that if we hadn't wanted you to come we'd have said no. We've felt very deprived, seeing so little of our grandchildren. We love having you. It's a very different life from what you've been used to—"

"Oh, Grand, I love it. I'm happy here. Grand, why did Mother have so many kids?"

"Would you want any of you not to have been born?"

"No, but—"

"But it doesn't answer your question." Mrs. Murry pushed her fingers through her still damp hair. "If a woman is free to choose a career, she's also free to choose the care of a family as her primary vocation."

"Was it that with Mother?"

"Partly." Her grandmother sighed. "But it was probably partly because of me."

"You? Why?"

"I'm a scientist, Polly, and well known in my field."

"Well, but Mother—" She stopped. "You mean maybe she didn't want to compete with you?"

"That could be part of it."

"You mean, she was afraid she couldn't compete?"

"Your mother's estimation of herself has always been low. Your father has been wonderful for her and so, in many ways, have you children. But . . ." Her voice drifted off.

"But you did your work and had kids."

"Not seven of them." Her grandmother's hands were tightly clasped together. Then, deliberately, she relaxed them, placed them over her knees.

Polly slid down in the bed to a more comfortable position. Suddenly she felt drowsy. Hadron, who had taken to sleeping with Polly, curled in the curve between shoulder and neck, began to purr.

"Women have come a long way," her grandmother said, "but there will always be problems—and glories— that are unique to women." The cat's purr rose contentedly. "Hadron certainly seems to have taken to you."

"A hadron," Polly murmured sleepily, "belongs to a class of particles that interact strongly. Nucleons are hadrons, and so are pions and strange particles."

"Good girl," Mrs. Murry said. "You're a quick learner."

"Strange particles . . ." Polly's eyes closed.—You'd think human beings would be full of strange particles. Maybe we are. Hadrons are—I think—formed of quarks, so the degree of strangeness in a hadron is calculated by the number of quarks.

"Were druids strange?" She was more than half asleep. "I don't know much about druids." Polly's breathing slowed as she pushed her face into the pillow, close to Hadron's warm fur. Mrs. Murry rose, stood for a moment looking at her granddaughter, then slipped out of the room.

In the morning Polly woke early, dressed, and went downstairs. No one was stirring. The ground was white with mist which drifted across the lawn. The mountains were slowly emerging on the horizon, and above them the sky shimmered between the soft grey of dawn and the blue which would clarify as the sun rose.

She headed outdoors, across the field, which was as wet with dew as though it had rained during the night. At the stone wall she paused, but it was probably too early for Louise the Larger. Polly continued along the path toward the star-watching rock. She had pulled on the old red anorak, and she wore lined jeans, so she was warm enough. She looked up at the sky in surprise as there was a sudden strange shimmering in the air. Then there was a flash as though from lightning, but no thunder. The ground quivered slightly under her feet, then settled. Was it an earthquake? She looked around. The trees were different. Larger. There were many more oaks, towering even higher than the Grandfather Oak. As she neared the star-watching rock she saw light flashing on water, and where the fertile valley had been there was now a large lake.

A lake? She reeled in surprise. Where had a lake come from? And the hills were no longer the gentle hills worn down by wind and rain and erosion, but jagged mountains, their peaks capped with snow. She turned, her flesh prickling, and looked at the rock, and it was the same star-watching rock she had always loved, and yet it was not the same.

"What's going on?" she asked aloud. Wreaths of mist were dissipating to reveal a dozen or more tents made of stretched and cured animal skins. Beyond them was an enormous vegetable garden, and a field of corn, the stalks recently cut and gathered into bunches. Beyond the cornfield, cows and sheep were grazing. On lines strung between poles, fish were hanging. Between stronger poles, beaver skins were being dried and stretched. In front of one of the tents a woman was sitting, pounding something with mortar and pestle. She had black hair worn in a braid, and she was singing as she worked, paying no attention to Polly or anything going on around her, absorbed in the rhythm of the pestle and her song. She looked like a much older version of the girl who had come to the pool.

In the distance Polly heard the sound of a drum, and then singing, a beautiful melody with rich native harmony. The rising sun seemed to be pulled up out of the sky by the beauty of the song. When the music ended, there was a brief silence, and then the noises of the day resumed.

What on earth was happening? Where was she? How could she get home?

She turned in the direction where the Murry house should have been, and coming toward her was a group of young men carrying spears. Instinctively, Polly ran behind one of the great oak trees and peered out from behind the wide trunk.

Two of the men had a young deer slung onto their spears. They continued past her, beyond the tents and the garden and the cornfield and pasture. They wore soft leather leggings and tunics, similar to the clothes worn by the girl who had come to Polly at the pool.

After they were out of sight on the path she leaned against the tree because her legs felt like water. What was happening? Where had the huge forest behind her come from? What about the lake which took up the entire valley? Who were the young men?

Her mind was racing, reaching out in every direction, trying to make some kind of sense out of this total dislocation. Certainly life had proven to her more than once that the world is not a reasonable place, but this was unreason beyond unreason.

Up the path came a young man with hair bleached almost white. He carried a spear, far larger than those of the hunters. At the haft it was balanced by what looked like a copper ball about the size of an apple or an orange, and just below this was a circle of feathers. She hid behind the tree so that he would not see her, dressed in jeans and a red anorak.

In one of the great oaks a cardinal was singing sweetly, a familiar sound. A small breeze blew through the bleached autumn grasses, ruffled the waters of the lake. The air was clear and pure. The mountains hunched great rugged shoulders into the blue of sky, and early sunlight sparkled off the white peaks.

She drew in her breath. Coming along the path toward her was the girl she had seen at the pool, her black braid swinging. She carried an armful of autumn flowers, deep-blue Michaelmas daisies, white Queen Anne's lace, yellow golden glow. She walked to a rock Polly had not noticed before, a flat grey rock resting on two smaller rocks, somewhat like a pi sign in stone.

The girl placed her flowers on the rock, looked up at

the sky, and lifted her voice in song. Her voice was clear and sweet and she sang as simply and spontaneously as a bird. When she was through, she raised her arms heavenward, a radiance illuminating her face. Then she turned, as though sensing Polly's presence behind the tree.

Polly came out. "Hi!"

The girl's face drained of color, and she swirled as though to run off.

"Hey, wait!" Polly called.

Slowly the girl walked toward the star-watching rock.

"Who are you?" Polly asked.

"Anaral." The girl pointed to herself as she said her name. She had on the same soft leather tunic and leggings she had worn the night before, and at her throat was the silver band with the pale stone in the center. The forefinger of her right hand was held out a little stiffly, and on it was a Band-Aid, somehow utterly incongruous.

"What were you singing? It was beautiful. You have an absolutely gorgeous voice." With each word, Polly was urging the girl not to run away again.

A faint touch of peach colored Anaral's cheeks, and she bowed her head.

"What is it? Can you tell me the words?"

The color deepened slightly. Anaral for the first time looked directly at Polly. "The good-morning song to our Mother, who gives us the earth on which we live"—she paused, as though seeking for words—"teaches us to listen to the wind, to care for all that she gives us, food to grow"—another, thinking pause—"the animals to nurture, and ourselves. We ask her to help us to know ourselves, that we may know each other, and to forgive"— she rubbed her forehead—"to forgive ourselves when we do wrong, so that we may forgive others. To help us walk the path of love, and to protect us from all that would hurt us." As Anaral spoke, putting her words slowly into English, her voice automatically moved into singing.

"Thank you," Polly said. "We sing a lot in my family. They'd love that. I'd like to learn it."

"I will teach you." Anaral smiled shyly.

"Why did you run off last night?" Polly asked.

"I was confused. It is not often that circles of time overlap. That you should be here—oh, it is strange."

"What is?"

"That we should be able to see each other, to speak."

Yes, Polly thought. Strange, indeed. Was it possible that she and Anaral were speaking across three thousand years?

"You do not belong to my people," Anaral said. "You are in a different spiral."

"Who are your people?"

Anaral stood proudly. "We are the People of the Wind."

"Are you Indians?" Polly asked. It seemed a rude question, but she wanted to know the answer.

Anaral looked baffled. "I do not know that word. We have always been on this land. I was born to be trained as—you might understand if I said I was a druid."

A native American who was a druid? But druids came from Britain.

Anaral smiled. "Druid is not a word of the People of the Wind. Karralys—you saw him yesterday by the great oak—Karralys brought the word with him from across the great water. You understand?"

"Well—I'm not sure."

"That is all right. I have told you my name, my druid name that Karralys gave me. Anaral. And you are?"

"Polly O'Keefe. How do you know my language?"

"Bishop."

"Bishop Colubra?"

Anaral nodded.

"He taught you?" Now Polly understood why the bishop had been concerned when she talked to him about Anaral and Karralys. And it was apparent that he had not told her grandparents or his sister everything he knew about the Ogam stones and the people who walked the land three thousand years ago.

"Yes. Bishop taught me."

"How do you know him?"

Anaral held out her hands. "He came to us."

"How?"

"Sometimes"—Anaral swung her black braid over

her shoulder—"it is possible to move from one ring to another."

Polly had a vision of a picture of an early model of a molecule, with the nucleus in the center and the atoms in shells or circles around it. Sometimes an electron jumped from one shell or circle to another. But this picture of the movement of electrons from circle to circle in a molecule didn't help much, because Anaral's circles were in time, rather than space. Except, Polly reminded herself, time and space are not separable. "You came to my time yesterday," she said. "How did you do it?"

Anaral put slim hands to her face, then took them down and looked at Polly. "Karralys and I are druids. For us the edges of time are soft. Not hard. We can move through it like water. Are you a druid?"

"No." Polly was definite. "But it seems that I am now in your time."

"I am in my time," Anaral said.

"But if you are, I must be?"

"Our circles are touching."

"Druids know about astronomy. Do you know about time?"

Anaral laughed. "There are more circles of time than anyone can count, and we understand a few of them, but only a few. I have the old knowledge, the knowledge of the People of the Wind, and now Karralys is teaching me his new knowledge, the druidic knowledge."

"Does the bishop know all of this?"

"Oh, yes. Do you belong to Bishop?"

"To friends of his."

"You belong to the scientists?"

"I'm their granddaughter."

"The one with the crooked fingers and lame knees—Bishop tells me he knows something about time."

"Yes. More than most people. But not about—not about going back three thousand years, which is what I've done, isn't it?"

Anaral shook her head. "Three thousand—I do not know what three thousand means. You have stepped across the threshold."

"I don't know how I did it," Polly said. "I just set out to walk to the star-watching rock and suddenly I was here. Do you know how I can get back?"

Anaral smiled a little sadly. "I am not always sure myself how it happens. The circles overlap and a threshold opens and then we can cross over."

As Anaral gestured with her hands, Polly noticed again the Band-Aid anachronistically on Anaral's finger. "What did you do to your finger?"

"I cut myself with a hunting knife. I was skinning a deer and the knife slipped."

"How did you get that Band-Aid? You don't have Band-Aids in your own time, do you?"

Anaral shook her head. "Dr. Louise sewed my finger up for me, many stitches. That was more than a moon ago. It is nearly well now. When I could take off the big bandage, Bishop brought me this." She held up the finger with the Band-Aid.

"How did you get to Dr. Louise?"

"Bishop brought me to her."

"How?"

"Bishop saw me right after the knife slipped. The cut was deep, oh, very deep. I bled. Bled. I was scared. Crying. Bishop held my finger, pressing to stop the blood spurting. Then he said, 'Come,' and we ran—Bishop can really run—and suddenly we were in Dr. Louise's office."

"You don't have anybody in your own time who could have taken care of the cut for you?"

"The Ancient Grey Wolf could have. He was our healer for many years, but he died during the cold of last winter. And his son, who should have followed him, died when the winter fever swept through our people a few turns of the sun ago. Cub, the Young Wolf, who will become our healer, still has much to learn. Karralys of course could have helped me, but he was away that day, with the young men, hunting."

"Karralys is a druid from Britain?"

"From far. Karralys is he who came in the strange

boat, three turns of the sun back, blown across the lake by a hurricane of fierce winds. He came as we People of the Wind were mourning the death of our Great One, felled by an oak tree uprooted in the storm, picked up like a twig and flung down, the life crushed out of him. He was very old and had foretold that he would not live another sun turn. And out of the storm Karralys came, and with him another from the sea, Tav, who is almost white of hair and has skin that gets red if he stays out in the sun."

Tav. That must be the young man with the spear.

"Where did they come from, Karralys and Tav?"

"From the great waters, beyond the rivers and the mountains. And lo, at the very moment that Karralys's boat touched the shore, the wind dropped, and the storm ended, and a great rainbow arched across the lake and we knew that the Maker of the Stars had sent us a new Great One."

"And Tav?" Polly asked.

Anaral continued, "Tav was in the canoe half dead with fever. Even with all their skill, Karralys and Grey Wolf had a hard time bringing the fever down. Night after night they stayed with Tav, praying. Cub, the Young Wolf, was beside them, watching, learning. The fever went down with the moon and Tav's breathing was suddenly gentle as a child's and he slept and he was well. They are a great gift to us, Karralys and Tav."

"Is Tav a druid?"

"Oh, no. He is a warrior. He is our greatest hunter. We have not had to worry about having enough meat since Tav came."

Polly frowned, trying to sort things out. "You were born here, in this place?"

"Yes."

"But you're a druid?"

Anaral laughed. "Now. That is what I am called now. For this I was born. And Karralys has trained me in his wisdom. And now there is danger to our people, and Karralys thinks you have been brought across the threshold to help us."

"But how could I possibly—" Polly started.

There was a sharp sound, as of someone stepping on and breaking a twig, and Anaral was off, swift as a deer.

Polly looked around, but saw no one. "You have been brought across the threshold to help us," Anaral had said. What on earth did she mean? And how was Polly to get back across the threshold to her own time? Without Anaral, how could she possibly get home?

She ran after the other girl. Polly had long legs and she ran quickly, but she was not familiar with the path, which zigzagged back and forth, always downhill. Anaral was nowhere to be seen.

Polly continued on, past the village, around the garden and the cornfield, across the pasture, and then picked up a path which led through a grove of birch and beech trees. She followed it until it opened out at a large flat stone, not quite as large as the star-watching rock. But in this terrain which had been covered by glaciers the topsoil was thin, the bones of the earth close to the surface. She continued on, listening, as she heard water plashing. Then she was standing on a stone bridge under which a small brook ran. She had been here before during her exploring, and it was a lovely place. Trees leaned over the water, dropping golden leaves. She was surrounded by rich October smells, decomposing apples, leaves, hickory nuts, acorns, pinecones, all sending their nourishment into the earth.

And suddenly she realized that the trees were the trees of her own time, not those of a primeval forest. She was home.

Chapter Three

In her own time. Weak with relief, Polly sat on the stone bridge, dangling her legs over the brook, trying to return to normalcy.

—Why do northern trees shed their leaves? she asked herself.—Is it to reduce their exposure to extreme cold?

That sounded sensible, and she wanted things to be sensible, because nothing about the morning had been sensible, and inside her warm anorak she felt cold. She got up and continued along the path, looking for the slim girl with a heavy dark braid. But Anaral had been in that other time, not the now of Polly's present. Nevertheless, she pushed along the path cut through low bushes, and on to a high precipice, from which she could look over the swampy valley to the hills beyond.

Her uncles, Sandy and Dennys, had cut paths through the brush when they were young, and the wildlife had more or less kept them open. She would need to come out with clippers to cut back some of the overgrowth. She stood on the high rock, looking westward. The landscape rippled with gentle color, muted golds now predominating, green of pine suddenly appearing where fallen leaves had left bare branches.

Then, below her, down where the bed of the brook should be, she saw a flash of brightness, and Bishop Colubra appeared out of the bushes, wearing a yellow cap and jacket and carrying a heavy-looking stone. A steep path led down the precipice which would have been easy to follow had it not been crisscrossed by bittersweet and blackberry brambles that caught at her as she plunged downhill toward the bishop, scratching her legs and hands, catching in her clothes.

The bishop was hailing her with pleasure, holding out the stone, and explaining that he hadn't been looking for Ogam stones but there was one, right there in an old stone wall, and wasn't it a glorious morning?

"Bishop!" she gasped as she came up to him. "I've been back!"

He stopped so abruptly and completely that the air seemed to quiver. "What?"

"I crossed the threshold, or whatever Anaral calls it. I went back to her time."

His voice was a whisper. He looked as though he were about to drop the stone. "When?"

"Just now. I've just come out of it. Bishop, while it

was happening it was all so sudden and so strange I didn't have time to feel anything much. But now I think I'm terrified." Her voice quavered.

He put the stone down, touched her arm reassuringly. "Don't be terrified. It will be all right. It will work out according to God's purpose."

"Will it?"

"I didn't expect this. That you—You saw her yesterday, at the pool?"

Polly felt cold, though the sun was warm. "She says that she and Karralys—he's the one by the oak—she says that they can cross the thresholds of time because they're druids."

"Yes." The bishop kept his hand on Polly's shoulder, as though imparting strength. "We've lost many gifts that were once available." He bent down to pick up the stone. "We'd better head back to your grandparents' house. This is the shortest way, if you want to follow me." He was definitely wobbly on his long, thin legs, trying to tuck the stone under one arm so that he could balance himself with the other, reaching for small trees or large vines to help pull himself along. They came to another curve of the brook and he stopped, looked at the water flowing between and around rocks, and made a successful leap across, dropping the stone, which Polly retrieved.

"I'll carry it for a while," she offered. She followed

the old bishop, who scurried along a nearly overgrown path, then turned sharply uphill, scrabbling his way up like a crab. At their feet were occasional patches of red partridge berries. A spruce branch stretched across their path, and he held it aside for Polly, continuing along his irregular course until he pushed through a thicket of shadblow and wild cherry, and they emerged at the star-watching rock.

"Bishop," Polly said. "This—what happened—it's crazy."

He did not speak. The sun rose higher. A soft wind moved through the trees, shaking down more leaves.

"Maybe I dreamed it?"

"Sometimes I don't know what is dream and what is reality. The line between them is very fine." He took the Ogam stone from her and set it down on the star-watching rock. Folded his legs and sat down, indicated that she was to sit beside him. "Tell me exactly what happened."

"I got up early and went for a walk, and as I came near the star-watching rock, everything changed. The ground quivered. I thought it was an earthquake. And then I saw that the trees, the mountains—the trees were much bigger, sort of primeval forest. And the mountains were huge and jagged and snow-topped."

He nodded. "Yes."

"And I know you've been there—back—"

"Yes."

"Is it real?"

He nodded.

"Do my grandparents know about this? Dr. Louise?"

He shook his head. "They don't believe in such things."

"They believe in the Ogam stones."

"Yes. They're tangible."

"But haven't you told them?"

He sighed. "My dear, they don't want to hear."

"But, Bishop, you took Anaral to Dr. Louise when she cut her finger."

"How do you—"

"Anaral told me."

"Yes. Oh, my dear. I didn't know what to do. I didn't stop to think. I just took her and ran, and thank heavens Louise was in her office."

"So she does know."

He shook his head. "No. I told her, and she thought I was joking. Or out of my mind. I've tended periodically to bring in waifs and strays for her to mend, and she thinks Annie was just another. Because that's what she wants to think. Have you had breakfast?"

"No."

"Let's go on back to your grandparents' and have some coffee. I need to think. Thursday is All Hallows' Eve . . ."

Halloween. She had completely forgotten.

He scrambled to his feet. Picked up the Ogam stone. "That may partly explain—the time of year—"

"Bishop, my grandparents don't know you've done what I did—gone back three thousand years?"

"Do you realize how extraordinary it sounds? They've never seen Karralys or Anaral. But you've seen them. You've crossed the threshold. If you hadn't, would you believe it?"

He was right. The whole thing did sound crazy. Time thresholds. Three thousand years. Circles of time. But it had happened. She didn't see how she and the bishop could have dreamed the same dream. "Bishop—how long have you been going—going back and forth? Between then and now?"

"Since last spring. A few months after I came to live with Louise."

"How often?"—Often enough to teach Anaral to speak English, she thought.

"Reasonably often. But I can't plan it. Sometimes it happens. Sometimes it doesn't. Polly, child, let's go. I really feel the need to confess to your grandparents, whether they believe me or not."

"They're pretty good at believing," Polly said. "More than most people."

The bishop shifted the stone from one arm to the other. "I never thought you'd become involved. I never dreamed this could happen. That you should—I feel dreadfully responsible—"

She offered, "Shall I carry the Ogam stone?"

"Please." He sounded terribly distraught.

She took the stone and followed him. When they crossed the wall that led to the field, Polly saw Louise the Larger watching them, not moving. The bishop, not even noticing the snake, scrambled across the wall and started to run toward the house.

Polly's grandparents were in the kitchen. Everything was reassuringly normal. Her grandfather was reading the paper. Her grandmother was making pancakes. Breakfast was usually catch-as-catch-can. Mrs. Murry often took coffee and a muffin to the lab. Mr. Murry hurried outdoors, working about the yard while the weather held.

"Good morning, Polly, Nason." Mrs. Murry sounded unsurprised as they panted in, Polly scratched and disheveled from her plunge down the precipice. "Alex requested pancakes, and since he's a very undemanding person, I was happy to oblige. Join us. I've made more than enough batter."

"I hope I'm not intruding." The bishop seated himself.

Polly tried to keep her voice normal. "Here's another Ogam stone. Where shall I put it?"

"If there's room, put it beside the one Nase brought

in last night," her grandmother said. "How many pan-cakes can you eat, Nase?"

"I don't know. I'm not sure I can eat anything. I don't think I'm hungry."

"Nason! What's wrong? Don't you feel well?"

"I'm fine." He looked at Polly. "Oh, dear. What have I done?"

"What have you done?" Mr. Murry asked.

Polly said, "You didn't do anything, Bishop. It just happened."

Mrs. Murry put a stack of pancakes in front of him, and absently he lavished butter, poured a river of syrup, ate a large bite, put down his fork. "I may have done something terrible."

"Nason, what's going on?" Mr. Murry asked.

The bishop took another large bite. Shook his head. "I didn't think it would happen. I didn't think it could."

"*What?*" Mr. Murry demanded.

"I thought the time gate was open only to me. I didn't think—" He broke off.

"Polly," her grandfather asked, "do you know what all this is about?"

Polly poured herself a mug of coffee and sat down. "The man by the oak, the one both Zachary and I saw, lived at the time of the Ogam stones." She did her best to keep her voice level. "This morning when I went off for a

walk, I—well, I don't know what it's all about, but somehow or other I went through the bishop's time gate."

"Nase!"

The bishop bent his head. "I know. It's my fault. It
must be my fault. *Mea culpa.*"

Mrs. Murry asked, "Polly, what makes you think you
went through a time gate?"

"Everything was different, Grand. The trees were
enormous, sort of like Hiawatha—*this is the forest primeval.*
And the mountains were high and jagged and snow-
capped. Young mountains, not ancient hills like ours.
And where the valley is, there was a large lake."

"This is absurd." Mrs. Murry put a plate of pancakes
in front of her husband, then fixed a plate for Polly.

"Nason!" Mr. Murry expostulated.

The bishop looked unhappy. "Whenever I've tried to
talk about it, you've been disbelieving and, well—
disapproving, and I don't blame you for that, so I've kept
quiet. I wouldn't have believed it, either, if it hadn't kept
happening. But I thought it was just me—part of being
old and nearly ready to move on to—But Polly. That
Polly should have—well! of course!"

"Of course what?" Mr. Murry sounded more angry
with each question.

"Polly saw Annie first at the pool." The bishop used
the diminutive of Anaral tenderly.

"Annie who?"

"Anaral," Polly said. "She's the girl who came to the pool last night."

"When you were digging for the pool," the bishop asked, "what happened?"

"We hit water," Mr. Murry said. "We're evidently over an aquifer—an underground river."

"But this is the highest point in the state," Polly protested. "Would there be an underground river this high up?

"It would seem so."

The bishop put down his fork. Somehow the stack of pancakes had disappeared. "You do remember that most holy places—such as the sites of the great cathedrals in England—were on ground that was already considered holy before even the first pagan temples were built? And the interesting thing is that under most of these holy places is an underground river. This house, and the pool, are on a holy place. That's why Anaral was able to come to the pool."

"Nonsense—" Mrs. Murry started.

Mr. Murry sighed, as though in frustration. "We love the house and our land," he said, "but it's a bit far-fetched to call it holy."

"This house is—what?—" the bishop asked, "well over two hundred years old?"

"Parts of it, yes."

"But the Ogam stones indicate that there were people here three thousand years ago."

"Nason, I've seen the stone. I believe you that there is Ogam writing on them. I take them seriously. But I don't want Polly involved in any of your—your—" Mr. Murry pushed up from his place so abruptly that he overturned his chair, righted it with an irritated grunt. The phone rang, making them all jump. Mr. Murry went to it. "Polly, it's for you."

This was no time for an interruption. She wanted her grandparents to put everything into perspective. If they could believe what happened, it would be less frightening.

"Sounds like Zachary." Her grandfather handed her the phone.

"Good morning, sweet Pol. I just wanted to tell you how good it was to see you yesterday, and I look forward to seeing you on Thursday."

"Thanks, Zach. I look forward to it, too."

"Okay, see you then. Just wanted to double-check."

She went back to the table. "Yes. It was Zachary, to confirm getting together on Thursday."

"Something nice and normal," her grandfather said.

"Is it?" Polly asked. "He did see someone from three thousand years ago."

"All Hallows' Eve," the bishop murmured.

"At least he'll get you away from here," her grandmother said. "Strange, isn't it, that he should know about the Ogam stones."

Polly nodded. "Zachary tends to know all kinds of odd things. But what happened this morning is beyond me."

The bishop said gently, "Three thousand years beyond you, Polly. And, somehow or other, I seem to be responsible for it."

Mr. Murry went to the dresser and picked up one of the Ogam stones. "Nason, one reason I've tended to disbelieve you is that, if what you say is true, then you, a theologian and not a scientist, have made a discovery which it has taken me a lifetime to work out."

"Blundered into it inadvertently," the bishop said.

Mr. Murry sighed. "I thought I understood it. Now I'm not sure."

"Granddad. Please explain."

Mr. Murry sat down again, creakily. "It's a theory of time, Polly. You know something about my work."

"A little."

"More than Nase, at any rate. You have a much better science background. Sorry, Nase, but—"

"I know," the bishop said. "This is no time for niceties." He looked at Mrs. Murry. "Would it be possible for me to have another helping of pancakes?" Then, back to Mr. Murry: "This tesseract theory of yours—"

Mrs. Murry put another stack of pancakes on the bishop's plate.

Mr. Murry said, "Tessering, moving through space without the restrictions of time, is, as you know, a mind thing. One can't make a machine for it. That would be to distort it, disturb the space/time continuum, in a vain effort to relegate something full of blazing glory to the limits of technology. And of course that's what's happening, abortive attempts at spaceships designed to break the speed of light and warp time. It works well in the movies and on TV but not in the reality of the created universe."

"What you ask is too difficult," the bishop said. "How many people are willing to take lightning into their bodies?"

Mr. Murry smiled, and to Polly it was one of the saddest smiles she had ever seen. "You are," her grandfather said.

The bishop said softly, "*It was as if lightning flashed into my spirit . . . and with the light such a profound peace and joy came into my heart. In one moment I felt as if wholly revitalized by some infinite power, so that my body would be shattered like an earthen vessel.*" He sighed. "That's John Thomas, a Welshman in the mid-1700s. But it's a good description, isn't it?"

"Very good," Mr. Murry agreed. "But it also shocks me."

"Why?" the bishop asked.

"Because you know more than I do."

"No—no—"

"But you don't know enough, Nase. You've opened a time gate that Annie—Anaral, whatever her name is— seems to be able to walk through and which has drawn Polly through it, and I want it closed."

Close it! How could it be closed!

The door had been opened, and the winds of time were blowing against it, keeping it from closing, almost taking it off the hinges.

"No!" Polly cried, stopping her grandfather in mid-sentence. "You can't forbid me to go to the star-watching rock!"

Her grandfather sighed heavily. "What a lifetime of working with the nature of the space/time continuum has taught me is that we know very little about space, and even less about time. I don't know whether you and Nase have actually gone back three thousand years, or whether those young snow-capped mountains are some kind of hallucination. But I do know that you're in our care, and we are responsible for you."

The bishop poured more syrup onto his pancakes. "Certainly some of the responsibility is mine."

Polly looked into his eyes, a faded silver that still held light, but there was nothing of the fanatic, of the mad-man, in his steady gaze.

Mr. Murry said, "Nase, you've got to keep Polly out of this. You don't know enough. We human creatures can make watches and clocks and sensitive timing devices, but we don't understand what we're timing. When something has happened—"

"It doesn't vanish," the bishop said. "It makes waves, as sound does. Or a pebble dropped into a pond."

"Time waves?" Polly suggested. "Energy waves? Something to do with $E = mc^2$?"

Nobody responded. Mr. Murry started clearing the table, moving creakily, as though his joints pained him more than usual. Mrs. Murry sat looking out the window at the distant hills, her face unreadable.

"I don't know what to do about this." Mr. Murry turned from the sink to look directly at Polly. "When we told your parents we'd love to have you come stay with us, it never occurred to your grandmother and me that you might get involved with Nase's discoveries."

"We didn't take them seriously enough," her grandmother said. "We didn't want to."

"Under the circumstances," her grandfather said, "should we send Polly home?"

"Granddad!" Polly protested.

"We can't keep you prisoner here," her grandmother said.

"Listen." Polly was fierce. "I don't think you can send me away. Really. If I'm into this tesseract thing that Bishop Colubra has opened—because that's what's happened, isn't it?—then if you try to take me out of it, wouldn't that do something to—maybe rip—the space/ time continuum?"

Her grandfather walked to the windows, looked out across his garden, then turned. "It is a possibility."

"If time and space are one—" the bishop suggested, then stopped.

"So it might," Polly continued, "rip me, too?"

"I don't know," her grandfather said. "But it's a risk I'd rather not take."

"Look"—the bishop clapped his hands together softly—"Thursday is All Hallows' Eve. Samhain, as Annie and Karralys might call it. The gates of time swing open most easily at this strange and holy time. If Polly will be willing to stay home just until after Thursday night—"

"Zachary's coming Thursday afternoon," Polly reminded them. "I can't very well tell Zachary that I can't go anywhere with him because Bishop Colubra's opened a tesseract and somehow or other I've blundered into it." She tried to laugh. "Is Zachary in it, too?"

The bishop shook his head slowly. "I think not. No. His seeing Karralys when he came to our time is one thing. Going through the time gate himself is quite another."

"If Zachary hasn't gone through the time gate, then he's not in the tesseract?"

"I think not," the bishop repeated. "Nor is Louise, even if—whether she believes it or not—she saw Annie."

"Polly," Mr. Murry queried, "you're sure Zachary saw this person?"

"Well, Granddad, yes."

Her grandfather had the hot water running, and he held his hands under the tap, nodding slowly. "Going somewhere with Zachary should be all right. Away from here, but not too far away. Nowhere near the star-watching rock."

"Just lie low till after Samhain," the bishop urged. "And don't go swimming unless one of your grandparents is with you."

She nodded. "Okay. Samhain. What does that mean?"

"It's the ancient Celtic New Year's festival, when the animals were brought down from their grazing grounds for the winter. The crops were harvested, and there was a great feast. Places were set at the festival dinner for those who had died during the previous year, as a sign of honor and faith in the continuing of the spirits of the dead."

"It sounds like a sort of combination of Halloween and Thanksgiving," Polly said.

"And so it was. Pope Gregory III in the eighth century dedicated November 1 All Saints' Day, and October 31 was All Hallows' Eve."

"So," Mr. Murry said dryly, "the Christian Church, and not for the first time, took over and renamed a pagan holiday."

The phone rang again, interrupting them. Mr. Murry went to it. "Yes, Louise, he's here. It would seem that somehow or other Polly walked into three thousand years ago this morning, if such a thing is to be believed . . . No, I find it difficult, too . . . Yes, we'll call." He turned back to the table.

"My little sister is a doctor," the bishop said.

"All right, Nason. We know your sister is a doctor."

"I made the mistake—if it was a mistake—Annie cut her finger deeply, badly. It needed stitching, and Cub, the young healer, is not experienced enough, and Karralys was away, so I brought Annie home with me."

"To now—to the present?" Incredulity, shock, and anger combined in Mr. Murry's voice.

"Just long enough for Louise to fix her finger. I took her right back."

"Oh, Nase." Mr. Murry groaned. "You can't play around with time that way."

"I couldn't play around with Annie's finger, either."

"Did Louise go along with you in this—this—"

"She wasn't happy about it, but there we were in her office and—to tell you the truth—she had never seen Annie before, so it didn't occur to her to think in terms of three thousand years ago. Her first reaction was that Annie needed help, and quickly, so she did what had to be done. When I told her who Annie was, she didn't really believe me, and I didn't press the point. She just told me to get Annie back to wherever or whenever it was she came from as quickly as possible."

"Nason." Mr. Murry stood up, sat down again. "This isn't *Star Trek* and you can't just beam people back and forth. How did you do it?"

"Well, now, I'm not exactly sure. That's part of the problem. Don't shout at me, Alex."

"I'm beyond shouting."

"Granddad." Polly tried to calm things down. Now that her grandparents were taking charge, the adventure began to seem exciting rather than terrifying. "Your tesseract thing—what you've been working on—space travel—it's to free us from the restrictions of time, isn't it?"

"Yes. But purely for the purpose of extra-solar-system exploration. That's all. We don't know enough to play around with it, as I know from my own experience."

The bishop spoke softly. "We climbed the Matterhorn because it was there. We went to the moon because it was there. We're going to explore the farther planets in our own solar system and then in our own galaxy and look toward the galaxies beyond because they're there. I didn't come to live with Louise with any idea of finding Ogam stones, but when I found one—well, I was interested because they were there."

"Here," Mr. Murry corrected.

"Here. I may have been foolish. But neither did I expect what has happened to Polly. Child, can you lie low till the weekend? Yes, go off somewhere on Thursday with your young man. Not that I think there's any real danger. But don't go to the star-watching rock—can you wait until Sunday?"

"I don't know." Polly looked troubled. "I don't know if that would do any good, because the first time I saw Anaral it was right here, last night while I was swimming."

The bishop held up his long, thin hands in a gesture of disclaimer, shook his head. Sunlight flashed off the topaz in his ring. "I'm sorry." Then he looked at Polly. "Or am I? We may be on to something—"

"Nason!" Mr. Murry warned.

Mrs. Murry hit the palm of her hand softly against the table. "This is Polly's study time. I think a little return to normalcy would be a good thing. There are some books up in her room she needs to look at."

"Good," Mr. Murry said. "Perhaps this morning was just an aberration. By all means let's try to return to normal."

Polly rose, went to the bishop. "This Ogam writing. You said it's an alphabet. Do you have it written down? I mean, so that I could make sense of it?"

"Yes. At home."

"Could I see it, please?"

"Of course. I have what may be no more than my own

version of Ogam in a notebook, but it's helped me translate the Ogam stones. I'll bring it over this afternoon."

Mrs. Murry started to intervene, then closed her mouth.

"Thanks, Bishop," Polly said, and turned to go upstairs.

Up in her room Polly simply sat for a few minutes in the rocking chair, not reaching for the books. What she would have liked to do was go out to the star-watching rock. She was no longer afraid of being trapped in past time. Somehow the threshold was open to her, as it was to Anaral. But her grandparents would be upset and angry. Would it truly help if she stayed around the house until after Thursday?

Polly turned toward her night table and reached for the books. Studying for her grandparents was a tangible reality, a relief after the almost dream world of the lake and village of three thousand years ago. Yes, she wanted to learn Ogam. If Anaral could learn English from the bishop, Polly could learn Ogam.

Meanwhile, she would study. The Murrys were more demanding than her teachers at Cowpertown High had been, and she was delighted at their challenge.

She turned to the first book in the pile. All the books had been marked with slips of paper. The first was by John Locke, a seventeenth-century philosopher—she knew that much, thanks to Max, who had frequently augmented whatever Polly was given at Cowpertown High. These were Locke's impressions of America, idyllic and, she thought, a little naïve. But Locke was writing from the far past (though only centuries ago, not millennia) when the new continent was fresh and still uncorrupted by the accumulated evils of the Old World. The naked Amerindians seemed to Locke to live a life as innocent as Adam and Eve in the Garden. They lived without external laws, did not buy or sell or pile up wealth. They were, Locke implied, without shame, not burdened by the guilts of the past.

The book on her lap, Polly rocked, thought. There was no evidence that there had ever been Celts or druids on these shores when the early settlers landed. Had they been assimilated into the local tribes, as Karralys and Tav seemed to have been taken into Anaral's people? Gone back to Britain? If there really were druids in New England three thousand years ago, what had happened to them?

She sighed, opened the second book to the page her grandmother had marked. It was by Alexis de Tocqueville, writing in the troubled period of Andrew Jackson, when the Indians were treated with terrible unfairness, and yet Tocqueville wrote that the settlers in America "had arrived at a state of democracy without having to endure a democratic revolution" and that they were "born free without having to become so."

Still true? Polly thought of herself as having been born free, and yet in the short span of her life she had witnessed much abuse of freedom. Surely the lusts and guilts and greeds of the Old World had taken root in the New. And despite her affection for the natives of Gaea, for the Quiztano Indians in Venezuela, she was leery of the concept of the "noble savage." People, in her experience, were people, some good, some bad, most a mixture.

Next in the pile was *Lectiones geometricae*, published by Isaac Barrow in 1670, and despite Polly's proficiency with languages she could not concentrate on the Old Latin, so she put it aside for when she could focus better. She read a marked chapter in a history of the sixteenth century, learning that Giordano Bruno had been burned at the stake for heresy, including the proposal, horrifying to the Church establishment of those days, that there are as many times as there are planets.

—And even one planet, Polly thought,—has many time zones, and when we try to cross them too quickly we get jet lag. And even in one zone, time doesn't move at a steady rate.

She remembered a day of lying in bed with flu and fever, every joint aching, and the day dragged on and on, far longer than an ordinary day. And then there was a New Year's Eve party at Max's beautiful plantation house, Beau Allaire, with Max sparkling as brightly as the crystal chandeliers, and there had been singing and charades and the evening passed in the twinkling of an eye. Poor Giordano Bruno. He was probably right about time. How many people have been burned at the stake for being right?

Then came a book by an eighteenth-century philosopher, Berkeley. She sat with the book unopened on her lap. Max had talked to her about this philosopher, who was also a bishop (was he anything like Bishop Colubra?), who had had the idea, amazing in his day, that the stairs outside his study were not there unless he was aware of them, that things had to be apprehended to *be*. "The anthropic principle," Max had called it, and had seen it as both fascinating and repellent.

If Polly did not believe that she had seen and talked with Anaral, would that keep the other girl in the past where she belonged? Would it close the threshold? But she had seen Anaral, and there was no way she could pretend that she hadn't. The threshold was open.

Last in the pile was a copy of the *New England Journal of Medicine* with an article by her grandmother on the effect of the microscopic on the macroscopic universe. What might seem to have been a random assortment of books was beginning to reveal a pattern, and the pattern seemed to Polly to have something to do with Anaral and the Ogam stones, though she did not think that her grandmother had had either Anaral or the Ogam stones in mind when she had chosen the readings, any more than she had had Polly in mind when she redecorated the bedroom.

Polly studied for a couple of hours, making notes, absorbing, so that she would be able to answer her grandparents' questions. She was fully focused in the present moment, and she did not know what made her look at her watch. It was after eleven. One of her jobs was to drive to the post office for the mail. If something was needed for lunch or dinner, her grandmother would leave a note with the outgoing mail.

She went downstairs. No one in the living room or kitchen. Her grandmother's lab door was closed, but Polly knocked.

"What?" came the not very gracious response.

"It's Polly. Is it all right if I get the mail and go to the store?"

"Oh, Polly, come in. I didn't mean to snarl. I suppose it's no use wishing Nase had never retired and come to live with Louise." Her grandmother was sitting on her tall lab stool. There was an electron microscope in front of her, but the cover was over it and looked as though it had not been removed in years. She wore a tweed skirt, lisle stockings, a turtleneck, and a cardigan—a down-to-earth country woman. And yet Polly knew that her grandmother delved deep into the world of the invisible, the strange sub-microscopic world of quantum mechanics. Her grandfather looked most comfortable in an old plaid flannel shirt, riding his tractor; and yet he had actually gone into space, orbiting the earth beyond the confines of the atmosphere. Her grandparents seemed to live comfortably in their dual worlds, the daily world of garden, kitchen, house, and pool, and the wider world of their scientific experiments. But Bishop Colubra had thrown them completely off course, Bishop Colubra and Polly's own unexpected journey through time.

"Grand?"

"I don't know, Polly. I don't know what your parents would say . . ." Her voice trailed off.

"Just to the post office and the store, Grand. I didn't want to go without asking you."

Her grandmother sighed. "Have I been living in a dream world? The only piece of equipment in my lab that gets any real use is the obsolete Bunsen burner, because it's become family tradition. Like your grandfather, I've been doing thought experiments." As Polly looked at her questioningly she continued, "Alex and I have sat in our separate worlds, doing experiments in our minds."

"And?" Polly prodded.

"If a thought experiment is capable of laboratory

proof, then we're apt to write a paper about it, and then either we or another scientist will put it to the test. But quite a few thought experiments are so wildly speculative that it will be a long time before they can be proven."

Which was more of a dream? The thought experiments in the minds of her grandparents and other scientists? Or the world of three thousand years ago which was touching on their own time?

The lab was damp. Polly wondered how her grandmother stood it. The floor was made of great slabs of stone. There was a faded rag rug in front of two shabby easy chairs, and the lamp on the table between them gave at least an illusion of warmth. Only the permeating cold grounded her in present reality. "Grand?"

"What is it, Polly?"

"The post office?"

"I suppose so. We can't keep you wrapped in cotton wool. I'm not even sure what we're afraid of."

"That I'll get lost three thousand years ago? I don't think that's going to happen."

"Neither do I. I still haven't given it my willing suspension of disbelief. But just the post office."

"We're out of milk."

"All right. The store. But check in with me when you get back."

"Sure."

Polly would keep her word and go only to the post office and the store. What she wanted was to talk to Anaral again. Go to the Grandfather Oak and see Karralys and his dog and hope that this time he would stay and talk with her.

Thursday was All Hallows' Eve and Bishop Colubra took it with great seriousness. Samhain. A festival so old that it predated written history. Polly's skin prickled, not with fear now, but with expectation, though for what she was not sure. All she knew was that she was touching on that long-gone age as it rose out of the past to touch on another age, a present that was perhaps as brutal as any previous age, but was at least familiar.

Her grandparents' car was elderly, and it took a few tries before the engine turned over and she shifted into reverse and pulled out of the garage. She went to the post office, to the store, speaking to the postmistress and the checkout girl, who were curious and friendly and already knew her by name.

When she got home, her grandmother had left the lab and was making toasted cheese sandwiches for lunch. They had just finished eating and were putting the dishes away when they heard a car pull up noisily. Bishop Colubra.

"Just a quick visit," he said. "Louise made me promise to come right back. I just wanted to bring Polly my Ogam notebook." He sat down at the table, indicated the chair next to him, and spread out the book between them.

It was tidily and consistently done, vocabulary, and simple rules of grammar, and a few phrases and idioms. "Druids had a vast amount of information in their memories after long years of training, but Ogam was an oral language rather than a written one. What I have here is in no way pure Ogam. It's what Anaral and Karralys and the People of the Wind speak today—their today, that is."

In three columns he had listed words used by Anaral's people before Karralys and Tav came; then there were words which were strictly Ogam and which Karralys and Tav had brought to the language; plus a short column of words which were still recognizable today; such as mount, glen, crag, bard, cairn.

"You can read my writing?" he asked.

"Yes, it's lots clearer than mine."

"Fascinating, isn't it, to see how language evolves. I wonder how many of our English/American words will still be around in another thousand years or so." He stood up. "I must go."

Polly picked up the notebook. "Thanks a lot, Bishop. I'm glad you've written out the pronunciation phonetically." She turned the pages, nodding, while he stood on one leg, scratching his shin with the other foot, looking more like a heron than ever.

"It's pretty arbitrary of me to call it Ogam, but it seems simplest. The language has evolved fairly easily, a sort of lingua franca."

"Bishop, you did teach Anaral to speak English?"

"Shh." He put his foot down and glanced at Mrs. Murry, who was feeding the fire, and at Mr. Murry deep in an article in a scientific journal. He leaned over the chair toward Polly "She's very bright. She learned amazingly quickly."

"But you've spent a lot of time with her."

He glanced again at her grandparents, sighed deeply. "This is no time for secrecy, is it? Yes. Whenever the time gate has opened for me, I've gone through. But you—" He shook his head. "I have to go." He ambled toward the pantry door. "You will stay close to your grandparents?"

She, too, sighed. "Yes, Bishop. I will."

Chapter Four

Polly spent several hours with Bishop Colubra's Ogam notebook. In the late afternoon her grandmother went swimming with her. Nothing happened. Anaral did not come. The evening passed quietly.

On Tuesday the bishop asked her over for tea.

"Go along," her grandmother said. "I know you're going stir-crazy here, and even though I don't think anything will happen while I'm with you, refusing to believe that three thousand years ago can touch directly on our own time, I'm just as happy to have you away from the pool."

"You don't need the car?"

"I'm not going anywhere. Louise's house is no distance as the crow flies. Our land is contiguous with hers. But by car you have to go down to the main road, drive west a couple of miles, and then turn uphill to the right the first chance you get."

The phone rang. Zachary. Obviously wanting to talk. "Polly, I'm just so glad to be in touch with you again. You're like a bright light in these filthy days."

"Autumn seems pretty glorious to me."

"Not in an office that's a small box with no windows. I can't wait to see you."

"I'm looking forward to it, too."

"Polly, I don't want to hurt you."

Her grandmother had left the kitchen and gone out to the lab, leaving Polly alone with the phone. "Why should you hurt me?"

"Polly, it's my pattern. I hurt every girl I get involved with. I hurt you last summer."

"Not really," she protested. "I mean, it turned out all right."

"Because your friends came and rescued us after I'd upset that idiot little canoe. But you're right. That was minor, compared to—"

He sounded so desperate that she asked, gently, "Compared to what, Zach?"

"Polly, I'm a self-protective bastard. All I think of is my own good."

"Well, don't we all, to some extent?"

"To some extent, yes. But I take it beyond some extent."

"Hey, are you at work?"

"Yah, but don't worry, I'm alone in my box and

things are slow today. I'm not goofing off. There's nothing for me to do right now. I just want to say that I'm going to try really hard not to hurt you."

"Well. Okay. That's good."

"You don't believe me."

"Sure I believe you, that you're not going to hurt me."

"No, what I mean is, how self-serving I am. Listen. Once I was with a girl I really liked. Her grandfather was sick, dying, really, and we went to the hospital to get blood for him, and she was upset, of course, really upset. And there was a little kid she knew there, and the little kid was having a seizure—well, Polly, the thing is that I really don't know what happened because I ran out on it."

"What?" She kept her voice gentle.

"I ran away. I couldn't take it. I got into my car and drove off. I just left her. That's the kind of putrid stinker I am."

"Hey, Zach, don't put yourself down. That's in the past. You wouldn't do it again."

"I don't know what I'd do, that's the point."

"Listen, Zachary, don't get stuck in the past. Give yourself a chance. We do learn from our mistakes."

"Do we? Do you really think so?"

"Sure. I've made plenty. And I've learned from them."

"Good, then. All I wanted to say is that I think you're terrific, and I want us to have a good time on Thursday, and I don't want to do or say anything to hurt you."

"We'll have a good time on Thursday," she promised.

"Okay, then. Till Thursday. I'm glad you're on this earth, Polly. You're good for me. Goodbye."

She was baffled by his call. What on earth was he afraid he would do that would hurt her? She shrugged, went out to the pantry, and took the red anorak off the hook, knocked on the lab door. "Grand, can I help with anything before I go?"

"Not a thing. Just be back in plenty of time for dinner. I'm sorry to be having an attack of mother hen-ism, but I can't wipe out your experience of crossing a time threshold just because it's totally out of the context of my own experience."

"I keep asking myself—did it really happen? But, Grand, I think it did."

"Go have tea with Nase." Her grandmother's voice was slightly acid. "Perhaps he'll see fit to tell you more than he's told us."

As Polly drove up the hill to Dr. Louise's yellow house, surrounded by maples and beeches dropping yellow leaves, the bishop came out to meet her, led her in, took the red anorak.

Dr. Louise's kitchen was smaller than the Murrys', and darker, but large enough for a sizable oak table by the window, and brightened by a surprising bouquet of yellow roses as well as copper pots and pans. The bishop took something lopsided out of the oven.

"Alex's breadmaking challenged me. This is supposed to be Irish soda bread, but I don't think it's a success."

"It'll probably taste wonderful," Polly said, "and I'm hungry."

The bishop put the bread out, with butter, jam, and a pitcher of milk. "Tea, milk, or cocoa?"

"Cocoa would be lovely. It's cold today."

"Perfect autumn weather, pushing sixty. Sit down, be comfortable."

Polly sat, while the bishop puttered about making two steaming mugs of cocoa, slicing the soda bread, which did indeed taste better than it looked, especially with homemade rose-hip jelly.

"What happens to what's happened?" Polly asked him.

"It's a big question," the bishop said. "I seem to have found one time gate. There may be countless others."

"What was going on three thousand years ago?" she continued.

"Abraham and Sarah left home," the bishop said, "and went out into the wilderness. But there were already Pharaohs in Egypt, and the Sphinx was asking her riddles."

"What else?"

"Gilgamesh," the bishop continued. "I think he was around then."

"But he wasn't from anywhere around here."

"Uruk," the bishop said. "Way on the other side of

the world. And there was Sumerian poetry, lamenting the death of Tammuz, the shepherd god." He sliced more bread. "Tammuz's mother was the goddess Innini. Let me see. Back to Egypt. That wasn't anywhere around here, either. The great pyramid was built at Giza. The Cheops pyramid conforms in dimensions and layout to astronomical measurements—like Stonehenge, in astronomy, if not in architecture. The stars have taught us more than we realize." He was rambling on happily. "I wonder what it would be like on a planet where the atmosphere was too dense for the stars to shine through? This bread isn't that bad, after all."

"Bishop, please." Polly smoothed jam onto her bread. "Maybe you've told my grandparents, but how did you meet Anaral and Karralys? When?"

"It started last spring." The bishop folded his legs and made himself comfortable, a piece of bread and jelly in his hand. "I'd never before been so unbusy in my life, and I was wandering around looking for odd jobs to do and came across an old root cellar behind the barn where Louise parks her car. At least, it was called a root cellar, and in the days when it was assumed that one could protect oneself from a nuclear attack some of the old root cellars came into reuse as bomb shelters."

"Fat lot of help they'd be," Polly said.

"Louise never bothered with hers. She always said that when she retired she'd have a garden and put it back to its original use, a storage place for tubers. But the thing is, some of the old root cellars were not built as root cellars."

"What, then?"

"They were dug centuries before the people we know as the first settlers came over from England, and they were dug to be holy places, where the priests or druids or whoever they were could go to commune with the dead, and with the gods of the underworld. They believed that those who had died were still available for advice and help, back for countless generations."

"Oh, I like that," Polly said. "Do my grandparents have a root cellar?"

"They used to, but when they put in the pool it got dug up, so I had only Louise's to excavate, and I spent weeks on it, with a trowel, then a shovel. And there I found the first of the Ogam stones, and the only one not on your grandparents' land. Over the years, the root cellar had filled in with leaves, loose dirt, other debris, and this had protected the stone. The writing on that first one was far clearer than those I've found in the stone walls."

"What did it say?"

"It was a memorial marker honoring our foremothers."

A car door slammed outside, and Dr. Louise came in, calling, "Hallo, I'm earlier than I thought I'd be. I hope there's tea left for me."

"Plenty," the bishop said. "I made a large pot, and Polly and I've been drinking cocoa instead."

Dr. Louise shucked off her heavy jacket and then her white coat, both of which she hung on deer antlers to the side of the door. "I inherited the antlers with the house."

Polly laughed. "You don't strike me as a hunter."

"Hardly." The doctor helped herself to bread and butter. "Nase, you're really becoming domesticated in your old age. This isn't half bad."

"It looks better now than when I took it out of the oven."

"Bishop," Polly said softly, "please go on."

"If I am right about root cellars, and of course I may not be, they were ancient time devices, a way the druids could commune with their past, with their gods, with powers of both good and evil long lost to us. You might call the root cellar a three-thousand-year-old time capsule."

"Have you been watching too much TV?" Dr. Louise asked.

"It's probably affected my metaphors," her brother agreed. "All spring the root cellar kept drawing me, but also sending me out. I found other Ogam stones in Alex and Kate's stone walls, worked on translating their hieroglyphs. Found three in a small cairn of stones near your star-watching rock, Polly. I knew there was something special about the star-watching rock. That it was a place of power. Benign power."

Polly said, "It was always a special place to my mom and her sibs. Go on, please, Bishop."

"In mid-June, as the days lengthened toward the summer solstice, an early heat wave hit us, and the root cellar was cool, so I spent more time there. Not digging anymore. Just sitting. Often moving beyond thought into the dark and timeless space of contemplation."

"I was afraid you were becoming a pagan," Dr. Louise remarked with irony.

"No, Louise, no. I was not then and am not now turning to the old gods. No, the God I have tried to serve all my life is still good enough for me. Christ didn't just appear as Jesus of Nazareth two thousand years ago, don't forget. Christ is, will be, and certainly was at the time the druids dug the root cellar three thousand years ago, just as much as now. But we rational and civilized people have turned our backs on the dark side of God because we are afraid of the numinous and the unexplainable. Forgive me, I'm preaching. I've spent so much of my life giving sermons that it's a habit I find hard to break."

"You're a good preacher," Dr. Louise said with sisterly pride.

"So, please," Polly urged.

"Midsummer's Eve," the bishop continued, "I was in the root cellar. When I called it a three-thousand-year-old time capsule, I was in a way joking. It's a metaphor that seems right. You see, what happened was that I was in the root cellar, and then, without transition, I was on the star-watching rock, and there was Anaral."

"And—"

"That first time we couldn't understand each other, except by gestures. I jumped to some conclusions, because she obviously wasn't an ordinary girl. There was a dignity, a nobility about her that set her apart. But it was a while before we knew each other's language well enough to communicate and I could truly believe that I had moved through a great deal of time."

"Bishop," Polly asked, "can you just go in and out of the time gate whenever you want to?"

"Oh, no." He shook his head. "I'm not sure how it happens when it happens. There is a feeling, just as you said, of lightning, and the earth quivering, if not quaking, and something seems to happen to the air. After that first time it has never again been from the root cellar, always from the star-watching rock. I go there and wait, and sometimes Annie or Karralys will come to me. But there will be weeks when nothing happens."

Dr. Louise said, "Thanks for the tea. I have some charts to go over."

The bishop was stiff. "I know it offends you, Louise. I try not to talk about it in front of you."

"That's not the solution, either," the doctor said. "I

keep wondering what Polly's family would make of your madness." She turned to Polly. "Are you going to tell them about this?"

"Of course. But not yet. I need to understand more, first. And I don't want to worry them."

"You may have to," the doctor said.

The bishop's eyes were closed, as though he was listening. "One of the stones from the cairn by the star-watching rock had a lovely rune on it. *Hold me in peace while sleeping. Wake me with the sun's smiling. With pure water slake my thirst. Let me be merry in your love.* That's a simplicity that's gone, at least in our so-called higher civilization."

"Don't knock our civilization," his sister warned. "Cataracts used to make people blind, and still do, in many parts of the world. Your lens implants have you seeing like a much younger man."

"That's technology, not civilization." The bishop was testy. "I'm grateful every day that I can read and write. I don't underestimate knowledge. But we get into trouble when we confuse it with truth."

"All right, Nase."

"Truth is eternal. Knowledge is changeable. It is disastrous to confuse them."

"My dear, I don't," Dr. Louise said. "But I can conceive of your adventures as having little to do with either knowledge or truth. They're beyond reason. And now I'm afraid they've made Kate and Alex terribly upset."

"I'm sorry," the bishop said. "I didn't expect Polly to become involved. If I've been closemouthed up till now, it has been not only because of your distaste for what has been happening but because I thought it was my own, unique adventure. I never expected that Polly—I simply have to have faith that all this has meaning."

Dr. Louise sighed, rose. "I really do have to go over charts."

Polly, too, stood. "I'd better get on back. I promised I wouldn't be late."

She drove off down the long dirt road. The tree frogs were singing their autumn farewell to summer. A few lingering insects chirred away. Above her flew a great gaggle of geese, honking their way south. Their haunting cry was new to Polly, and she found it both exciting and sad. On either side of the road, bushes were red and rust-colored. There was some dry-looking goldenrod and joe-pye weed. As she turned into a curve, she could see the hills shadowed in purple. Low hills weathered by centuries. Comforting hills.

When her grandmother came in to say good night, Polly was deep in Bishop Colubra's notebook.

"This Ogam's really not too difficult, as long as I don't try to connect it to Latin or Greek roots but think of it as a made-up language."

"Polly." Her grandmother sat on the edge of the bed.

"It is my hope that you are not going to have any opportunity to speak this language."

"I love languages, Grand. They're fun. You know how Granddad loves to do his puzzle in the paper every day? It's the same sort of thing."

Her grandmother ruffled her hair. "I want you to have fun, my dear, but not to get yourself into any kind of danger. I hope you'll have fun with Zachary on Thursday. But he strikes me as a complex young man, and I'm very uncomfortable with the idea that you think he's seen someone from the past."

"I find it pretty uncomfortable, too."

"And you'll stay away from the pool and the star-watching rock?"

"Yes. We will." Polly sighed, then indicated the pile of books still on her bed table. "I went through the parts you marked and took notes. I love learning from you, Grand."

"You don't miss school?"

"I didn't much like it. I was used to being taught by Mother and Daddy when we lived on Gaea, and the Cowpertown school was pretty boring after that. I wasn't that great at school. Okay, but not great."

"Your mother must have understood that. School was disastrous for her till she went to college."

"I find that hard to believe."

"Believe it."

"But she's so brilliant."

"She's good at the difficult stuff, but not with the easy, and I guess you're not unlike her in that."

"Well—maybe. Like Zachary, I'm better if I'm interested. The only teacher I really liked left. And last year I could go to Beau Allaire and do homework there and Max could make it interesting."

"Her death must be a great grief to you." Her grandmother touched her gently on the knee.

"Yes. It is. But Max would want me to get on with life, and that's what I'm trying to do. But I do miss . . ." For a moment her voice trembled.

"Max was very close to Sandy and Rhea, too. Sandy says her death has left a big hole in their lives."

"I guess the planet is riddled with holes, isn't it? From all the people who've lived and then died. Do the holes ever get filled?"

"That's a good question."

"Grand, those people I saw when I went back— Anaral and—Maybe you don't want to talk about it?"

"Go on."

"They've been dead maybe three thousand years." She shuddered involuntarily. "What about their holes? Are the holes just always there, waiting to be filled?"

"You have always tended to ask unanswerable questions. I don't know about those holes. All I know is that Max gave you great riches, and we would, all of us, be less than we are if it weren't for those we love and who've loved us who have died." Her grandmother rose, bent down, and kissed Polly. "Good night, my dear. Sleep well."

Polly woke up, freezing. Her quilt had slid to the floor. She was caught in a dream, not quite a nightmare, of Zachary driving along a winding road in the bishop's blue pickup truck. She was in the back of the truck and icy rain was drenching her. Every time Zachary hit a bump, she was nearly thrown out. To one side of the road was a cliff, to the other a drop down to a valley far below. The truck hit a bump and—

She woke up. Hadron's warm body was not by her. She picked up the quilt and huddled under it. Her feet were like ice. There was no way she was going to be able to escape the dream and go back to sleep until she warmed up.

The meaning of the dream was apparent to her. It was simply her reaction to Zachary's phone call and had, she thought, no particular meaning of its own. She had dreamed of the rain chilling her because the quilt had slid off the bed and she was frozen. The wind hit against the house, emphasizing the cold.

The pool. It was by far the warmest place in the house. Forgetting her promises, forgetting for the moment the reason for them, aware only that she was shivering, she tiptoed downstairs. All the fires were banked. The house was cold. She opened the door to the room with the pool and was met with a humid warmth and a green smell from all the plants which flourished there.

Moonlight was coming through the skylights. The plants hanging in the windows made strange shadows. Then, as her eyes adjusted, she saw an unexpected shadow, a darkness in one of the poolside chairs. Someone was sitting there.

Terrified, she reached for the light switch and the room was flooded with light.

Anaral leapt from the chair like a wild gazelle, more frightened than Polly. Surely Anaral's world knew electricity only as lightning unleashed and dangerous.

Polly's heart stopped pounding in her throat. "Lights. Electric lights. Don't be afraid."

Anaral capsized, rather than sat back down. "Bishop told me about lights. Yes. Still, it frightens me. No one can hear us?"

"Not if we're quiet. How did you get here?"

"I came from our great standing stones to this place of water in a box." Anaral was referring to the pool, the pool that was over an underground river. "Where your water in the box is in your time circle, in my circle it is our most holy ground, the stones that stand over the scent of water. I lay on the sarsen and I thought about you and I called myself to you. And I came." She looked at Polly with a delighted smile. Then she got up and walked slowly around the room, looking at the poolside chairs, the stationary bike Polly's grandmother used when the weather was too inclement for walking outside. "Bishop says you live in house. We are in house?"

"Yes. This is the new wing, built for the pool—the water in a box." Of course Anaral would know nothing about a house or its contents.

Anaral picked up a paperback book lying on a small table by the chair where she had been sitting. "One day Bishop brought book to show me. Bishop says you have stories in books."

"Many stories."

"Karralys says that for stories the writing has to be more—more full than ours, less simple."

"Yes, more complex."

Anaral touched her forehead. "Druids have stories here. Many stories. We keep the memory. Without our memory we would be—less. I do not know the word."

"Our books are like keepers of the memory. In them we have the stories of many people, many times, many cultures."

"Cultures?"

"People who live in different circles of place, as well as time."

Anaral nodded. "You are certain you are not a druid?"

Polly laughed. "Positive."

"But you have gifts. You cross the threshold of time. To do that requires much training, and Karralys was concerned that, though I have the training, no threshold was open to me. But then I saw Bishop before he did, and now I am practicing using the gift and the training by coming to you. And you crossed into my time."

Polly spread out her hands. "I don't know how I did it, Anaral. I haven't any idea. I don't know if I could ever do it again."

"Karralys has been to many places, to many different times. I have crossed only one threshold, seen only you and Bishop. Karralys says that there is meaning that you have come, meaning for the pattern."

"What pattern?"

"The pattern of lines drawn between the stars, between people, between places, between circles, like the line between the great stone and the water in a box."

Polly thought of the book of constellations in her room, with the lines drawn between the stars.

Anaral looked at her, smiling. "It is nice, what I sit on."

"A chair."

"At the great stones there are chairs, but very different, carved out of stone. This holds my body with more ease."

Polly wondered what Anaral would think of the rest of the house, of the bedroom, the kitchen. All the things that Polly took for granted, hot running water, toilets, refrigerators, microwave, food processor—would they seem like miracles to Anaral, or would she think them magic, perhaps evil magic? "Anaral, I'm very glad to see you, even in the middle of the night. But—why have you come?"

"To see if I could," Anaral said simply. "Everybody else was asleep, so I could practice the gift all alone. I came and I called you. To know you. To know why you can come to my circle of time. To know if you have been sent to us by the Presence."

"The Presence?"

"The One who is more than the Mother, or the goddess. Starmaker, wind-breather, earth-grower, sun-riser, rain-giver. The One who cares for all. Karralys says that it happens only once or twice in a pattern where the lines touch so that circles of time come together with the threshold open in both directions. When this happens, there is a reason."

"Have you asked the bishop?"

"Bishop, too, says there is a reason. But he does not know what. Do you?"

Polly shook her head. "Haven't the foggiest."

"The—"

"I don't know the reason, Anaral. But I like you. I'm glad you're here. I would like to get to know you better."

"Friends?"

"Yes. I'd like to be friends."

"It is lonely for druids, sometimes. Friends care for each other."

"Yes."

"Protect each other?"

"Friends do everything they can to protect each other."

"But it is not always possible." Anaral shook her head. "In a terrible storm, or when lightning starts fire, or when other tribes attack."

"Friends try," Polly said firmly. "Friends care." She felt deeply drawn to Anaral. Was it possible to develop a real friendship with a girl from three thousand years ago? "I would like to be your friend, Anaral."

"That is good. I am your friend." Anaral stood up. "Bishop calls me Annie."

"Yes. Annie."

"I willed for you to wake up, to come here, to water in a box. And you came. Thank you."

"The quilt fell off my bed. I was cold." Quilt. Bed. It would make no sense to Anaral.

"You came, Polly. Now I go." Anaral went to one of the north windows. "See? Now I know how to open it." She jumped lightly down and ran off into the night.

Polly looked after her until she disappeared into the woods. Then she closed the window. She stayed by the pool for several more minutes, but nothing happened.

The water was quiet. She sat in one of the poolside chairs, wondering, until she grew drowsy and her eyelids drooped. She was warm now. Even her toes. Had Anaral been part of a dream? She went upstairs. Perhaps she would understand more in the morning.

She woke later than usual, dressed, and went downstairs. Her grandfather was sitting at the table drinking coffee and doing his puzzle. Polly poured herself half a cup of coffee, filled it with milk, and put it in the microwave. For the moment she had forgotten her bad dream, forgotten going down to the pool to warm up, forgotten Anaral's visit. "This does make *café au lait* much easier. I hate washing out a milky saucepan."

"Polly." Her grandfather looked up from the paper. "Tell me what you know about time."

She sat down. "I don't know that much."

"Tell me what you know."

"Well, there's the—uh—the space/time continuum, of course."

"And that means?"

"Well, that time isn't a separate thing, apart from space. They make a thing together, and that's space/time. But I know that there isn't any time at all if there isn't mass in motion."

Her grandfather nodded. "Right. And Einstein's famous equation?"

"Well, mass and energy are equivalent, so any energy an object uses would add to its mass, and that would make it harder to increase its speed."

"And as it approached the speed of light?"

"Its mass would be so enormous that it couldn't ever get to the speed of light."

"So in terms of space travel?"

"You can't separate space travel from time travel."

"Good girl. So?"

"I don't know, Granddad. How did I go back three thousand years?" Suddenly she remembered Anaral's visit the night before, but this was not the moment to talk about it.

The pantry door opened and her grandmother came in.

Her grandfather said, "That's the billion-dollar question, isn't it?"

"And I seem to have broken Einstein's equation. I mean, didn't I get there faster than the speed of light? I mean, I was here, and then I was there."

"Department of utter confusion," her grandfather said.

Mrs. Murry sliced bread and put it in the toaster. "One theory I find rather comforting is that time exists so that everything doesn't happen all at once."

"What a picture!" Polly had ignored the microwave timer's ping. Now she opened the door, took out her cup, and sat at her place. Hadron got up from his scrap of rug at the fireplace, greeted her by twining about her legs, purring, then returned to the warmth.

Mrs. Murry took the bread from the toaster and put it on a plate in front of Polly. "Eat."

"Thanks. Granddad's bread makes wonderful toast."

Her grandmother continued, "Your grandfather and I have lived with contradictions all our lives. His interests have been with the general theory of relativity, which is concerned with gravity and the macrocosm. Whereas I have spent my life with the microcosm, the world of particle physics and quantum mechanics. As of now these theories appear to be inconsistent with each other."

"If we could find a quantum theory of gravity," Mr. Murry said, "we might, we just might resolve the problem."

Polly asked, "Would that explain the space/time continuum?"

"That's the hope," Mrs. Murry said, and turned to answer the phone.

And now Polly remembered her dream. Zachary. She hoped it would be Zachary on the phone.

But her grandmother said, "Good morning, Nason . . . Yes, we're all here in one place and one time . . . That's dear of you, but why don't you two come here? You know you and Louise like to swim . . . Nase, I like to cook . . . No, don't bring anything. See you this evening."

She turned to her husband and Polly. "As you gathered, that was Nason. Louise has filled him with chagrin and remorse, as a result of which she hasn't been able to talk him out of feeling that he can protect Polly from the past if he's here with her, which is certainly logic nohow contrariwise. They're coming over for dinner."

Mr. Murry smiled. "That was at least partly his motivation in calling."

His wife smiled back. "Cooking has never been Louise's thing. She's a perfectly adequate cook, but it's not foremost on her mind."

"And Nase has rather gourmet tastes," he added.

"And you're a terrific cook," Polly said.

Her grandmother flushed. "Oh, dear, it does look as though I was fishing for a compliment."

"A well-earned one," her husband said.

"I enjoy cooking. It's therapy for me. Louise's therapy is her rose garden. You may note, Polly, that we don't have any roses."

"Accept it graciously, my love," her husband said. "You're a good cook."

"Thanks, dearest." She sat down, elbows on table, chin in hands. "Polly, there is the matter of your parents."

Polly looked at her questioningly.

"Your grandfather believes that you are right, that it would not be safe to take you out of the tesseract, to send you back to Benne Seed. And if I didn't take his fear seriously, you'd be with your parents right now."

"How far can I go?" Polly asked. "How far away from the time threshold?"

Her grandfather folded his paper. "I'm not sure. About ten or so miles, I'm guessing. Maybe more. Maybe as far as Anaral and her people ranged. But not up in a plane. Not across the country."

"Well, I really am in the tesseract." And she told them about Anaral's visit.

Her grandparents gave each other troubled looks.

"Don't tell Mother and Daddy," Polly urged. "Not yet. We don't know enough. It sounds too impossible."

Her grandfather said, "If I know your father, he'd come and get you and there'd be no reasoning with him. And that could be fatal."

"I hate secrets," her grandmother said. "But I agree it would be best to keep silent for a few days."

"Till after Halloween," her grandfather said.

"Tomorrow," her grandmother added.

"Samhain," Polly said.

"We'll tell them everything on Sunday when they call," her grandmother said.

Both grandparents looked at Polly, and then at each other, unhappily.

*　*　*

The morning passed without incident. Polly spent an hour with her grandmother in the lab, till her toes grew too cold. Then she went to her room, to sit at her desk and write out responses to some of the questions her grandmother had asked her. She found it unusually difficult to concentrate. At last she shut her notebook and went downstairs. It was time for a brisk walk before lunch.

She had promised not to walk across the field to the woods and the star-watching rock, so she walked along the dirt road the house faced. Originally it had been one of the early post roads, but with the changing of demographics it was now only a lane. The garage led to a paved road, with farms above, a few dwellings below. The lane wandered along, past pastures, groves, bushes. It was a pleasant place to walk, and Polly ambled along, picking an assortment of flowering autumn weeds.

When she got home, Dr. Louise had called to say that she had an emergency and would not be able to get away for dinner. Could they come the next day? Nase very much wanted to be with Polly on Thursday.

Thursday came, crisp and beautiful. The autumn days were perfect, blue and gold, with more and more leaves falling. Polly worked with her grandfather in the morning, studying some advanced mathematics. Around eleven he took off for town to get his chainsaw sharpened, and her grandmother as usual was in the lab.

She walked to the end of the lane and back. A little over a mile. Then she crossed the field to the stone wall. She would go no farther than that. Surely just to the stone wall should be all right.

Louise the Larger was there, basking in the sun. Polly was used to all kinds of odd marine animals, and her father had once had a tank of eels for some experimental purpose, but she knew little about snakes. Polly looked at Louise, lying placidly in a puddle of golden light, but did not feel enough at ease to sit down on the wall beside her.

As though aware of her hesitancy, Louise raised her head slightly, and Polly thought the snake nodded at her kindly before sliding down into the wall and out of sight. Or was she anthropomorphizing, reading human behavior into the snake?

Snake in Ogam was *nasske*. It was on the bishop's vocabulary list. So that meant that the people who used that language knew about snakes. She continued to stare at the wall, but when there was no sign of Louise after a few minutes, Polly sat down. The stones felt warm and comforting. This was as far as she could go without breaking her promise. The breeze ruffled the leaves remaining on the trees which leaned over the wall, making shifting patterns of light and shadow. The day was gold and amber and russet and copper and bronze, with occasional flashes of flame.

A rustling sound made her turn around and there, on the other side of the wall, stood the tow-headed young man, holding his spear. He beckoned to her.

"I can't come. I'm sorry, I promised," she explained, and realized that he could not understand her.

He smiled at her. Pointed to himself. "Tav." She returned his smile.

"Polly," she replied, pointing to herself.

He repeated after her, "Poll-ee." Then he looked up, pointed at the sun, then pointed at her hair, and clapped his hands joyfully.

"I'm just an old carrot top." She blushed, because he was obviously admiring her hair.

Again he indicated the sun, and then her hair, saying, "Ha lou, Poll-ee."

She visualized a page of Bishop Colubra's notebook. Ha lou was a form of greeting. Easy enough to remember. The bishop's notebook had contained various greetings used throughout the years: hallo, hello, hail, howdy, hi. The negative, na, was also simple. No in English, non in French, nicht in German, nyet in Russian. The n sound seemed universal, she thought, except in Greek, where the neh sound meant yes.

Tav beamed, and burst into a stream of incomprehensible words.

She smiled, shaking her head. "Na." She did not have the vocabulary to say "I don't understand."

Carefully, tenderly, he placed his great spear on the ground. Then he sat beside her on the wall. Pointed to the sun. "*Sonno.*" Then, with utmost delicacy, his fingertips touched her hair, withdrew. "*Rhuadd.*" He held out his hand, spoke a word, and touched his eyes. Spoke again, and touched his nose. He was teaching her words of Ogam. Some of the words, such as *sun* and *red*, she recognized from Bishop Colubra's vocabulary list. Others were new to her. Polly was a quick study, and Tav laughed in delight. After they had worked—or played—together for half an hour, he looked at her and spoke slowly, carefully. "You, *sonno.* Tav"—he touched his pale hair—"*mona.* You come tonight."

She shook her head.

"It is big festival. Samhain. Music. Big music. Much joy."

She could understand him fairly well, but she could not yet put enough words together to explain to him that she had promised not to cross the wall, not to go to the star-watching rock. And did Tav understand that they were separated not only by the stone wall but by three thousand years?

Suddenly he leaped to his feet. Louise had come out of her hiding place. Tav reached for his spear.

"No!" Polly screamed. "Don't hurt her! She's harmless!"

If Tav did not understand her words, he could not

miss her intent. She thrust herself between the snake and the young man.

He put down the spear, careful not to bruise the feathers. "I would only protect you," he told her, in sign and body language as much as in words. "Snake has much power. *Mana* power, good power, but sometimes hurting power."

Fumblingly, Polly tried to explain that Louise was a harmless black snake, and a special one, a family friend.

Tav let her know that Louise's friendship was good. "You are gift. The Mother's gift. You will come? Tonight?"

"I cannot. I—" What was the word for promise? Or for grandparents? Mother was something like *modr*. "Mother says no." That was the best she could do.

He laughed. "Mother sent you! You will come!" He bent toward her again and delicately touched her hair with the tips of his fingers. It was like a kiss. Then he picked up his spear and walked along the path in the direction of the star-watching rock.

Polly went back to the house. His touch had been gentle, pleasing. He had actually compared her red hair to the sun. Her fear of him had vanished. But she also felt confused. Why had he been ready to kill Louise? Did he really think the snake was about to strike? What had he meant by good power and hurting power? His intent had certainly not been to kill for killing's sake, but only to protect her.

At lunch she told her grandparents about Tav. They listened, made little comment. It was evident that they were deeply concerned. "I won't cross the field to the stone wall again," she promised. "But he was nice, really he was."

"Three thousand years ago?" her grandfather asked wryly.

Her grandparents did not scold her for going to the stone wall. They were all unusually silent as they ate lunch.

Chapter Five

Promptly at two, Zachary drove up in his red sports car. It struck Polly again how sheerly felicitous he was to behold, like Hamlet, she thought, Hamlet in modern dress. Black jeans and a pale blue cashmere turtleneck, his black jacket over his arm. Dark hair framing a pale face. Tav had likened Polly to the sun, and himself to the moon. Although Zachary's hair was a dark as Tav's was fair, he was far more a moon creature than a sun creature.

He greeted her grandparents deferentially, pausing to sit and tell the Murrys a little about his work in the law office in Hartford. "Long hours at a desk," he said. "I feel as though I've come out from under a stone. But I'm lucky to have got an internship, and I'm learning a lot."

Again he was making a good impression, she thought.

"I've done some research on this Ogam stuff," he said. "As a language, it isn't that difficult, is it? It really does look as though this land was visited three thousand years ago, long before anyone thought. Primitive people weren't nearly as primitive as we'd like to think, and they did an incredible amount of traveling to all kinds of places. And druids, for instance, were not ignorant savages who did nothing but slit the throats of sacrificial victims. They could navigate by the stars, and as a matter of fact, their knowledge of astronomy was astounding."

"Bishop Colubra would agree with that," Polly said.

Her grandparents were polite, but not enthusiastic.

Zachary said, "I'd really like to talk with the bishop. My boss, whom I've been pumping, is erudite and dull."

Mr. Murry smiled. "Let's keep Polly in the twentieth century." But his smile was strained.

Zachary said, "Fine with me. Is there someplace around here we can go?"

As far as she knew, the village consisted of post office, store, church, filling station, and a farm-equipment place.

Her grandfather suggested quickly that they go to the country club, that he'd already called ahead to arrange a guest pass. Polly knew that her grandfather occasionally played golf when he needed to talk to a colleague without fear of being overheard. "It's a lovely drive," he told Zachary, "especially right now when the colors are still bright. But there's not much going on at the club this time of year if you're not a golfer."

"My pop is," Zachary said. "I plan to take it up when I'm rich and famous."

"The swimming pool is closed for the winter. But you can get a soda and there are some nice walks." It was obvious that he wanted them away from the house. And that, under the circumstances, was understandable.

"Do I look okay for the country club?" She was wearing jeans and a flannel shirt.

"You're fine," Zachary and her grandparents assured her simultaneously.

"But take a jacket," her grandmother added.

Polly and Zachary went out through the pantry and she took the red anorak off one of the hooks. Zachary pointed to the door to her grandmother's lab. "What's in there?"

"Grand's lab."

"Can we have a peek? I'm really honored to have met your grandmother, Pol, and I'd love to see where she works."

"Just a peek." She opened the door. "It's verboten to go into the lab without Grand, but she won't mind if we just look."

Zachary peered in with interest, looking at the counter with its equipment. "What's that?"

"It's an electron microscope."

"What's it for?"

"Oh, lots of things. It proved, for instance, the existence of a plasma membrane bonding each cell, separating it from the internal environment. But I don't think Grand's used it in years. Most of her work is in her head."

"Your parents are scientists, too, right?"

"My father's a marine biologist. That's why we've tended to live on islands. My mom does all his computer work. She's a mathematical whiz." She stepped back and shut the door carefully.

Zachary had not parked his car in the driveway but had left it on the dirt road which the house faced, so they walked across the lawn. "Listen," he said. "I didn't mean to turn you off with that phone call."

"You didn't." But she looked at him questioningly.

He was looking at the house. "This is beautiful, your grandparents' place. We don't have any houses anywhere near this old in California."

"I love it," she said. "I'm really happy here."

"I can understand that." He held the car door open for her. As they started off, he pointed to the wing. "Hey, is that a swimming pool?"

"Yah, a small one. The doctor recommended it for Granddad's arthritis."

"That's terrific. It's the best exercise in the world, my doctor says. Is there good skiing around here?"

"Yes. Do you ski?"

He drove slowly along the dirt road. "Oddly enough,

I do. Being a totally non-kinetic person, I'm not very good at it, but given time, I might improve. You ski?"

"I've spent my life in warm climates. But Grand says she'll go skiing with me this winter."

Once they were out on the highway, Zachary's driving reminded her of Bishop Colubra's, though it was probably a little less erratic.

"Gad, the fall's glorious," he said. "A couple of my prep schools weren't far from here. But the colors always catch me in the throat. Look at that golden tree there. There aren't many elms left. Isn't it gorgeous?"

"That it is. And there's one maple we see from the kitchen windows that's almost purple. I've never seen autumn colors before and I'm overwhelmed."

"I'm glad you were here a week ago. It's past its first glory now," Zachary said, "but it's still breathtaking."

"Here we are." Polly pointed to a sign that indicated the long driveway to the country club. At the top of the hill was a large white building with a gracious view across the valley—that valley which had been covered by a lake three thousand years ago.

Zachary led her into the bar, where he asked her what she wanted. "Don't worry, sweet Pol. I'm driving, so I'm having a Coke. Do I remember that you like lemonade?"

"You do. How nice of you to remember."

"There's not much about you I've forgotten." He ordered their drinks and they sat on high bar stools and the slanting autumn sunlight reached through the windows and touched Polly's hair. Zachary whistled. "I'd forgotten how gorgeous you are."

She could feel herself blushing. She understood that she was far better-looking now than she had been as an early adolescent, but she did not think of herself as beautiful, or even pretty, and now both Tav and Zachary were telling her that she was.

"You were lovely last summer in Greece," Zachary said, "but you're even better now. I'm glad I was able to find you."

"Me, too." She sipped at her lemonade, which was nicely tart. It had been an amazement to her the past summer in Athens that Zachary had wanted so much of her company; it was still an amazement to her.

"What do you do with yourself all day?"

"Oh, lots of things. Grand and Granddad worry about my being bored, but the days slide by so full it's hard to realize at bedtime that another day has passed."

"Full of what?"

"I study with my grandparents in the mornings. I hike. I swim. We've had friends over for dinner. It may not seem exciting, but it's just what I need." It didn't sound exciting as she told it, but although Zachary had surprised her by knowing about the Ogam stones and, even more surprising, had seen Karralys, she was not ready to tell him about Anaral or Tav.

Then he reached into his leather pouch. "I brought you a present."

"An unbirthday present!" Polly exclaimed. "Terrific."

He handed her something flat and rectangular wrapped in wrinkled pink tissue paper. She removed the paper and there was a picture, backed by a thin piece of wood, of an angel, immensely tall, with great wings, bending protectively over a small child.

"A guardian-angel icon! It's beautiful! Thank you!"

"I found it in a funny junk shop in Turkey, not long after I left you at Athens airport last summer. When I looked back to wave at you, you looked so sort of lost that I thought then that you needed a guardian angel. So, when I saw this, it made me think of you, and I got it, and thought I'd give it to you if ever we met again, and here we are."

"Thanks, Zachary. Really. Thanks a lot."

"It's not an original or anything. I don't suppose it has any real value."

"I love it." She put it carefully into the largest of the anorak pockets. "It was really nice of you to think of it."

"Why do you sound so surprised? Is it because it's a picture of an angel?"

"Well—sort of."

"I suppose I made it quite clear that I don't believe in anything."

She nodded.

"Take what you can get. Right now. Because that's all there is. That's still my policy. But I had a grandmother who really believed in angels, and that they care for us." He stopped, drained the dregs of ice from the bottom of his glass. "She loved me. Me, Zachary, not some projection."

"Grandmothers are marvelous. Mine is. And Granddad, too."

"I didn't know my grandfather that well. Pa's parents died young. The ones I knew were Ma's parents, and they lived near us. My grandfather was a champion polo player, but he was thrown from his horse and his spine was crushed. And Grandma went right on believing in angels—and in me—while he cursed from his wheelchair till the day he died. Another lemonade?"

"No, thanks."

"Shall we just drive around and see what we can see?"

"Sure. That would be nice."

For the first few miles he was silent, and Polly thought that Zachary had just revealed to her, in talking of his grandparents, more than he had been willing to show when they were together in Athens. She glanced at his face, and it seemed very thin.

"Have you lost weight?" The question slipped out before she realized that it was a personal one and shouldn't be asked.

"Some. Look, that maple's completely bare." He whistled a few notes, then said, "If autumn comes, can winter be far behind?"

"Where's the whistle you had the other day?" she asked.

"Oh, I gave it to one of the office boys. I found it used too much wind." He apologized quickly. "Sorry, Polly, sweet, sorry. I spend my days in an office, ruining my eyes and getting no exercise. At this point I don't know why I'm doing it, but I still seem to want to learn all about insurance and all the legal ramifications." He turned off onto a side road that wound through a pine forest.

"What about college?" she asked.

"I hope I can go back next semester. I'm not sure I think a college degree is really necessary, but law schools do. It's a rough world out there, and I've always been determined to equip myself for it, and college is part of the deal."

A plane droned by, far above them. She looked up but could not see it. It must have passed overhead before its sound followed it. Their road turned sharply uphill.

"What about you, Polly?"

"What about what?"

"You *are* planning to go to college?"

"Sure."

"Planning to be a scientist?"

"I don't know. I'm interested in a lot of things. One problem is—well, Max said I have too many options."

"Are you over it?"

"Over what?"

"Your friend's death."

"Zachary, you don't get over someone's death. Ever. You just learn to go on living the best way you possibly can."

"I got over Ma's death." He sighed.

Did he? Really? she wondered. And what about the grandmother who had believed in him? "I don't want to get over Max's death. She'll always be part of me and I'll be—more—because she was my friend."

"Oh, Polly." He took his hand off the steering wheel and reached out to touch her shoulder gently. "You teach me so much, and I love you for it, Polly. Polly, if I'm going to see as much of you as I want to these next few months, there's something I ought to tell you." Then he fell silent. The road came out of the woods, went past a farm, and then offered them a wide view across a valley to ranges of mountains beyond, a far more spectacular view than her grandparents' gentle one. He pulled the car over, stopped it, and sat there, staring out.

She waited. Decided he was not going to tell her whatever it was, when he said softly, "Polly, if I died, would you get over me?"

She turned to look at him.

"I've always been my own worst enemy, and now it's coming back at me." She saw his eyes fill with sudden tears.

"Zachary. What is it?"

"My heart. It's never been very good. And now——"

She looked at his white face, at the slight blueness about his lips, at his eyes trying to blink back tears. She reached out to touch him.

"Don't touch me. Please. I don't want to cry. But I don't want to die. I'm not ready. But I've only got—oh, nobody will be specific, but it's not likely I'll make it to law school."

"Oh, Zachary." She sat, not touching him, honoring his wish. "What about open-heart surgery?"

"It wouldn't help that much."

"If you take care of yourself, don't work too hard . . ."

He shook his head, reached up, and fiercely rubbed away his tears with the heel of his hand.

"Oh, Zach——"

"See, I'm hurting you just by being. I don't mean to use emotional blackmail. Polly, sweet, what I'm doing is living as though I'm going to go on living. Working in Hartford this semester. Planning on going back to college. To law school. My doctors say that's the best thing. Take it moderately easy, but live while I can. So what I'd really like is to see you sort of on a regular basis. Would that be possible?"

"Well, of course, Zach." Words seemed totally inadequate.

He started the car again and took off, far too fast. He'd

said that he didn't want to die, that he wasn't ready. He'd said that he didn't want to hurt her. "Slow down a bit, hey?" she suggested.

He took his foot off the accelerator and drove at a more moderate speed. In silence. She did not break it because there was nothing to say. When they got to her grandparents' land, he turned onto the dirt road the house faced and stopped his car by the wing with the pool.

"I've been horrible," he said. "I'm sorry."

"You haven't been horrible."

He groped toward her to kiss her and she let his lips touch hers, then gently turned away. She felt deep sympathy for him, but kissing out of sympathy could only lead to trouble.

Instead of trying to kiss her again, as she expected, he stared out the windshield. "Hey, who's that girl?"

She stared, but saw nobody. "Who?"

"She just went around the corner of your pool." He pointed.

"Who?" Polly asked again.

"A girl with a long black braid. She turned and ran."

Polly stared. There was the white wing of the addition, with lilacs planted beneath the windows, their leaves turned grey with autumn and slowly dropping to the ground. There was nobody there.

Zachary explained, "She was just walking toward

your pool. A good-looking girl. But when she saw me and I smiled at her, she took off. Like a deer."

Anaral. It had to be Anaral Zachary had seen. There was nobody else it could be. First Karralys and now Anaral—why?

"Is it someone you know?" he asked.

"Well, yes, but—"

"Listen, I didn't mean to upset you by telling you about myself. I'm sorry."

Of course she was upset. Upset in all directions.

"Polly, you know the last thing I want in the world is to hurt you. But I thought you ought to know about me. I know I've often been self-destructive, but I didn't ex-pect—" Again his dark eyes were bright with tears. Fiercely he blinked them back. "I'm sorry. This isn't fair of me. I'd better take off, and I'll see you again soon—maybe this weekend?"

She nodded slowly. Now Zachary had seen Anaral. What would her grandparents think? Bishop Colubra? She unfastened her seat belt. She was badly shaken, both by what Zachary had told her about his heart and by his having seen Anaral. Her ears were cocked for the Colubras. Perhaps if they drove up, Zachary would talk with the bishop. "Listen, are you busy this evening? Could you stay for dinner?"

"Tonight?"

"If that's okay. Dr. Louise and Bishop Colubra are

coming, and Bishop Colubra knows Anaral really well—the girl you saw." Dr. Louise, she thought, might be able to check on Zachary's doctors, see if there might be some better hope for him.

"No, sorry. I wish I could, I really do. But I promised my boss I'd have dinner with him and let him go on about Ogam. Fortunately, he doesn't try to order dinner in Ogam. He'd drop a gourd if he knew I'd seen an Ogam stone."

—If he knew Zachary had seen a girl from Ogam days . . .

"I'm free on Saturday," he continued. "Shall I come on over?"

"Yes, please do."

"Maybe we'll just go for a walk around your grandparents' place. It'll be good just to be with you. But now I really need to get back to Hartford."

Zachary got out of the car and came around to her. "Don't worry overmuch, pretty Pol. I'm not going to drop dead on you. That wouldn't be fair. I do have some time left." He hugged her briefly, and he felt painfully thin. The Colubras had not come, and probably weren't even expected for another hour.

It was All Hallows' Eve. Samhain. That made a difference. At least she was sure that the bishop would think that it did. Samhain must be why Zachary was able to see Anaral. And yet he had seen Karralys, too. Was it that, as the time of Samhain approached, the doors started opening?

She walked slowly round the house, scuffing fallen leaves, walked around the wing with the pool. The house faced south. The wing was on the east end, with windows on all three sides and skylights north and south. She crossed to the field by the northeast corner, although she was not going to cross the field. She would not go near the stone wall.

Coming across the field toward her was the young man with the intensely blue eyes. He did not have the dog with him this time, but a grey wolf. When he saw Polly, he spoke to the wolf, who turned and ran back across the field and disappeared into the woods.

Mesmerized, Polly stood still and waited. He walked toward her unhurriedly, smiling slightly. There was no telling how old he was. Certainly older than she, but there was a serene agelessness to his face.

"Karralys—"

He nodded. "You will be Poll-ee." Like Anaral, he spoke slowly and carefully, with an indeterminate trace of accent. Probably Bishop Colubra had taught him English, too. "It is time we talked. I am sorry Anaral didn't summon me when you came to us."

She stared at him. "Who are you?"

"As you said. Karralys."

"A druid?"

He nodded gravely.

"You came from England—from Britain?"

Again the slight nod. The blue of his eyes was serene.

"Why did you come?"

"I was banished."

She looked at him in astonishment.

"For heresy," he said quietly. "You have heard of punishment for heresy?"

"Yes." She thought of Giordano Bruno being burned at the stake for his understanding of time, and also because he did not believe that planet earth was the center of all things. She wondered what Karralys's heresy could have been, that he had been expelled from Britain and sent so far from home. What did druids believe?

He said, "I have been here, on this land, for what you would call three years. It is good land. Benign. The great underground river flows from the place of our standing stones"—he waved toward the wing—"to the lake, with its beneficence. I believe this land, these mountains, the lake, to be the place where the Presence has called me to be. When I was banished, I held on to the hope that there was a reason for my leaving home and that I would find a new home waiting for me, and so I did. The Presence calmed the storm that blew me here, and the promise of the rainbow came, and I knew that I was where I was meant to be." He smiled at her. "And you? You, too, were banished?"

She laughed. "No, not banished. I needed more education than I could get at the local high school, so my parents sent me here. But it wasn't banishing. It's wonderful here."

"I, too, find it wonderful." Above Karralys, high in the sky, flew an eagle. "Here you have"—he pointed to the addition with the pool—"water that is held in on all four sides, and it is in the same space as our great standing stones, our most holy place, even more holy than the rock and the altar by the lake. But for you the lake is gone, and the great stones, and there is no snow on the hills. I see you, and I wonder."

"I wonder, too."

"Bishop Heron—"

"Bishop Colubra." She laughed with delight that Karralys, too, thought of the bishop as a heron.

"Yes. He is, I believe, a kind of druid."

The eagle soared up, up, until it was lost in blue. Polly watched it disappear, then asked, "Bishop Colubra's spent lots of time with you?"

"When he can. The threshold does not always open for him, and he cannot leave his own circle. He is wise in the ways of patience and love. He has turned his loss to compassion for others."

—What loss? Polly wondered fleetingly.

But Karralys continued, "He has much knowledge of the heart, but he does not understand why it is that you were able to see me by the oak tree, or why the young man saw me. He does not understand how it is that you walked into our time."

"I don't understand, either."

"At Samhain, more is possible than at other times. There has to be a reason. Anaral says you are not a druid."

"Heavens, no."

"There has to be a reason for you to have come. Perhaps the Heron opened the time gate especially for you."

"But I'm not the only one. Oh, Karralys—" She took in a deep gulp of fresh air. "Karralys, Zachary was here with me just a few minutes ago, and he saw Anaral."

Karralys looked shocked, frozen into immobility. "Who saw Anaral?"

In her urgency, Polly sounded impatient. "The one you saw by the oak tree. His name is Zachary Gray. He's a young man I met last summer in Greece."

"In—"

"Greece. It's far away, in the south of Europe, near Asia. Never mind. The point is, he's someone I met last summer, but I don't know him very well. He told me, this afternoon, that his heart is giving out, that he's going to die. And then he saw Anaral."

Karralys nodded several times, soberly. "Sometimes when death is near, the threshold is open."

Suddenly Zachary's words rang frighteningly true.

She had not completely understood or believed him before. Now she did. "But he hasn't crossed the threshold."

"No," Karralys said. "No. He has glimpsed us when we have crossed the threshold and come into your circle. But you—you have come into our circle, and that is a very different thing."

"But—" She was not sure what she wanted to ask.

"When we are in your circle, we are not invisible," Karralys said. "People do not expect to see us, so we are translated, as it were, to people of your own time."

"You mean, people don't know what—who—they've seen? I mean, I didn't, when I saw you by the oak tree."

"Exactly," Karralys said.

"And when I first saw Anaral, at the pool, I thought she was just some girl—"

"Yes."

"But then, when I was walking to the star-watching rock, and everything changed, and I was in your time . . ." Again her voice trailed off.

"There is a pattern," Karralys said. "There are lines drawn between the stars, and lines drawn between places, and lines drawn between people, and lines linking all three. It may be that Zachary is indeed as you are."

Polly frowned. "It does seem weird that his boss should be so interested in Ogam stones. But, Karralys, what about Dr. Louise? She saw Anaral."

"That was by chance, by emergency. Anaral does not fit into her worldview, so she does not believe. But you, Polly. You must be part of the pattern. There is a strong line drawing you from your circle to ours. I am afraid for you."

"Afraid? Why?"

"You have spoken with my countryman? Tav?"

"Yes." She smiled. Both Zachary and Tav thought her red hair was beautiful. Tav tried to teach her Ogam and it was a game and they had laughed and been happy.

"You must not speak with him."

"Why not? I've been studying Bishop Colubra's notebook of Ogam, and Tav taught me some more."

"The hand that feeds the chicken ends up wringing its neck."

"What?"

"If Tav likes you, and you like him, it will be even harder."

"What will be?"

"Do not cross the threshold again. There is danger for you."

"I don't understand."

"Anaral has come to you too often. She is very young, and she must learn not to waste her power. Speak with the Heron. Tell him. Tell him about this—his name again, please?"

"Zachary. Zachary Gray."

"He alters the pattern. Tell Bishop Heron. You will?"

"Yes." Suddenly she remembered the bishop saying that Zachary did not look well. Dr. Louise had said that he was too pale.

"I must go." Karralys bowed to her, turned, and walked away across the field. She watched after him until she heard a car drive up, too fast, skidding on the macadam as it came to a stop. Bishop Colubra.

The bishop and Dr. Louise had brought their bathing suits, but they all sat around the table and listened as Polly told them about Zachary. About Karralys.

"I didn't totally believe Zachary—about his heart being that bad, until Karralys . . ." Her voice faltered.

"Now, wait," Dr. Louise said. "I'd like to speak to his doctor. Someone in the last stages of heart failure doesn't work in a law office or drive around in sports cars. He'd be pretty well bedridden. He looks pasty, as though he doesn't get outdoors enough, but he doesn't look as if he's on his deathbed."

"He didn't say he was actually on his deathbed," Polly said. "He didn't give any time limits. Only that he wasn't likely to make law school. And that's at least a couple of years away."

"It still sounds a little overdramatic to me."

"Well, I thought so, too, but Karralys—"

Dr. Louise spoke sharply. "Karralys is not a physician."

"He's a druid," the bishop said, "and I take him seriously."

"Really, Nason. I thought you were more orthodox than that."

"I'm completely orthodox," the bishop expostulated. "That doesn't mean I have to have a closed mind."

"Since when has this odd faith in druids been part of your orthodoxy? Weren't they involved in the esoteric and the occult?"

"They strike me as being a lot less esoteric and occult than modern medicine."

"All right, you two," Mr. Murry broke in.

"And if you're going to have a swim before dinner," Mrs. Murry suggested, "have it. Did you two squabble when you were kids?"

"We drove our parents crazy." Dr. Louise smiled.

The bishop rose. He was a good foot taller than his sister. "But on the big things, the important things, we always stuck together. By the way, Louise, St. Columba speaks of Christ as his druid. You scientists can be terribly literal-minded. There's really not that much known about druids, and I think they were simply wise men of their time. Caesar considered that all those of special rank or dignity were druids."

"Nase, let's go swimming." Dr. Louise was plaintive.

"Of course. I'm running off at the mouth again. Alex, shall I change in your study?"

"Fine. And Louise can have the twins' room. I'll just go out and bring in some more wood for the fire. It's a never-ending job."

"I'll set the table," Polly said.

Her grandmother was washing broccoli. "First thing tomorrow morning I'm going to take those Ogam stones off the kitchen dresser and put them outside somewhere. I'd move them tonight, but Alex and Nase—Nase particularly—would object."

"Why?" Polly asked. "I mean, why move them?"

"The kitchen dresser's cluttered enough already. Large stones are not the usual kitchen decor. And if that Ogam writing was carved into them three thousand years ago, they may have something to do with Anaral's and Karralys's ability to come to our time and our place. And your ability to go to theirs. I'll go out to the lab and get the casserole. It's one of my Bunsen Burner Bourguignons."

As the door closed behind her grandmother, Polly remembered that Karralys had warned her of some kind of danger. In her concern for Zachary she had forgotten, and she did not take it very seriously because she could not believe that Tav with his laughter as he taught her Ogam, with his fingers gently kissing her hair, was any kind of menace to her.

She opened a drawer in the kitchen counter and pulled out table mats, which she began to place on the table. Slowly she added silver, china, glasses. Had she ever studied English history? She thought back to some of the books, historical novels mostly, that she had read. Britain, she remembered, was made up of a lot of warring tribes in the early, pre-Roman days, and they impaled the heads of their enemies on poles and, yes, had practiced human sacrifice, too, at least in some of the tribes. Ugh. That was a time long gone, and a way of seeing the universe that was completely different from today's.

She was folding napkins as her grandmother came in, bearing a steaming casserole.

"Grand, do you have an encyclopedia?"

"In the living room. It's the 1911 Britannica, which was supposed to be particularly fine. It's totally obsolete as far as science goes, but it should be all right for druids, if that's what you want to check out. It's on the bottom shelf, to the right of the fireplace."

Polly got the encyclopedia, the D volume. There was only one page on the subject of druids. But yes, there was a mention of Caesar, the bishop was right. Druids went through extensive training, with much memorizing of handed-down wisdom. Anaral had told her that.

Her grandmother called from the kitchen, "Found anything?"

Polly took the volume and went into the kitchen. "Some. Druids studied astronomy and geography and whatever science was known in their time. Oh, and this is fascinating. There's a suggestion that they might have been influenced by Pythagoras."

"Interesting, indeed." Her grandmother was slicing vegetables for the salad.

"Oh, listen, Grand, I like this. Before a battle, druids would often throw themselves between two armies to stop the war and bring peace."

"Armies must have been very small," her grandmother remarked.

Polly agreed. "It's hard to remember in this over-populated world that two armies could be small enough for a druid to rush in and stop war."

"They were peacemakers, then," her grandmother said. "I like that."

Polly read on. "Oak trees were special to them. I can see why. They're the most majestic trees around here. That's about it for information on druids long ago. Later on, after the Roman Empire took over, druids and Christians didn't get along. Each appeared to be a threat to the other. I wonder if they really were."

"Even Christians are threats to each other," her grandmother said, "with misunderstandings between Protestants and Catholics, liberals and fundamentalists."

"Wouldn't it be great," Polly suggested, "if there

were druids to throw themselves between the battle lines of Muslims and Christians and Palestinians and Jews in the Middle East, or Catholics and Protestants in Ireland?"

"And between Louise and Nason when they spat," her grandmother said, as the doctor and her brother came downstairs in bathing clothes, carrying towels.

Polly put the encyclopedia away. She had learned a little something, at any rate.

The bishop, evidently continuing a train of thought, was saying, "The people behind the building of Stonehenge were asking themselves the same questions that physicists like Alex are asking today, about the nature of the universe."

Mr. Murry was coming in with a load of wood in a canvas sling. He set it down beside the dining-room fireplace. "We haven't come up with a Grand Unified Theory yet, Nase, not one that works."

The bishop ambled toward the pool, his legs showing beneath his robe. "The motive was certainly religious— behind the building of Stonehenge, that is—more truly religious than the crude rituals and 'worship services' that pass for religion in most of our churches today."

"Coming from one who has spent his life in the religious institution, that's a rather sad remark," his sister commented.

The bishop opened the door, speaking over his shoulder. "Sad, perhaps, but true. And not to be surprised at. Come on. I thought we were going swimming."

"And who's holding us up?" The two of them went through the door to the pool, shutting it carefully behind them.

Mr. Murry put a sizable log onto the fire.

"Polly looked druids up in the encyclopedia," Mrs. Murry said. "The article wasn't particularly enlightening."

"We need more than an encyclopedia to explain Nase's opening a time threshold." Mr. Murry blew through a long, thin pipe and the flames flared up brightly. "And Polly's involvement in it. It's incomprehensible."

"It's not the first incomprehensible thing that's happened in our lifetime," his wife reminded him.

"Have things ever been as weird as this?"

Her grandmother laughed. "Yes, Polly, they have, but that doesn't make this any less weird."

Mr. Murry stood up creakily. "Polly's friend Zachary strikes me as adding a new and unexpected component. Why is this comparative stranger seeing people from three thousand years ago that you and I have never seen?"

"Nobody told him about her," Mrs. Murry said, "so he didn't have time to put up a wall of disbelief."

"Is that what we've done?"

"Isn't it? And isn't it what Louise has done?"

"So it would seem."

"Remember Sandy's favorite quotation? *Some things have to be believed to be seen?* Louise doesn't believe, even though she's seen. Zachary, it would seem, has no idea what— or who—he has seen."

Mr. Murry took off his glasses and wiped them on his flannel shirt, blew on them, wiped them again, and put them on. "Why on earth did I think that old age would mean less unexpectedness? Wouldn't a glass of wine be nice with dinner? I'll go down to the cellar and get a bottle." In a moment he came back up, carrying a rather dusty-looking bottle. "There's a dog barking outside."

There was— a dog barking with steady urgency.

"Dogs bark outside all the time," his wife said.

"Not this way. It's not just ordinary barking at a squirrel or a kid on a bike. He's barking at our house." He put the bottle down and went out the pantry door. The dog kept on barking. "It's not one of the dogs from the farms up the road," he said as he returned. "And it doesn't have a collar. It's sitting in front of the garage and barking as though it wants to be let in."

"So?" Mrs. Murry was wiping off the bottle with a damp cloth. "Do you want me to open this to give it a chance to breathe?"

"Please. Louise thinks we ought to have another dog."

"Alex, if you're going to let the dog in, for heaven's sake let it in, but remember we have company for dinner."

"Polly, come out with me and let's study the situation. I agree with Louise. This house doesn't feel right without a dog. A dog is protection." He walked through the pantry and garage, and Polly followed him. In the last rays of light, a dog was sitting on the driveway, barking. When they appeared, it stood up and began wagging its tail hopefully. It was a medium-to-large dog, with beautiful pricked-up ears, tipped with black. There was a black tip to its long tail. Otherwise, it was a soft tan. Tentatively it approached them, tail wagging. Mr. Murry held out his hand and the dog nuzzled it.

"What do you think?" he asked Polly.

"Granddad, it looks like the dog I saw with Karralys." But Karralys had had a wolf rather than a dog with him that afternoon. She could not be sure.

"He looks like half the farm dogs around here," her grandfather said. "I doubt if there's any connection. He's a nice-looking mongrel. Thin." He ran his hands over the rib cage and the dog's tail wagged joyfully. "Thin, but certainly not starved. We could at least bring him in and provide a meal."

"Granddad." Polly put her arm about her grandfather's waist and hugged him. "Everything is crazy. I went back three thousand years, and Zachary saw Anaral, and—and—you're thinking of adopting a stray dog."

"When things are crazy," her grandfather said, "a dog can be a reminder of sanity. Shall we bring him in?"

"Grand won't mind?"

"What do you think?"

"Well, Granddad, she's pretty unflappable, but—"

"I don't think a dog is going to overflap her." Mr. Murry put his hand on the dog's neck where a collar would be, and went into the garage, and it walked along with him, whining very softly, through the pantry, and into the kitchen, just as the Colubras were coming in the other direction, wrapped in towels.

"I see you're taking my advice about another dog," Dr. Louise said.

"Oh, my." Bishop Colubra's voice was shocked.

Mrs. Murry looked the dog over. "He seems clean. No fleas, as far as I can tell, or ticks. Teeth in good condition. Healthy gums. Glossy coat. What's wrong, Nase?"

"I'm not sure, but I think I've seen that dog before."

"Where?" his sister asked.

"Three thousand years ago."

Chapter Six

The silence in the kitchen was broken by Dr. Louise drumming on the table.

Mr. Murry put a bowl of food by the pantry door. "Are you sure?"

The bishop rubbed his eyes. "I could be wrong."

Hadron, asleep on his scrap of rug, watched with one suspicious eye. The dog ate hungrily, but tidily. When it was finished, Hadron minced over to inspect the bowl, licking it for possible crumbs, while the dog stood, wagging its long tail.

Mrs. Murry took an old blanket out to the garage. "He can stay there for tonight. If he's a dog from three thousand years ago, I don't want him to . . ." Her voice trailed off.

Dr. Louise laughed. "If he's from three thousand years ago, do you think keeping him either in or out of the house would make any difference?"

Mrs. Murry was chagrined. "You're right, of course. But somehow I feel he's freer to come and go if he's outside. For tonight, at any rate. Tomorrow we'll see. This evening we're going to sit around the table and eat a civilized meal with a very nice glass of burgundy." She washed her hands. "All right. We're ready. Let's gather round."

The kitchen curtains were drawn across the long expanse of windows. The fire in the open hearth crackled pleasantly. The aroma of Mrs. Murry's casserole was tantalizing. It should have been a normal, pleasant evening, but it wasn't.

"Bishop, tell us about the dog, please," Polly asked.

He lifted his glass of wine so that the light touched the liquid and it shone like a ruby. "I'm getting old. I'm not sure. I'm probably wrong. But Karralys has a dog like that."

"Yes," Polly agreed. "The first time I saw Karralys, by the big oak, there was a dog with him."

"Was it that dog?" her grandfather demanded.

"That kind of dog, with big ears tipped with black."

"You're sure Karralys has a dog?"

"Yes. Why?" the bishop asked.

"It just seems very unlikely. Three thousand years ago there were very few domesticated dogs. There were wolves, and dog-wolves. But domesticated dogs were just beginning to be mentioned in Egypt."

148

"We don't know exactly how long ago Karralys lived. Three thousand years is just a convenient guess. Anyhow, how do you know?"

"I'm a fund of useless information."

"Not so useless," his wife said. "This dog appears to have no wolf blood. It's unlikely your Karralys would have had a dog like this."

"Unless," the bishop said, "he brought him to the New World with him?"

"What's all the fuss?" Dr. Louise raised her eyebrows. "If you're seeing people from three thousand years ago, why get so excited about a dog?"

"It's one more thing," the bishop said. "I think it's a sign."

"Of what?" His sister sounded impatient.

"I know, I know, Louise, it's against all your training. But you did take care of Annie, you have to admit that."

"I took care of a girl whose badly lacerated finger needed immediate attention. She wasn't that different from all the other fallen sparrows you seem to think it's your duty to rescue."

"Louise," Mrs. Murry said, "I find it hard to believe that Nase actually brought Anaral to your office and that you treated her as an ordinary patient."

"As an ordinary patient," Dr. Louise said firmly. "Whether or not the girl whose finger I took care of was from three thousand years ago or not, I have no idea."

"You told me to take her back," the bishop said.

"To wherever. Whenever."

"Louise, it all started in your root cellar with the first Ogam stone."

"I'm only a simple Episcopalian," Dr. Louise said. "This is too much for me."

"You aren't a simple anything, that's your problem." The bishop looked over to the Ogam stones on the dresser. "And noting the fall of the sparrow is an activity not unknown to you, Louise. Maybe you should come to the star-watching rock with me. Maybe if you crossed the time threshold—"

Dr. Louise shook her head. "No, thanks."

The bishop's plate was empty and he took a large helping from the bowl Mrs. Murry held out. The quantity of food he managed to put away seemed in direct disproportion to his long thinness. "This is marvelous, Kate. And the wine—you don't drink this wine every night?"

Mr. Murry refilled the bishop's glass. "All in your honor."

The bishop took an appreciative sip. "The words on the Ogam stones, if I have deciphered them correctly, are peaceable, gentle. Memorial markers. And occasionally something that sounds like part of a rune. The one Polly carried in for me, for instance: *Let the song of our sisters the stars sing in our hearts to*—and there it breaks off. Isn't it beautiful? But, alas, in Annie's time, as now, sacred things were not always honored. Words—runes, for instance—were sometimes misused. They were meant to bless, but they were sometimes called on for curses. And they were used to influence weather, fertility, human love. Yes, runes were sometimes abused, but it was never forgotten that they had power."

"You're lecturing again," his sister commented.

But Polly, interested, asked, "You mean the old rhyme 'Sticks and stones may break my bones but words can never hurt me' is wrong?"

The bishop agreed. "Totally."

Mrs. Murry pushed her chair back slightly and Hadron, taking this as an invitation, left his place by the hearth and jumped into her lap.

The bishop continued, "That little rhyme doesn't take into account that words have power, intrinsic power. I *love you*. What could be more powerful than that small trinity? On the other hand, malicious gossip can cause horrible damage."

Mr. Murry said, "If Dr. Louise tells me I look awful, my joints are going to feel hot and inflamed."

"Whereas, happily, I can say you're doing very well indeed," Dr. Louise said.

"Swimming definitely helps," Mr. Murry said, "but we do respond to suggestion."

Dr. Louise pursued her own train of thought. "I'm an

internist, not a cardiologist, but I'd like to have a look at Zachary. I thought he seemed a charming young man and I don't like the sound of this."

"He's coming over on Saturday," Polly said. "I'd like you to see him, too, Dr. Louise, I really would."

"Is he a special friend of yours?" she asked.

"He's a friend. I don't know him that well. I don't even know him well enough to know whether or not he's likely to exaggerate. I know he was scared."

"One of the Ogam stones"—the bishop frowned slightly, remembering—"goes: *From frights and fears may we be spared by breath of wind and quiet of rain.*"

"Is a rune a sort of prayer?" Polly asked.

"If one truly believes in prayer, yes."

"Like the Tallis Canon?" she suggested.

"*All praise to thee my God this night*"—the bishop nodded— "*for all the blessings of the light.* Yes, of course. And then there's: *Let all mortal flesh keep silence.* Oh, indeed, yes."

Mrs. Murry brought the salad bowl to the table. "What a conversation for a group of pragmatic scientists—with the exception of you, Nase."

"Alas." Bishop Colubra took a piece of bread and wiped up his gravy. "Bishops all too often limit themselves to the pragmatic. And there are times when pragmatism is essential. The trouble is that then we tend to forget that there's anything else. But there is, isn't there, Louise, even in the most pragmatic of sciences?"

"Louise has a fine reputation as a diagnostician," Mrs. Murry said, "and—am I right, Louise?—her diagnoses are made not only from observation and information and knowledge but also on a hunch."

Dr. Louise agreed.

"Intuition." The bishop smiled at his sister. "The understanding of the heart, rather than the mind."

"You were always wise, big brother." Dr. Louise suddenly sounded wistful. "You were the one I could always turn to for reason when things got out of hand. And now I'd think you've gone completely off your rocker if these eminently sane people sitting around the table didn't take you seriously. And Polly, who strikes me as a most sensible person, is having the same hallucinations that you are."

"Mass hallucinations—though two people are hardly a mass," Mrs. Murry said. "It's a possibility, but not a likelihood."

"I wish I didn't feel so outraged," Dr. Louise apologized. "It's making me inordinately grumpy. When Nase brought Annie to me, did I just move into his hallucination? If it weren't for that possibility, I could wipe the whole thing out and return to my rational world."

Mrs. Murry took the casserole to the counter and brought back a bowl of fruit. "I couldn't eat another thing," Polly said, "not even an apple. Anyhow, I like our funny-looking gnarled ones better than these pretty ones."

The bishop reached into the bowl and helped himself.

No one wanted coffee and Dr. Louise rose and announced that it was time to go home.

Polly and her grandparents went outdoors to give the Colubras the traditional farewell. The northwest wind was cold, but the sky was high and clear, the stars dazzling like diamonds. The Milky Way streamed its distant river across the sky.

The bishop raised his face to the starlight. "How many millions of years are we seeing, Alex?"

"Many."

"What is the nearest star?"

"Proxima Centauri, about four light-years away."

"And how many miles?"

"Oh, about 23 million million."

The bishop's breath was cloudy in the light over the garage door. "Look at that star just overhead. We're seeing it in time as well as space, time long gone. We don't know what that star looks like now, or even if it's still there. It could have become a supernova. Or collapsed in on itself and become a black hole. How extraordinary to be looking at a star in this present moment and seeing it millions of years ago."

Dr. Louise took her brother's arm affectionately. "Enough fantasizing, Nase."

"Is it?" But he got into the car, behind the steering wheel.

"Louise shows both courage and trust to let Nason drive," Mrs. Murry murmured.

Dr. Louise, getting into the passenger seat, laughed. "He used to fly a lot, too."

"Terrifying thought," Mrs. Murry said.

They waved as the bishop took off in a cloud of dust.

"Well, Polly." Mrs. Murry sat on the side of her granddaughter's bed.

"Grand, there isn't any point keeping me cooped up. Zachary saw Anaral just outside the pool wing, he really did, even if we find it strange. And I saw Karralys." She thought of Karralys's warning, but said firmly, "I don't think there's any danger."

"Not from Annie or Karralys, perhaps. But wandering about in time doesn't strike me as particularly safe."

"It really isn't wandering about in time," Polly persisted. "It's just one particular sort of circle of time, about three thousand years ago, to now, and vice versa."

"I don't want you getting lost three thousand years ago."

"I really don't think that's going to happen, Grand."

Mrs. Murry gently smoothed back Polly's rumpled hair. "Bishop Colubra suggested that you not go to the star-watching rock till after the weekend. Please abide by that suggestion. For my peace of mind. And not to the stone wall, either."

"All right. For you."

Her grandmother kissed her good night and left. The wind continued to rise and beat about the house. One of the shutters banged. Polly heard her grandparents getting ready for bed. She herself was not sleepy. Anything but sleepy. She shifted from one side to the other. Curled up. Stretched out. Flopped over onto her back. Sighed. Insomnia was something that very seldom troubled her, but this night she could not sleep. She turned on her bed lamp and tried to read, but she could not keep her mind on the book. Her eyes felt gritty, but not sleepy. She could not get comfortable in bed because something was drawing her out of it.

The pool. She had to go to the pool.

—Nonsense, Polly, that's the last place in the world you should go. You promised. Don't be crazy.

But the pool kept drawing her. Maybe Annie was there. Maybe Annie needed her.

—No. Not the pool. She lay down, pulled the quilt over her head.—No. No. Go to sleep. Forget the pool.

And she could not. Almost without volition, she swung her legs out of bed, pushed into her slippers. Went downstairs.

When she got out to the pool, the moon, which was only a few days off full, was shining through the skylights, so there was no need to turn on the lights. She pulled off her nightgown and slid into the water, which felt considerably colder than it did during the day. Swam, backstroke, so that she could look up at the night sky, with only a sprinkling of the brightest stars visible because of the moonlight. Then she swam the length of the pool underwater, thought she saw metal glistening on the bottom of the pool at the deep end.

She dove down and picked up something hard. Shining. It was a silver circlet with a crescent moon. At first she thought it was a torque, but there was no opening, and she realized that it was meant for the head. She put it on over her wet hair, and it felt cool and firm. Took it off and looked at it again. She did not know much about jewelry, but she knew that this small crown was beautiful. What was a silver crown with a crescent moon doing in her grandparents' pool?

She got out of the water, wrapped a large towel around herself, and sat down to dry off before going to her cold bedroom. She still felt wide awake. In the moonlight she could see the big clock at the far end of the pool. It was not quite midnight. She put on her warm nightgown, intending to go right back upstairs. But the silver circlet caught the light and she picked it up and looked at it again, and once more placed it on her head, with the crescent moon in the center of her forehead.

The webbing of her chair no longer felt soft and resilient under her, but hard, and cold, and a sharp wind was blowing.

She shuddered.

She was sitting on a stone chair, slightly hollowed, so that her hands rested on low arms. A circle of similar chairs surrounded a large altar, similar to the one before which Anaral had sung her song of praise to the Mother, but several times bigger. Behind each chair was a large standing stone. The place was reminiscent of pictures she had seen of Stonehenge, except that at Stonehenge there were no thrones or jagged mountains in the background, no snow on peaks white with moonlight.

She should never have gone to the pool.

Her breathing was rapid, frightened. Her heart thumped painfully. Karralys was sitting on one of the thrones, about a quarter of the way around the circle from Polly. He wore a brass torque set with a stone she thought was a cairngorm, which reminded her of the topaz in Bishop Colubra's ring. He wore a long robe that looked like white linen but was probably very soft, bleached leather. His dog was beside him, sitting upright, ears pricked at attention, his dog which looked like the dog Mr. Murry had brought into the house. Anaral was at his right, wearing a silver circlet similar to the one Polly had found in the pool and which was still on her head.

Across the altar from Karralys was Tav, who wore a short, light tunic, a wildcat skin over one shoulder, and leather straps around his wrists and upper arms. His great spear was leaning against his chair. There were several other men and women, some young, some old, many wearing animal skins or cloaks of feathers. Only Anaral and Polly wore the silver circlets. The chair at Karralys's left was empty.

The moon was setting directly behind the standing stone that backed Karralys's chair, and above the moon was a bright star. No, not a star, Polly thought; a planet. She started to speak, to question, but Anaral raised a hand to silence her.

In the background there were more people, and she heard the low, almost subliminal throbbing of a drum. In the distance the sound was echoed. Otherwise, there was silence. All the faces in the circle were grave. Expectant.

Karralys and Anaral rose and went to the outside of the circle, where a large fire was laid in a shallow pit. Anaral gave Karralys a flintstone and he struck a spark and ignited the fire. The two druids raised their arms in a wide gesture of praise, and together they danced slowly and majestically, first around the now blazing fire, and after that around the circle of standing stones. Then, one by one, each person in the circle took a brand and lit it from the fire, and handed it to one of the people who were outside the circle.

When the passing of the fire was complete, there was a burst of song, rich in harmony, joyous in melody. Polly's heart soared with the voices of the people in and around the circle, so that she forgot her fear. Slowly the song died away into a gentle silence.

Then Karralys spoke in his low, ringing voice. "The year has been kind." He indicated the empty chair next to his. "The Ancient Grey Wolf was full of years and was gathered to the ancestors on the sixth day of the moon during the night. His spirit will continue to care for us, joined to the spirits of all of the People of the Wind who are among the stars but whose concern is never far from us." A soft breeze touched Polly's cheeks, moving over the great circle of standing stones. Behind them shadows swayed, purple, silver, indigo, shadows of men and women so tall that they seemed to reach to the stars. Polly could not understand all of what was said, but she felt wrapped in loving strength.

Karralys continued, "The Cub is still young, but he has the gift, and he will learn under the guidance of those who have gone before."

A young man, indeed very young, wearing a grey-wolf skin, rose. "And from you, Karralys." He turned around slowly, bowing to the assembly.

Then Tav spoke, standing and leaning on his great spear. The moonlight touched his hair and turned it to silver. His grey eyes glinted silver. Moonlight touched the ruffling of feathers on his spear. "We have honored the ritual. The fire burns. It flames as brightly as the head of the one who has been sent us by the Mother." He indicated Polly, and his face was solemn.

"Tav, you assume too much and too quickly," Karralys chided.

"The Mother has kept her promise," Tav said. "And so have I. She has come." Again his spear pointed toward Polly.

"You brought her." Karralys spoke sternly.

"I did what the Mother bade. I put the diadem on the altar and she translated it to the place of sacred water."

"Time is fluid at Samhain," Karralys said. "This may not have been the Mother's will."

"Listen to me." Tav leaned forward earnestly. "The Mother speaks in the dark, in the waters, in the womb of the earth. She is never to be understood directly."

"She does not ask for blood!" Anaral's voice rang out clearly.

"No," Tav agreed. "The Mother does not want the blood of her children. Her children. Hear me! This sun-headed child is not one of hers, nor of ours. She has been sent us so that the Mother may be nourished and her demand fulfilled."

Tav spoke more rapidly than Karralys and the implications of his speech did not fully reach Polly because she was struggling to understand the Ogam phrases. If she listened carefully she could make out each word, but it took several beats before the sentences had meaning. The fire had something to do with Samhain, a sacred fire that was passed to each family of the tribe. The dancing had been beautiful and serene, and the singing had been pure joy, taking away her fear, but now Tav was bringing in a different note, a somber note, and her skin prickled.

"And what does the goddess say?" Karralys demanded.

Tav looked up at the moon. "The goddess says that there is danger for us. Grave danger. There has been no rain for the People Across the Lake. Last week a raiding party took sheep from us, and two cows. Their drums tell us that their crops wither. The earth is dry and must be nourished."

Karralys replied, "Ah, Tav, it is not blood that our Mother demands, nor do the gods across the lake. What is asked from us is nurture, our care for the crops, that we not overuse the land, planting the same crops in the same place too many years in a row, not watering the young shoots. Our Mother is not a devouring monster but a loving birth-giver."

"And for such strange ideas you were sent away from home. Excommunicated." The moonlight struck against Tav's eyes.

"And you, Tav? Why were you sent from home?" Karralys demanded.

"You have not forgotten that there was a time when there was no rain, and the little people from the north came and stole our cattle. Our own crops withered, as the crops of the People Across the Lake are withering. Then I understood that blood was demanded, not the blood of a lamb, but real blood, human blood. A raider came by night and I fought him in fair combat and I took him. And so we had the necessary sacrifice. I put him on the altar, yes, I put him on the altar because you would not, nor would you permit the others. I, only I, obeyed the Mother. And so we had the blood that brought the rain, though I was expelled for taking upon myself the sacrificial role of a druid. And so we were both sent away—you for refusing, I for doing what you should have done. Blood was demanded by the Mother then, and it is demanded now. If we do not take care, tribes who are stronger than we are will come and drive us away from our land."

Anaral rose. "Tav, here on my land you and Karralys have lived together in harmony for three turns of the sun. Do not start the old quarrels again, especially on this night."

Tav's voice was urgent. "There will be more raids. And we ourselves have had no rain since the last moon."

"Our crops are harvested. Corn was plentiful." Karralys smiled.

"The water of the lake is low. The rivers run dry. Even

our underground river which gives water to our crops flows less swiftly."

"As always at this time of year. When the winter snows come, the rivers will be refilled."

"The winter snows may not come," Tav warned, "if the earth is not given what she demands."

"Tav." Karralys looked at him sternly. "Why bring up again what was resolved when we became one with the People of the Wind? Those of this land who have welcomed us into their lives forbid such sacrifice. As do I."

"There are other peoples, across the lake, beyond the mountains, who do not think as you do, or as the People of the Wind. We must protect ourselves. Can you not hear the drums which echo ours and are not merely an echo? It is the People Across the Lake. Do you think they will stop at one small raid? Please understand. I know you do not like the sacrifice. Nor do I." He looked at Polly and his face was anguished. "But unless we obey, our land is doomed."

Behind Karralys the moon slipped below the great standing stones, leaving the star to shine brightly just above it, almost like a jewel touching his fair hair.

Tav's voice grated with urgency. "Will one war spear be enough if others want our land?" He raised his great spear. "And why, Karralys, why have we been sent this sunlit stranger?"

"Sunlit, yes," Karralys said. "Life, not death."

"A time gate has been opened," Anaral said.

"And why? A time gate opens once in how many hundred years? Why now? Why here? And when the time is needful?"

Anaral rose again. "She has been sent for good, not ill. This girl and also the old Heron. They have come for our good. We must treat them with courtesy and hospitality until we understand."

"I understand!" Tav cried. "Why are your ears closed?"

"Perhaps it is your ears that are closed," Karralys reprimanded gently.

"I long for home," Tav said. "Around our standing stones were poles and on the poles were the skulls of our enemies. Blood ran from the altar into the ground and the summers were gentle and the winters short. Here we wither from the heat of the sun, or our bones are brittle from the ice and cold. Yes, we have been treated gently by the People of the Wind, but their ways are not the old familiar ways. And now a time gate has been opened and if we are not careful it will close again, and we will have lost the one we have been sent."

Behind Karralys the star, too, was slipping below the great stone. He rose, walked slowly around the table, and took the silver circlet from Polly's head. "Go home," he commanded. "Go home."

Chapter Seven

She jerked upright, as though out of sleep. She looked around. There was no silver circlet with crescent moon. She wore only her damp nightgown. The pool rippled in the starlight. The moon was gone. The distant sound of the village church bell came to her, twelve notes, blown and distorted by the wind. She shivered.

All she knew was that it had not been a dream.

When Polly woke up, it was broad daylight and the sun was streaming into her room. She lay in bed debating. How could she explain to her grandparents what had happened to her? On Samhain. All Hallows' Eve. It was over. Today was Friday, All Souls' Day.

She heard them coming up from the pool. She dressed and went downstairs, feeling weary and anxious. Coffee was still dripping through the filter into the glass carafe. She got a mug from the dresser. The Ogam stones were still there. She wondered where her grand-mother was going to take them. She waited till the cof-fee had stopped dripping, then filled her mug and added milk. She was too tired to make *café au lait*.

Her grandparents came downstairs and into the kitchen. Greeted her. Then: "What's the matter?"

She started to spill out her story.

"Wait," her grandfather said, and poured himself a cup of coffee and sat at his place.

Her grandmother, too, sat down. "Go on."

They listened without interrupting. They did not tell her she should not have gone down to the pool. When she had finished, they looked at each other.

"We'd better call Nase," her grandfather said.

While they were waiting for the bishop, they had breakfast. Mrs. Murry had made oatmeal the night be-fore, and it was on the back of the stove, hot, over a double boiler. Automatically she set out brown sugar, raisins, milk. "Help yourselves."

"I don't like the implications of this," Mr. Murry said. "There seems to be no way we can protect Polly, except by chaining her to one of us."

They stopped talking as they heard urgent barking outside. Mr. Murry put his hand to his forehead. "I'd al-most forgotten—" He went out through the pantry door and came in with the dog, who pranced about ex-citedly. "Polly, is this Karralys's dog?"

"I think so."

Mr. Murry shook his head, went back out to the garage, and returned with the blanket, which he put down near the wood stove. The dog flopped down on it, tail thumping, and Hadron leaped upon him, playing with his tail as though with a mouse. The dog sighed with resignation.

"Three thousand years don't seem to make much difference to Hadron," he said. "Somehow I find that comforting. But maybe I'm grasping at straws."

The bishop arrived with Dr. Louise. "I want to make sure that sanity outweighs my brother's fantasy," she said. "I don't have to be at the hospital for another hour."

"The dog's still here." The bishop petted the animal's head, stroked the great ears.

"He was with Karralys last night," Polly said, "whenever last night was . . ."

"Have you had breakfast?" Mrs. Murry asked.

"Long ago," Dr. Louise replied.

The bishop looked at the stove. "Very long ago."

Mrs. Murry handed him a bowl. "Help yourself, Nason. It's only oatmeal this morning."

He filled his bowl, heaped on brown sugar and raisins, added milk, and sat at the table. "I find it comforting that the dog is here. I'm sure he's protection. Now, Polly, tell me exactly what happened last night. Don't leave anything out."

"I couldn't sleep," she started, "and it was as though the pool was pulling me. I can't explain. I knew I shouldn't go to the pool. I didn't want to go to the pool. But it kept pulling me. And I went."

The bishop listened carefully, eating all the while, looking up as she described the silver circlet with the crescent moon. "Surely," he said, "a symbol of the moon goddess. You said Annie had one, too?"

"Yes."

"The moon goddess. And the Mother, the earth. What we have, you see, is a mixture of Native American and Celtic tradition. They overlap in many ways. Go on."

After a while Mr. Murry interrupted, "You say that Karralys and this other person—"

"Tav."

"—have been here, in the New World, only three years?"

"I think so, Granddad. That's what Anaral and Karralys both said."

The bishop nodded. "Yes. That's what they told me. I've paid less attention to time than to the trip. Karralys and Tav came in a boat. Of course that would not be possible now with the lake long gone, along with the rest of the melt from the glaciers. But three thousand years ago it is quite possible that one could have come first across the ocean, and then by the rivers—and probably what are merely brooks and streams now would have been sizable rivers then—and so get to the lake and to this place. What do you think, Alex?"

"Possibly," Mr. Murry agreed. "Once they'd landed on this continent, they could probably have made their way inland in some kind of small boat."

"It's the ocean crossing that's hard to understand," Dr. Louise said.

"People did cross oceans, remember," her brother said. "Navigating by the stars. And the druids were astronomers."

The bishop helped himself to more oatmeal. "Go on, Polly."

When she had finished, the bishop's bowl was again empty. "All right. So you were part of the Samhain remembrance of the People of the Wind."

"And Karralys and Tav were assimilated by the native people—the People of the Wind?" Mr. Murry asked.

"Karralys became their new leader," the bishop said. "He and Tav were blown across the lake by a hurricane, which in itself would have seemed an omen." He took a handful of raisins. "Karralys and Tav were each sent from Britain for opposite heresies—Karralys for the refusal to shed blood, and Tav not so much for shedding it as for performing the sacrifice that should have been done by a druid. Tav believed that human sacrifice was demanded, that the earth cried out for blood, and he acted accordingly."

"Polly. Blood." Mr. Murry's voice was heavy. "He's thinking of Polly."

Until her grandfather put it thus baldly, Polly had not quite absorbed the import of Tav's words the night before.

Mrs. Murry asked, "Was blood sacrifice part of the druidic ritual?"

"It's not been proven," the bishop said. "There is a theory that it was believed the Earth Mother demanded blood and that each year, perhaps at Samhain, there was a human sacrifice. If possible it was a prisoner. If not, then someone, usually the weakest in the tribe, would be laid on the altar and blood given to the ground."

Polly shivered.

"What about the skulls?" Dr. Louise asked.

"That, I understand, was common practice among some of the tribes. The skulls of the enemies were placed on high poles in a circle around the altar or the standing stones. Remember, these were Stone Age people and their thinking was very different from ours."

"Bloodthirsty," Dr. Louise stated.

The bishop asked mildly, "Any more bloodthirsty than incinerating people with napalm? Or hydrogen bombs? We appear to be bloodthirsty creatures, we so-called human beings, and peacemakers like Karralys are in the minority, I fear."

"Meanwhile," Mr. Murry demanded, "what about Polly?"

"Samhain is over," the bishop said. "Karralys was able to send Polly safely home."

"You think the danger is over?"

The bishop nodded. "It should be. The time has passed."

The dog rose from the blanket and came over to Polly, sitting beside her and laying his head on her knee. She put her hand on his neck, which felt strong and warm. His hair, while not long, was soft.

The bishop nodded again. "Karralys and Annie will protect Polly. Karralys has sent his dog."

Mr. Murry spoke sharply. "It is not necessarily the same dog. I don't want Polly to see them again, not any of them. And as soon as your time gate is closed, I want Polly away from here."

"But, Granddad, if the time gate is closed, then there isn't any problem, and we don't have to worry about the tesseract one way or the other."

The bishop agreed, then said, "Samhain is over. This is All Souls' Day, when we remember those who have gone before. It is a quiet day when we can let our grief turn to peace."

"Nason." Mr. Murry's voice grated. "What do we do now? Can you guarantee that the danger to Polly is over?"

The bishop gazed at a last raisin in his bowl as though searching for an answer. "I don't know. If it weren't for that young man, Zachary."

"What about him?"

"His part in all this, whatever it is, has not been played out."

Mrs. Murry asked quietly, "Is Polly still in the tesseract?"

Again the bishop stared at the raisin. "There are too many questions still unresolved."

"Is that an answer?"

"I don't know." The bishop looked at Mr. Murry. "I don't understand your tesseract. Polly has been through the time gate, and if I am the one who opened it—forgive me."

"Bishop," Polly interrupted, "Tav. What about Tav?"

"Tav has reason for concern. There are neighboring tribes which are not as peaceable as the People of the Wind. There have been several summers of drought, far more severe across the lake, where there is no underground river to be tapped for irrigation. Raids have already begun. This land is eminently desirable. Tav is ready to fight to protect it."

"Is Karralys?" Mr. Murry asked.

"I'm not sure." The bishop rubbed his forehead. "He seeks peace, but peace is not easy to maintain single-handed."

Mr. Murry went to the dresser. "I wish you'd never found the Ogam stones, or opened the time gate."

"It was—it was inadvertent. It was nothing I planned."

"No? You opened the time gate thoroughly when you brought Annie to Louise." Mr. Murry's voice was level, but it was an accusation nevertheless.

Dr. Louise said quickly, "She would have lost the use of her forefinger. Infection would probably have set in if I had not used antibiotics. What might seem like a simple slip of the knife could well have proved fatal."

Mrs. Murry smiled slightly. "Brother and sister do stick together when push comes to shove," she murmured to Polly. "Anyhow, Alex, you and I were fascinated, disbelieving but fascinated, until Polly was involved."

Mr. Murry asked, "Is it safe for us to send Polly home to Benne Seed Island?"

"No—" Polly started, but the bishop interrupted, raising his hand authoritatively.

"I think not yet. Things have to be played out. But meanwhile we will keep her safe here. One of us must be with her at all times to prevent a recurrence of last night."

"Not you, please, Nase," Mrs. Murry said. "Sorry, but it's you who opened the gate."

"You're probably right," the bishop conceded, "but you, my dear. And Alex. Just be with her."

"What would happen," Mr. Murry suggested, "if you sealed up the root cellar?"

"Nothing, I fear. It was simply the closest root cellar

to the star-watching rock, and the place of your pool. These are the holy places."

"Holy?" Dr. Louise asked.

"Sacred. We have lost a sense of the sacredness of space as we have settled for the literal and provable. We remember a few of the sacred spaces, such as Mount Moriah in Jerusalem, or Glastonbury Abbey. Mount Moriah was holy before ever Abraham took Isaac there. So was Bethel, the house of God, before Jacob had his dream, or before the Ark of the Covenant was briefly located there, according to Judges."

"Nase," his sister said softly, "you're getting in the pulpit again."

But he went on, "One theory is that such sacred spaces were connected by ley lines."

She interrupted, "Nase, what on earth are ley lines?"

"They are lines of electromagnetic power, well documented in England, leading from one holy place to another, lines of energy. I suspect that there is a ley line between the root cellar and the star-watching rock, between the star-watching rock and the pool."

"What faddish rubbish," his sister said.

But Polly remembered Karralys talking about lines between the stars, lines between places, between people. It did not seem like rubbish.

"It can become a fad," the bishop told his sister, "but that doesn't make the original holiness any less holy."

"I don't want you falling for fads in your old age," Dr. Louise warned.

"Louise, I didn't ask for any of this. I wasn't looking for Ogam stones. But they can hardly be classified as rubbish. I had no idea that your root cellar was in fact not a root cellar at all. I didn't expect three thousand years to be bridged by Annie. But Annie is a lovely, innocent creature, and I feel a certain—a distinct— responsibility toward her."

"How can you be responsible for someone who has been dead for approximately three thousand years?" Dr. Louise demanded. "Her story is already told. Kaput. Finished."

"Is it?" the bishop whispered. "Is it?"

Dr. Louise went to the door. "I have to get along to the hospital. But I think it might be a good idea for all of you to come over to our house for lunch and perhaps the rest of the day. The greatest risk to Polly seems to come from right around here, and I think there's a certain safety for her from being with us pragmatists, who may well keep Nase's time gate closed because basically we still don't give it our willing suspension of disbelief."

This plan was readily agreed to, although there was considerable argument about whether or not Polly should be allowed to ride in the pickup truck with the bishop.

"There are no time gates on the highway," the bishop said. "We'll go directly to your house, Louise, and Kate and Alex can come right behind us."

"Why can't Polly go with Kate and Alex?"

"I feel responsible."

"Nase, you're the last person she should be with."

But the bishop was persistent and finally it was agreed that Polly could ride with him as long as he stayed within the speed limit and the grandparents followed directly behind him.

"I'll be home for lunch," Dr. Louise said. "I'll pick up some cold cuts on the way."

Polly climbed into the truck after the bishop. The dog whined and barked, not wanting to be left behind.

"Go," Mr. Murry ordered the dog. "Go to wherever you came from."

The bishop started the ignition. "Polly, I'm sorry."

She sighed. "Don't be. It wasn't anything you planned, and, Bishop, it may be scary, but it's also exciting."

"I wish I had something to give you for protection, a talisman of some kind."

She had put on the red anorak. Now she felt in the pocket and pulled out Zachary's icon. "Zachary gave me this yesterday afternoon."

The bishop took it, keeping one hand lightly on the steering wheel. "A guardian-angel icon! It's delightful, utterly delightful!"

Behind them the Murrys honked, and the bishop lightened his foot on the accelerator and gave the icon back to Polly. "It's a reminder that there are powers of love in the universe, and as long as you respond with love, they'll help you."

She put the icon back in her pocket. "Once my uncle Sandy gave me an icon of St. George and the dragon."

"And it didn't stop bad things from happening?" the bishop suggested. "An icon is not meant to be an idol. Just a reminder that love is greater than hate."

"Do you really and truly believe that?"

The bishop nodded calmly. Then he said, "You know a good bit of physics, don't you?"

"Is that a sequitur?"

"Indeed. Do you know what physicists call the very different interactions between the electromagnetic, the gravitational, and the strong and weak forces?"

"Nope."

"The *hierarchy* of interactions. Hierarchy was the word used by Dionysius the Aeropagite to refer to the arrangement of angels into three divisions, each consisting of three orders. Today the physicist arranges the fundamental interactions of matter into hierarchies instead. But it does go to show you that at least they've heard of angels."

"Why does it show that?"

"Your grandfather pointed it out to me."

"Does that mean he believes in angels?"

"Perhaps. I do, though not that they look like that beautiful angel in your icon. What is the first thing that angels in Scripture say when they appear before somebody?"

"What?"

"*Fear not!* That gives you an idea of what they must have looked like."

Once again the Murrys honked. Again the bishop slowed down, then turned up the hill to Dr. Louise's house in a burst of speed, stopped, and turned off the ignition. The Murrys drew up beside him.

They sat around Dr. Louise's kitchen table. "It's by far the warmest place in the house," the bishop said.

Polly felt a wave of unreality wash over her. In a way, she was as much out of the world staying with her grandparents, or here in Dr. Louise's kitchen, as when she moved into Anaral's time. Her grandparents were isolated in their own, special, scientific worlds. Their house was outside the village. She could go for days without seeing anyone else if she did not go to the post office or the store.

At home, although the O'Keefes' house on Benne Seed Island was as isolated as her grandparents' house, school and her siblings kept her in touch with the real world. How real was it? Drugs were a problem at Cowpertown High. So were unwed mothers. So was lack of motivation, a lazy conviction that the world owed the students a living.

She suddenly realized that although there was a television set in her grandfather's study, they had not turned it on. The radio was set to a classical music station. Her grandparents read the papers, and she assumed that if anything world-shattering was happening they would tell her. But she had, as it were, dropped out since she had come to them.

She looked at her grandparents and the bishop. "Zachary's coming tomorrow. What are we going to do about Zachary?"

"I want Louise to see him," Mrs. Murry said.

"She's not a cardiologist," Mr. Murry warned.

"She's been a general practitioner for so long in a place where there are few specialists that she has considerable knowledge based on years and years of experience."

"All right, I grant you that, but I suspect that Zachary would like us to treat him as normally as possible. His seeing Annie may have been an aberration. Or it may not have been Annie he saw at all."

"Who else could it be?" Polly asked.

They all looked up as they heard an urgent barking

outside. The bishop went to the door, opened it, and in came the dog, tail wagging, romping first to Mr. Murry and Polly, then the others.

The bishop put his hand on the dog's head. "We can't escape the past, even here."

"He's a perfectly ordinary dog." Mr. Murry was determined. "I'm still not certain he's anything but a stray."

"He's protection," the bishop said. "Don't take that lightly."

The dog pranced to Mrs. Murry and leaned his head against her knees. Absently she fondled the animal's ears. "We don't seem to have much choice about keeping this creature."

"You have been chosen." The bishop smiled. As though in response, the dog's ropy tail thudded against the floor. "Now you should name him."

Mr. Murry said, "If we name him, we're making a commitment to him."

"But we are, aren't we?" Polly asked.

Her grandmother sighed lightly. "So it would seem."

Polly added, "And Dr. Louise said you needed another dog."

The bishop suggested, "Would you like to name him, Polly?"

She looked at the dog, who, while he did not seem to belong to any known breed, was handsome in his own

way. His tan coat was sleek and shiny, and the black trac-
ing around his ears gave him a distinguished look. His
rope of a tail was unusually long, tipped with black. "He
ought to have a Celtic name, I suppose. That is, if he has
anything to do with Karralys."

"He may be just a stray." Mr. Murry was not going to
give in.

"Ogam. How about calling him Ogam?"

"Why not?" Polly's grandmother asked. "Naming a
dog is a normal, ordinary thing to do, and we need normal, ordinary things right now."

The dog settled at Polly's feet, snoring lightly and
contentedly.

"Okay, Polly," her grandfather said. "Let's have some
normal, ordinary lesson time. What is Heisenberg's un-
certainty principle?"

She sighed, relaxing into the world of particle
physics, which, strange as it was, was a welcome relief.
"Well, if you're measuring the speed of a particle, you
can't measure its position. Or if you measure its position, you can't measure its speed. You can measure one
or the other, but not both at the same time."

"Right. How many quarks does a proton have?"

"Three. One of each color."

"Position?"

"Two up quarks and one down quark."

"And quarks are—"

"Infinitely small particles. The word quark is out of *Finnegans Wake*."

"So Murray Gell-Mann, who named them, obviously read Joyce. I find that rather comforting."

So did Polly. Working with her grandfather was ordinary and normal, but it was not ordinary and normal to be sitting in Dr. Louise's kitchen.

Her grandparents felt the dislocation, too. The lesson petered out. Her grandmother took the wilting bunch of roses from the table and emptied the water from the vase. "I'll just go throw these on the compost and see if there are a few more to bring in."

Mr. Murry looked at his granddaughter. "You all right?"

"Sure. Fine."

"If I go out to the garden with your grandmother, you'll stay right here?"

"I won't go anywhere."

"Nor I," the bishop promised.

"We'll be only a few minutes."

As the door slammed behind Mr. Murry, the bishop said, "What happened last night—"

"It was very frightening."

"It was frightening?" he asked. "Are you frightened?"

"A little."

"A little is not enough. We can't have you going through the time gate again."

Polly looked down at the dog. Ogam. His black nose was shiny. His eyes were closed, and he had long, dark lashes. "I went through the time gate last night because I went down to the pool and put on the silver circlet."

"Don't do it again."

"Of course not, Bishop. But the first time I went through I was just walking along on my way to the star-watching rock."

"I wish you could go home."

"Bishop, I'm in a tesseract. Granddad believes it could really hurt me if I were taken out."

"He's probably right. Does he believe that Tav would put you on the altar for a sacrifice?"

"I don't know. I'm not sure I believe it."

"Believe it, child. The idea of blood sacrifice is gone from our frame of reference, but it's not that much different or worse than things that go on today. What else is the electric chair or lethal injection than human sacrifice?"

"We're told that it's to protect society," Polly said.

"Isn't Tav trying to protect his society in the only way he knows how? He believes that if the Mother isn't appeased, his land and his people are going to be taken over by stronger tribes."

"Tav likes me," Polly said softly.

"Who could help it?" the bishop asked. "His liking for you will just make it harder for him to do what he believes he is called to do. Do you understand? He has to obey the Mother whether he wants to or not."

"She doesn't sound very motherly," Polly said.

The bishop continued, "I don't want to speak this way in front of your grandparents. They're already distressed enough, and if it would be seriously harmful to you to send you away, there's no point in upsetting them further."

"I agree," Polly said, "and I promise not to do anything stupid."

"Now. About Zachary."

"I don't understand what he has to do with all this."

"Karralys may be right. If he's near death—"

"I don't think death is imminent, or anything. But he's scared."

"Of?"

"Death. He's frightened of death."

"Yes." The bishop nodded.

"He thinks death is the end. Poof. Annihilation."

"And you, Polly?"

"I can't imagine Max entirely gone from the universe. I don't need to know how she is being, somehow, Max— learning whatever it is she needs to learn, doing whatever she's supposed to do. But I can't just imagine her totally wiped out."

"What you believe is what I, too, believe," the bishop said. "It is enough."

The Murrys returned then, Mrs. Murry carrying a few yellow roses which were still blooming in a sheltered corner. She cut their stems, put them in the vase, and set it on the table. They were all on edge, out of place, trying to make normal that which was not normal.

"At least you take it seriously," Polly said. "You don't think the bishop and I are out of our tree."

"We would if we could," her grandmother said.

"I just wish"—Mr. Murry spread out his gnarled hands—"that we could be in this with you."

Dr. Louise came in with two brown paper bags, which she set down on the table; then shucked off her outer clothes, hanging them on the antlers. "Bread—not as good as yours, Alex, but reasonable. And an assortment of cold cuts."

The bishop unpacked the bags, setting out plates of bread and meat, while Dr. Louise took condiments from the refrigerator, and a pitcher of milk. "I'll make tea," the bishop offered.

They sat around the table, making sandwiches.—And we don't know what to say, Polly thought.

Dr. Louise sighed.

"All Souls' Day," the bishop said. "Always a poignant day for Louise and me."

There was a silence, and Polly looked questioningly at her grandparents. Mrs. Murry spoke in an even voice. "It was on this date that Louise's husband and baby boy, and

Nason's wife, were killed in a train accident. Louise survived. Nason was away."

"It was a long time ago." Dr. Louise's expression was
calm. "I was pregnant again and I miscarried. I thought
I had lost all that made life worth living, but Nason kept
prodding me, and I went to medical school, and I have
had a good life. I *have* a good life."

"And I," the bishop said, "with friends who keep the
stars in their courses for me, and a faith in God's loving
purpose and eventual working out of the pattern."

"And all this?" Dr. Louise asked. "This three-thousand-
year-old time capsule you've opened up, what does this
do to your faith?"

The bishop smiled. "Why, widens it, I hope."

Dr. Louise laughed softly. "Nason, if you'd been a
druid, you'd probably have been excommunicated for
heresy, just like Karralys."

"Yesterday's heresy becomes tomorrow's dogma," the
bishop replied mildly, and Polly thought once again of
Giordano Bruno.

After lunch they went for a walk in the woods behind
Dr. Louise's house, Ogam close at their heels, occasion-
ally tearing off in great loops, but always circling back.
"Behaving just like an ordinary dog," the bishop said.
"Bless Og."

"He may give you a sense of security, Nase," Dr.

Louise said, "but he reminds me of the reason we're keeping Polly here all day, and that's something I'd rather forget."

They found some beautiful pale pink mushrooms, saw the bright red clustered berries of jack-in-the-pulpit, and tried to pretend they were focused on a nature walk. The rising wind and their own restlessness drove them in. The bishop made tea from a selection of herbs in the garden. They played Botticelli and other word games, but they could not concentrate. When the sun slipped behind the mountains, Mr. Murry stood up. "It's time we went home. We'll keep a close eye on Polly. And, as you say, Nase, Samhain is over. Keep the dog here."

But not long after they were home there was a sharp, demanding bark outside.

"He stays in the garage," Mrs. Murry said.

They had a quiet dinner, with music in the background. Afterwards Polly helped her grandfather with the dishes. When they were through, he suggested, "Let's go for a brief stroll around the house."

They put on anoraks and as soon as they were out of the house Og pranced up beside them. "We always used to walk our dogs three times around the vegetable garden," her grandfather said. "We might as well continue the tradition. It helps keep the woodchucks away. I've plowed and composted half the garden, but we still have some good broccoli and sprouts and carrots and beets. The twins' garden was magnificent. After they left home for college they grew Christmas trees for a while, but when they were all sold I found I wanted a vegetable garden again. What time is your young man coming tomorrow?"

"Around two, I think."

Og chased off into the field and Mr. Murry whistled and he turned and ran back to them. "Good boy," Mr. Murry praised, "though whistling was a reflex. I should have let you go." He stood, raising his face to the sky. It was a clear night, with the Milky Way a river of stars. Polly tipped her head to look for the North Star.

"I can understand how people could see a big dipper or a little dipper," she said, "but not bears. And maybe if you draw lines between those stars you could make a crooked chair for Cassiopeia."—Ley lines between stars?

"There's Orion's belt," her grandfather pointed. "See those three bright stars?"

"Belt, okay," she said, "but I don't see Orion the hunter. Some night, could we have a plain old-fashioned astronomy lesson?" As she spoke, a falling star streaked across the sky and went out in a flash of green light.

"Of course. Let me do a little brushing up. It would be nice to have a dog again. It ensures a night walk, and that means a chance to look up at the sky."

"Granddad, where do you think Og came from?"

"I really don't think he came from three thousand years ago. We often have stray dogs in the village, dumped out of cars by people going back to the city."

"People don't do that!"

"People do. They have a puppy or a kitten for the summer and then, on the way back to the city, they let their summer pet loose. Maybe the city's got into their bloodstream and they're under the illusion that country dogs and cats can fend for themselves. I phoned around to see if anybody's lost a dog, but thus far, nobody has. He's a sweet dog. But he's going to sleep in the garage tonight. Not in the house."

Mrs. Murry came into Polly's room, wearing her night-clothes. "Polly, love. I'm glad this is a double bed. I'm going to sleep with you."

"Grand, it's all right. I won't leave. I won't go down-stairs. I promise."

"Your grandfather and I will feel better if I'm in here with you."

"But you won't be as comfortable—I'll keep you awake—"

"Please. For our sakes."

"Okay, Grand, but I really don't think it's necessary. I mean, it's fine with me, but—"

Mrs. Murry laughed. "Indulge your grandfather and me. We just want to make sure one of us is with you." She got into bed beside Polly. "Let's read for a while."

Polly picked up a book, but she could not concentrate. After half an hour her grandmother kissed her good night and turned over on her side to sleep. Polly switched off the light, but she was not sleepy. Hadron was stretched out between them, purring sleepily.

Again the pool was pulling her. Pulling. This time she would resist. She pressed up against her grandmother's back. Was it Tav's influence, pulling her toward the pool and the past as the moon pulls the tide?

Polly stiffened. No. No. She would not go to the pool. If she got out of bed, her grandmother would waken, would stop her.

What Tav cared about was protecting the land, the flocks, the people, and Polly could not help feeling sympathy for that. When the O'Keefes had had to leave the island of Gaea, with its golden beaches and azure waters, it had been because of developers, because of greed and corruption, and people lusting for money and power and ignoring the loveliness of the island, the birds and the animals and the natives, who lived much as they must have many centuries earlier. And Benne Seed Island was already being developed, and soon it, too, would be irrevocably changed, with no thought for the birds whose habitat had been the jungly forest, or for the great trees two and three hundred years old.

Is it all greed and corruption? she asked herself. We've become an overpopulated planet. People need places to live.

But the condos and resort hotels were for the rich, not the poor. Nobody was building condos in the Sahara or the Kalahari deserts. Not yet.

But three thousand years ago the planet was not over-populated. There was land enough for everybody. Was drought really bad enough to send tribes away from their home places and into land that belonged to others? Wasn't the history of the planet one of people taking over other people's lands? Didn't Jacob and his people take over the land of Canaan? The Romans and then the Saxons and then the Normans took over the British Isles, and then the British took over India, and if some of the American colonists wanted to live in peace with the Indians, others didn't. Others took over.

She sighed. There were no easy answers.

The pull of the pool had lessened. Polly nestled against her grandmother and went to sleep.

Chapter Eight

Polly slept late, and when she got up, both her grandmother and Hadron were gone. She hurried downstairs.

She had a stubborn determination to see this adventure through. All her senses were unusually alert. The smell of danger was in the air, and she had a strong feeling that, even if she wanted to, there was no way she could run away from whatever awaited her.

Could Tav really sacrifice her without Karralys's or Anaral's consent? They would never give it. They were the leaders of the tribe, and surely they would be listened to.

She sipped her coffee thoughtfully. Her grandparents came in from the pool. Her grandfather dressed and then came to the table with the morning paper. When her grandmother went out to the lab, bearing her cup of coffee, the dog came leaping in, jumped up, and greeted Polly and her grandfather. Then went to Hadron and licked the cat, who flicked his tail indifferently. Polly idly watched the big dog and the half-grown cat. Hadron had jumped to his feet and was thoroughly and diligently washing Og's face while the big dog sat patiently.

"Granddad, look."

He smiled at the two creatures. "Our animals have always been friends, but this is remarkable. I have a feeling we aren't going to be able to get rid of Og, and oddly enough, I don't want to. I wish I could hold on to the thought that he's only an ordinary stray." He picked up a ballpoint pen and began doing his crossword puzzle.

Dr. Louise arrived shortly after lunch. Clouds were scudding across the sky, and although it was warm in the sun, the wind was brisk.

"Where's Nase?" Mrs. Murry asked.

"I don't know where Nase is." Dr. Louise looked troubled. "He took off in hiking boots right after breakfast and said he'd meet me here."

"I think we have enough Ogam stones." Mrs. Murry glanced at the two on the dresser, which she still had not removed.

"I don't think he was looking for Ogam stones. He seemed unusually preoccupied. You know, Kate, it's really rather foolish, my coming here. I can't very well ask that young man to let me listen to his heart, and I'm not one for long-distance diagnoses. I need to know his history, talk to his doctor. But I, too, feel the need to protect

Polly. I don't have office hours on Saturday, and I have only one patient in the hospital, and I promised Nason I'd meet him here."

"I'm glad you've come," Mrs. Murry said, and Polly echoed her.

"And I'm curious," Dr. Louise acknowledged. "I think all this is folly, but at the same time I'm curious." She laughed at herself, then glanced at Polly, who was finishing the luncheon dishes. Mr. Murry was out, chopping more wood, a never-ending task, and they could hear the rhythmic stroke of his axe. The dog was with him, and occasionally barked in sheer exuberance. "Nothing new, I hope, Polly."

"No. I just wish the bishop were here."

"Why?"

"I want to ask him about blood."

"What about blood?"

"Well, I know that blood is important in all cultures. And in lots of Eastern religions women have to be set apart, away from everybody else, during their menstrual periods, because they're thought to be unclean."

"Maybe not unclean as you're thinking of it," the doctor said. "Remember, sanitary napkins and tampons are inventions of this century." Polly looked at her questioningly. "My grandmothers, and women before them, used old sheets, any old linens. Back in the Stone Age there weren't any cloths to use. Having women set apart during their periods was a simple sanitary measure, and a ritual that was often looked forward to, when women could be together and rest from the regular backbreaking work. It was a time of rejuvenation, of peace and prayer."

"I hadn't thought about that," Polly said. "I guess I took a lot for granted. But weren't men convinced that women were—I think I read somewhere—separated from God at that time?"

Dr. Louise smiled. "You will have to ask Nase about that. All I can tell you is that superstition has been around as long as human beings."

Polly still had a dish towel over one arm. "Okay. Yes. But what about blood sacrifice?"

"I suppose I think it's superstition," Dr. Louise said. "The earth doesn't need human blood in order to be fertile."

"But what about—what about—"

"What, Polly?" her grandmother urged.

"Well, Jesus. Aren't we supposed to believe that he had to shed his blood to save us?"

Dr. Louise shook her head decisively. "No, Polly, he didn't have to."

"Then—"

"Suppose one of your siblings was in an accident and

lost a great deal of blood and needed a transfusion, and suppose your blood was the right type. Wouldn't you want to offer it?"

"Well, sure . . ."

"But you'd do it for love, not because you had to, wouldn't you?"

"Well, yes, of course, but . . ."

"I'm a doctor, Polly, not a theologian, and lots of Christian dogma seems to me no more than barnacles encrusting a great rock. I don't think that God demanded that Jesus shed blood unwillingly. With anguish, yes, but with love. Whatever we give, we have to give out of love. That, I believe, is the nature of God."

"Okay," Polly said. "Okay. That's good. I don't quite understand it, but it makes some kind of sense." She looked at Dr. Louise and thought that she must be a good doctor, someone you could truly trust with your life.

"Polly," her grandmother said, "why these specific questions?"

"Oh—well—Tav does seem to believe in some kind of blood sacrifice."

"Tav lived three thousand years ago," her grandmother reminded her. "He didn't know what was going to happen a thousand years later."

There was the sound of a car outside on the lane, and

the toot of a horn. Ogam barked, telling them about it, tail swishing back and forth, ready to greet the guest.

Mrs. Murry patted his head, "Thanks, Og," and turned toward the door. "Must be Zachary."

"Bring him in," Dr. Louise suggested, "and we'll give him a cup of tea."

Once again Zachary had parked his car on the lane. He kissed Polly in greeting, then said, "Thanks for letting me come. It means a lot to me."

"It's good to see you. Come on in and say hello."

"Who's here?"

"My grandparents—though Granddad's working outdoors. And Grand's friend Dr. Louise. You met her."

"Yes. Nice. A bit formidable maybe, but nice. What kind of doctor is she?" They went in through the garage.

"An internist. But, she says, she's basically a country doctor, and they're almost a lost breed. Endangered, at any rate."

They passed Mrs. Murry's lab and climbed the three steps to the kitchen just as the kettle began to sing. Mrs. Murry went to the wood stove. "Hello, Zachary. Will you join us for a cup of tea?"

"Thanks. Tea would be fine. Hello, Dr. Colubra. Nice to see you again." Zachary shook hands courteously, then sat at the table.

Mrs. Murry poured tea. "Sugar? Lemon? Milk?"

"Just as it comes, please."

She handed him a cup. "It's another superb autumn day. Do you and Polly have plans?"

Zachary was wearing jeans and a bulky Irish-knit sweater, and new-looking running shoes. "I thought we might go for a walk."

"Oh, good. If you drive to the ski area, there are several excellent walking trails."

"Polly says there are good places to walk right around here."

"There are, but . . ."

—Now what? Polly thought.—How are they going to keep us away from here?

Mrs. Murry was busy adding more water to the teapot. "I gather there's a good movie on in town if you're interested. It's only half an hour's drive."

"No, thanks," Zachary said. "I can go to a movie anytime, and what I really want to do is just amble around and talk with Polly."

Polly perched on the stool by the kitchen counter, where her grandmother sat to chop vegetables, and waited. She knew she ought to say something, make some reasonable suggestion, but her mind was blank. How could she explain her trips to Anaral's time? Zachary had no idea that the girl he had seen was from the past, and if Polly cared anything about him, she would see to it that he didn't get drawn further in.

"Zachary," Mrs. Murry said, "I'm simply going to have to ask you to take Polly somewhere else for your walk. As I said, there are some good hiking trails near the ski area."

Zachary put down his cup. "That was excellent tea. Mrs. Murry, is something peculiar going on? Does it have something to do with that guy with the dog or the girl I saw the other day that Polly was so mysterious about?"

"Anaral? In a way, yes."

"I don't mean to push, but could you explain?"

Dr. Louise stood up, took her cup to the sink, rinsed it, and put it in the rack. "All right, Zachary. You would like an explanation?"

"Yes. Please."

"My brother, who is a retired bishop, has accidentally opened a time gate between the present and three thousand years ago, when there were druids living with the native people of this land." Her voice was calm, without emphasis. "The girl you saw on Thursday is a druid and belongs to that time. Her people are largely peaceable, but one of the Celts who came here from Britain believes that the Earth Mother needs human blood to stop the drought which is driving other tribes to this part of the world, tribes which are not peaceable."

Zachary stared at her and burst into laughter. "You're kidding!"

"Would that I were."

"But that's—"

"Crazy?" Dr. Louise smiled.

"Out of sight."

Dr. Louise continued, again in a cool, academic way. "It seems that there is at least one person back in that long-gone time who feels that Polly would be just the right human sacrifice. Naturally, we are not eager for Polly to be drawn through the time gate and into danger."

There was what seemed to Polly a very long silence. Then Zachary said, "This is absolutely the most off-the-wall—"

Mrs. Murry said, "You did see Anaral."

"I saw a beautiful girl."

"Describe her."

"She had a long black braid. And honey-colored skin, and eyes that weren't quite slanty, just—"

"A little exotic?" Dr. Louise suggested.

"Definitely. I'd like to see her again."

"Even if it means going back three thousand years?"

"That's an extraordinary suggestion," Zachary said, "especially coming from a—a—"

"A physician. Who totally rejects everything she's said, and yet on another level has to admit the possibility."

"Why? It's impossible."

"A lot of things my forebears would have considered

impossible, such as television, or astronauts, or much of modern medicine, are now taken for granted."

"Still—"

"Polly has been through the time gate. So has my brother. My brother may be eccentric, but he's no fool."

Mrs. Murry's voice, too, was quiet. "We don't want Polly in any kind of danger, real or imaginary. Perhaps the imaginary danger is the most frightening because it is the least understood."

Zachary looked at Polly, raising his brows at the story he was expected to take seriously.

Polly said, "Well, I know it sounds crazy, but there it is."

"In which case," Zachary touched her arm lightly, "I'd still like to go for that walk with you. I gather this time gate is somewhere on your land?"

"Yes. By the star-watching rock, where we were the other day. But also by the swimming pool. That's where you saw Anaral."

"A swimming pool hardly seems the likeliest place for a time gate, or whatever you call it." He sounded slightly dazed.

"The pool is over an underground river, and three thousand years ago there wasn't a pool, and there wasn't the house. It was a great circle of standing stones."

"If I didn't know you're an intelligent person, I mean highly intelligent—do you believe all this?"

"I've been there. Then."

"So—I can't just wipe it out, can I?" Suddenly he laughed. "I'm intrigued. Really intrigued. You think the girl I saw actually lived three thousand years ago?"

"Yes," Polly said.

"Mrs. Murry? Dr. Colubra?"

"It appears to be a possibility," Mrs. Murry said.

"Who knows, then?" He sounded suddenly wistful. He looked at Mrs. Murry and Dr. Louise. "Polly may have told you I'm having some problems with my health."

"She told us that your heart is troubling you," Mrs. Murry said.

"And my life expectancy isn't good. If I'm to take all you've been saying seriously, maybe it would be a good idea for me to drop back three thousand years."

"Not with Polly." Mrs. Murry was firm.

"Zach—" Polly was tentative. "Would you let Dr. Louise examine you—listen to your heart?"

"Sure," Zachary said. "But I don't think you"—he turned courteously to Dr. Louise—"can find much beyond a murmur and some irregularity."

"Probably not," Dr. Louise agreed. "I have my stethoscope with me, but that's all. Shall we go into the other room?"

Zachary followed her out, and Polly turned to her grandmother. "He's right, I guess. I mean, she can't find out much just this way, can she?"

"I doubt it. But Louise has a sixth sense when it comes to diagnosis. Polly, can't you suggest to Zachary that you go to the club, or hike by the ski trails?"

"I can suggest," Polly agreed, "but I don't think Zach's up to much in the way of hiking."

When Dr. Louise and Zachary came back, the doctor's face was noncommittal. "Zachary obviously has excellent doctors," she said, "who are doing everything I'd recommend. Now, my dears, I need to make a move-on. What are your plans?"

"We could amble along the lane toward the village," Polly suggested.

"Ambling is fine with me," Zachary said. Then, to Dr. Louise, "Thank you very much, Doctor. You're very kind." And to Mrs. Murry: "Would it be possible for us to have tea and some of that marvelous cinnamon toast when we get back?"

"Quite possible. Polly, just walk on the lane and the road to the village, please."

"Yes, Grand." She and Zachary went out through the pantry and Polly took the red anorak off the hook. "Are you warm enough?" she asked.

"Sure. This sweater is warm enough for the Arctic. Polly, I wish your doctor friend had been able to give me some good news. She didn't say anything."

"Well—as you said—she didn't have anything except her stethoscope."

"Polly, do you believe in angels?" He turned to follow her as she started down the dirt lane.

"I don't know. Probably."—But not, she thought, that they're fairies with magic wands who can hold back bullets or make new a maimed heart.

"I wish my grandmother were still alive—the one who was willing to let me be me, and didn't load all kinds of expectations on me. I've gone along with the expectations. I could follow in Pop's footsteps if I had a life expectancy in which to do it. Now I'm not sure that's what I want. Maybe there's more to life." He turned as there was a sound behind them and Og dashed to Polly, waving his tail, jumping up in joy.

"Down, Og," she said severely, and the dog obediently dropped to all four feet.

"Hey!" Zachary stared at Og. "Where'd that dog come from? I mean, haven't I seen him before?"

"Yes." Polly looked directly at him. "Remember that man you saw under the oak tree the day you came looking for me?"

"Yeah. He had a dog."

"This dog." Polly tried to keep her voice as dry and emotionless as Dr. Louise's.

"So how come he's here, obviously thinking he belongs to you?"

"Well. He just sort of appeared."

"What do you mean?"

"What I said. That's how my grandparents always get their dogs."

"Crazy." Zachary shrugged.

"Maybe," Polly said. "The thing is, he's come through the time gate, too."

Zachary sighed exaggeratedly, then looked again at Og, who stood by Polly, long tail moving gently back and forth. "Dogs going through time gates? That's as nuts as anything else."

"Yes," Polly agreed.

"He's sort of odd-looking. Reminds me of some of the dogs on the Egyptian friezes. Well, if he's three thousand years old, that would explain it all, wouldn't it?" He laughed, a short, unamused sound. "Does he have a name?"

"We're calling him Og, mostly. It's short for Ogam."

"It suits him, somehow." Zachary plucked a blade of grass and chewed on it. "Polly, this dog—it's just another sign. I want to go back to that place—the star-watching rock—and that oak tree—and the stone wall where I met you."

"I can't go there, Zach. I promised." Og nudged his head under her hand, and she scratched between his ears.

"I just have this strong feeling that if we go there, there will be things I need to find out."

"I don't think so, Zach. There are things to find out just walking along here. This is a beautiful place." She paused to watch a small stream, not more than a trickle, sliding under some water willows.

Suddenly fierce, he said, "I don't give a bloody zug if it's beautiful. What I want to know is if there's some way I can live a little longer. I don't think that's likely here, in this time. I don't like the way your doctor friend very carefully didn't say anything. But I saw her face. I saw the look in her eyes."

"You're projecting," Polly said firmly. "She didn't say anything because she didn't have enough to go on."

Just past the small stream there was a faint path to their left, probably made by wildlife. "Let's go this way," Zachary said.

"It doesn't go anywhere. It'll just end up in under-brush." Polly didn't remember having seen the small path before, but it ran roughly parallel to the orchard and the field that led to the stone wall.

"Polly." Now Zachary's voice was soft. She followed him along the path in order to hear, Og at her heels. "I want to see what all this Ogam stuff is about. If some-how I could go back three thousand years, what would happen? Would I be the same me? Or would my heart be okay?"

"I don't know." Polly watched Zachary push through browning blackberry brambles. Then the path widened out slightly and wound between grassy hummocks and across the ubiquitous glacial rocks.

"Am I right?" Zachary asked. "Is this path going toward the star-watching rock?"

"I've never been on it before. I don't think it goes anywhere."

He reached back and caught her hand. "Polly. Please. I need you to help me."

"This isn't going to help. Come on. Let's go home." She tried to release her hand.

"Polly. Please. Please. Don't pull against me. I need you to help me. Please."

Og had run on ahead of them, and circled back, tail swishing happily.

"See, the dog thinks everything's okay," Zachary said.

Now the path went under some wild apple trees and they had to bend low. Then it opened up and joined the path at the stone wall. Louise the Larger was lying there in the sunlight, but they were on the far side of the stone wall and Zachary hurried away from her, along the path to the star-watching rock.

"No, Zach, come back!"

Louise raised her head and several inches of body and began weaving back and forth.

"No, Zach!" Polly repeated. "Zach! Come back!"

But he was continuing along the path, calling, "Polly! Please! Don't desert me now!"

Og pushed against her, growling slightly, but she could not let Zachary go alone. Stumbling a little, she ran after him. "Zachary, this is foolish. Nothing's going to happen."

"Okay, so if nothing happens, we'll just go back for tea." He stopped, breathing rapidly and with effort. His face was very pale, bluish around the lips. He reached out his hand for hers, and she took it.

Under their feet the ground seemed to tremble. There was a faint rumble, as of distant thunder. The air about them quivered with concealed lightning.

"Hey! Polly!" Zachary's voice soared with surprise.

The trunks of the trees thickened, the branches reached upwards. Ahead of them, sunlight glinted off water.

"Well," she said flatly, "it's happened."

"What's happened?"

"We've gone through the time gate. Look at the trees. They're much older and bigger. And that's a lake that fills the whole valley. And look at the mountains. They're younger and wilder and there's still lots of snow on their peaks. I guess in geological terms the Ice Age wasn't so long ago."

Zachary stared around at the primeval forest, the jagged mountains. "Maybe I've had a heart attack and died?"

"No, Zach."

"In which case," he continued, "you'd have to be dead, too."

"No, Zachary. We aren't dead. We're three thousand years ago."

"So in our time we'd be dead, wouldn't we?"

"We're alive. Right now."

"I don't feel any different." He breathed in, deeply, disappointedly. "Hey, and the dog's still with us."

Polly put her hand on his arm as she saw Anaral running toward them.

"Poll-ee! Go back! It is not safe!" She looked suddenly at Zachary, her hand to her mouth. "Who—"

"Zachary Gray. He saw you the other day. I guess you saw him, too."

Zachary stared at Anaral. "Who are you?"

Anaral's eyes were veiled. Polly answered, "She's a druid."

"Holy zug."

"Go back, both of you. It's not safe."

"What's not safe?" Zachary demanded.

"Last night there was a raid. Several of our best sheep and cows were taken."

"What's that got to do—" Zachary started.

Anaral continued. "Tav is wild, and not only Tav. We are all in danger. Raiders may return at any moment."

"Tav?" Polly asked.

"Tav is not the only one who is ready to fight for our land. Karralys fears that there will be much blood shed. You understand?"

"No," Zachary said.

Polly still could not conceive of having fun with someone you were planning to sacrifice.

Anaral looked at her. "You understood what was being said—" She paused, looking for words. Continued, "—around the council table?"

"Most of it, I think."

"What did you understand, please?"

"I think—I think Tav believes that the Mother—Mother Earth?"

"Yes."

"That she demands a blood sacrifice, and that I have been sent—" Her skin prickled. "Do you and Karralys—?"

"No. Not us. For us, the Mother is loving and kind. Karralys, too, believes that you have been sent."

"Sent?"

"Not for the shedding of blood. Karralys lies on the great altar rock and prays, long, long, and he says the pattern is not yet clear."

"Hey, what are you talking about?" Zachary demanded.

"Well." Polly's face was stark. "Tav believes—perhaps—that the earth demands blood in order to be fertile, and that my blood . . ." Her voice trailed off.

Anaral said, "Karralys says that there is—is problem—across the great water where he and Tav come from. He says it used to be that the shedding of the blood of a lamb was—was—" She stopped.

"Enough?" Polly suggested. "Sufficient?"

"Yes, and the lamb was thanked, and mourned for, and then there was a great feast. But there came a time of no rain—you remember, Tav told—"

"Yes."

"The lamb's blood was not suff—"

"Sufficient."

"Sufficient. Rain did not fall. Crops died. People were hungry. And after Tav killed the man and his blood was spilled on the ground, rain came."

Zachary asked, "Do you think that was why the rain came?"

"No. We People of the Wind do not try to tell the Presence what to do, but to understand and use what is given, whether it seems good or bad. Some of my people think that there may be other gods across the water, gods who are angry and have to be—"

"Placated?" Zachary suggested.

Anaral looked at him questioningly.

Polly said, "The gods will be mad at you unless you give them what they want?"

"Yes."

Zachary scowled. "But you think your god loves you?"

Anaral smiled. "Oh, yes. We do not always understand our part in the working out of the pattern. And you see, it is possible for people to work against the pattern, to— to tangle the lines of love between stars and people and places. The pattern is as perfect as a spiderweb, and as delicate. And you"—her level gaze rested on Zachary— "we do not know where you fit in the pattern, which lines come to you, or which lines are from you, or where the lines that touch you touch us."

Og, who had been standing quietly by Polly, moved to Anaral, and she reached down and patted the dog's head. "Karralys has sent him to you. I am glad. Now go. Please go. To your own place in the spiral." She turned from them and ran swiftly away.

"Wow," Zachary said. "Let's go after her." He took a few hurried steps.

"No, Zach. Let's go home."

"Why?"

Polly was impatient. "You heard Anaral."

"Yes, and I'm fascinated. I want to know more."

"Zachary, it isn't safe."

"Surely you don't believe anybody is going to sacrifice you."

"I don't know what to believe. I know we should go home." She walked in the direction of the house, or what should be the direction of the house, but the trees continued to tower above them.

From behind one of the great oaks came a low whistle, and she froze. Og pressed against Polly's legs, ears up
and alert, tail down and motionless.

"Poll—ee." It was Tav's voice. He appeared from behind the tree, and Og's tail began to wave. "You've come."

"Who's that?" Zachary was startled. "I can't understand a word he's saying."

"It's Tav," Polly said, "and he's speaking Ogam."

"I know that." Zachary sounded irritated. "It's much
faster than when my boss tries it."

Polly turned back to Tav, and despite Anaral's warning,
she was absurdly glad to see him. "He's a Celt, a warrior
from ancient Britain." Og was pressed close against Polly,
but he was not growling. His long rope of a tail was
swishing back and forth.

Tav, holding his great spear firmly, pointed at Zachary. "Who?"

"His name is Zachary." Polly spoke slowly in Ogam,
sounding out Zach-a-ry carefully. "He is from my time."

Tav raised his eyebrows. "Zak?"

"Zachary."

"But we do not need another one!" Tav's eyes were
wide with surprise. "Why would the goddess send another one? I do not understand." The sun turned his pale
hair to silver.

Zachary interrupted, "What's he saying?"

Behind them came the throb of drums, low, menacing. Og's tail dropped, and he began to growl, his hair bristling.

Tav listened. "There is danger. Go back. Do you know that we have had a raid and some of our best animals taken?"

"Yes," Polly said. "I'm sorry."

"Go home," Tav said. "Quickly."

"I'm not going back," Zachary muttered.

Tav ignored him. "Oh, my Poll-ee, there will be another raid. You must go. I do not understand why this one"—he looked at Zachary—"this Zak one, has been sent."

The sound of the drums grew louder, closer. Og barked.

Polly turned to Tav. "I don't know how to get him to go back."

Tav shook his spear. "Go, then, Poll-ee. Go."

But suddenly the beating of drums was upon them, was joined by shouting, screaming, closer, louder, and up the path from the direction of the lake burst a group of men wearing skins, with feathers in their dark hair. Two of them were dragging Anaral with them, and two of them held Bishop Colubra. Anaral was screaming, and the bishop was shouting, trying to free himself.

Into their midst leapt Tav with his great war spear, one

man against a mob. Polly grabbed a branch from the ground and rushed after him. Og crouched low and then launched himself at one of the men who held Anaral. He let her go, clutching at his throat. But she was still held in the other warrior's arms. Polly hit at him with the branch, which was dry and broke off ineffectually. She began kicking, hitting, clawing, biting, whatever she could do to free Anaral. She must have seemed such an extraordinary apparition in her red anorak and with her flaming hair that she almost wrenched Anaral away from the warrior before he thrust her roughly to the ground.

"No!" Anaral screamed. "Go home, Poll-ee!"

The men were shouting, singing a high-pitched melody, each line ending with a shrill *"Hau!"*

Suddenly the bishop began to sing, too, his voice quavering but clear. *"Kyrie eleison! Christe eleison! Kyrie eleison!"*

There was a beat of silent surprise, then the clamor began again as the People of the Wind came running from all directions, carrying spears, clubs, bows and arrows, shouting as they rushed the raiders. The noise and confusion made Polly reel, but she continued her wild fighting.

Then, seemingly out of the blue, came Karralys, bearing a staff, trying to thrust it between the two groups. "Stop!" he was shouting. "Stop this madness!"

"You can't stop it!" Tav shouted back. "They have Anaral and the Heron!"

Polly was grabbed from behind and heaved up into the arms of one of the raiders. She grabbed at his hair, knocking his feathers askew. Og leaped to her defense, and was felled by the blow of a heavy club.

"Help!" Polly shrieked. "Help!" Then a hand slapped roughly against her mouth, and she bit at it.

"Help!"

Now Karralys was thrusting with his great staff fiercely, and his young warriors were shouting, too, and there was nothing but chaos and terror.

Polly wrenched her head free of the man's hand.

"Help!" she screamed again.

Then there was a strange hush, still as the eye of a hurricane. A harsh cry of terror. The raiders holding Anaral and the bishop let go abruptly, and to Polly's amazement they turned and ran away. She herself was dumped on the ground. She picked herself up and saw Louise the Larger slithering along the path, red tongue flickering.

As suddenly as it had begun, it was over.

The raiders were running away, bumping into each other in their fear.

The battle had been noisy and rough rather than lethal. The wounded were gathered together.

The raiders were in long, swift canoes, and were already well out into the lake, paddling fiercely.

Among the People of the Wind was a woman whose hair was white and who had a broken arrow still stuck in her shoulder. Karralys looked around and saw Polly. "Our Eagle Woman is hurt and cannot help with the wounded. Cub and I will have to have some assistance. What we need is a steady hand and head." He looked at her questioningly.

"Sure, I'll do what I can," Polly said. "I'm not afraid of blood." She looked around for Zachary but did not see him anywhere. Meanwhile, she was obviously needed. She turned to Karralys, who introduced her to a young man who had a grey-wolf skin over his shoulder, the young man who had been at the circle of standing stones on Halloween—Samhain.

"This is Cub, our young healer."

"I have not the experience of Karralys or the Old Wolf," the young man said. "I will be grateful for your help."

She did whatever Karralys and Cub told her to do when they took the arrow from Eagle Woman's shoulder, which had been broken from the impact. She clenched her teeth while they worked, and Polly kept wetting a soft piece of leather and wiping the sweat from her face. Then they moved on to set broken bones, stanch blood from a few wounds.

Mostly what was required of Polly was to hold a bowl

of clean water and replenish it from the lake after each use. One of the raiders was laid out with a concussion, and Karralys had him stretched out on a bed of moss, covered with skins to keep him warm. Another had been left behind with a compound of his leg, and Polly helped hold his head while Karralys and Cub set the leg. It was a bad break, and the young raider clutched her in pain. Cub gave him something to drink, telling him it would ease the pain, then poured a thick greenish liquid into the wound where the jagged bone had broken through the skin, explaining that this would help prevent infection.

When the leg was set and bound between two splints, the young raider was able to talk. Polly had difficulty in understanding him, and Karralys translated for her. "He says their crops have failed. There is no corn. Their grazing grounds are parched and the earth is dry and hard. They will not have enough to eat this winter. They will raid us again, with more men this time. They have no choice, he says. If they do not take our land and our crops and herds, they will starve."

"Couldn't they just come ask you to share with them?" Polly asked.

Karralys sighed. "That is not how it is done."

"Well." Polly sighed, too. "At least nobody was killed."

"This time," Karralys said. "Thank you for your help,

Poll-ee." He glanced over at the white-haired woman, who was still among the wounded, her shoulder held immobile by a stiff leather sling. "Eagle Woman is our—" He paused, searching for the right word.

"Medicine woman?" Polly suggested. "Witch doctor? Shaman?"

Karralys shook his head. None of these words had any meaning for him. "From what the Heron tells me, I think she is something like what you call doctor, and that you have no one like Cub, who is healer. She has knowledge of herbs and the cure of fevers and chills, and helps Cub nurse the sick or hurt. But the wound in her shoulder will keep Eagle Woman from work for some time. The bone is shattered where the arrow penetrated. You have done well. You did not need to turn away. You have training in the care of wounds?"

Polly shook her head. "I come from a large family, and when we lived on Gaea—an island far away—where there weren't any doctors, when anybody was hurt or sick I helped my parents. Karralys, where is Zachary?" She had followed Zachary out of a sense of responsibility, and now she had no idea where he was.

"Zak?"

"He was with me, the one I told you about, who saw Anaral. He was with me, and then when the fighting began, I forgot about him."

Karralys looked troubled. "He is here?"

"That's why I'm here," Polly said. "I tried to stop him—but then I couldn't let him come alone, so . . ."

"I do not understand why he is here," Karralys said.

"Neither do I."

"He is an unexpected complication. He may change the pattern."

"Karralys." Polly pondered the question. "If Zachary and I have come to your time, couldn't that change what happens in our time?"

"Yes," Karralys replied calmly. "The future is often changed by the past. There may indeed be many futures. But someone blundering into our time who is not part of the pattern may tangle and knot the lines."

"Unless," Polly questioned, "he is part of the pattern?"

"It is possible," Karralys said. "If it is so, then it will not be easy."

"But where is he?"

Anaral came up to them, hearing the question. "Zak? He is all right. He is with Bishop."

Polly then remembered that Dr. Louise had said her brother had gone off wearing hiking boots. Had he crossed the time threshold, knowing that he would be needed?

Anaral had brought a clean bowl of water so that Karralys and Polly could wash their hands. The druid looked at Polly gravely. "You were a very great help. You are brave."

"Oh, I didn't do anything much."

"Your hands have the gift," Karralys pronounced. "You should serve it. Now we must join the others at the standing stones. They will be waiting."

They sat on the stone chairs within the great ring of stones—Polly, Anaral, Karralys, Cub, Tav, Zachary, the bishop, and several others of the People of the Wind.

Polly still had a feeling of nightmare from the strange battle between two small armies, or bands of people—they could hardly be called armies. But if the skirmish had ended differently, Anaral could very well have been taken by the raiders.

And what about Bishop Colubra? What would have happened if the raiders had taken the bishop? How would that have affected the circles of time? She shook her head. What mattered right now was that she had helped Cub and Karralys with the wounded, and she had to understand that although this clash of two tribes was over, there was more danger to come.

She looked around at the circle of men and women, the leaders of the People of the Wind. Each one wore an animal skin or bird feathers or something representing a specific role in the affairs of the tribe. Eagle Woman was in her chair, her face white but composed, her arm held immobile by a leather sling and cushioned on a bed of moss and fern.

The bishop was sitting across from Polly, and beside him was Zachary, pale as alabaster. Karralys sat in his stone chair, looking unutterably weary. He wore the long white robe and the torque with the stone the same shade as the topaz in the bishop's ring. Og was lying beside him, bruised from the raider's blow, but, Karralys assured them, no bones were broken.

"The snake," Tav said. "How was it that the snake came to end the fighting?"

Karralys looked at Polly. "We have few snakes, and they are revered as gods. That you should have called a snake—you did call this snake?"

"No!" She was astonished. "I just shouted for help."

"But immediately the snake came."

"It had nothing to do with me," Polly protested.

"Maybe she was just coming—on her way somewhere."

"A snake does not willingly come through lines of battle," Cub said. "You called, and she came."

Tav hit the butt of his spear against the hard ground. "The snake came for you before, at the wall, when I was first speaking with you. She is your friend, that is what you said."

As Polly started to protest, again Karralys raised his

hand. "It must have seemed to the raiders that you called the snake, that you had special help from the goddess, and that you yourself had special powers."

"*Archaiai exousiai*," the bishop said.

It was Greek, Polly knew, something about powers. The bishop had called out the Kyrie. Could not Louise have come as much for that as for her own cry for help? Or was it not, most likely, coincidence that the snake had come along the path at just that moment?

"Principalities and powers," the bishop said. "It would have looked to the raiders as though you could call on the principalities and powers." He spoke gaspingly, as though he could scarcely breathe.

"Bishop!" Anaral's voice was sharp with anxiety. "Is something wrong?"

All attention was drawn to the bishop, who was breathing in painful gasps. The rapid fluttering of his heart could be seen through his plaid shirt.

Cub rose and went to the bishop. "Heron, our dear, it would please me if you would let me try to slow the beating of your heart. It is fast, even for a bird."

The bishop nodded. "Of course, Cub. It would be a great inconvenience to everybody if I died now, and it might produce a paradox that would distort the future."

Cub knelt beside the bishop, placing one hand under the plaid shirt, firmly against the bishop's chest.

Polly saw Zachary's eyes lighten with interest and hope.

Karralys watched Cub intently, nodding in approval.

Tav looked from Cub to Karralys, then to Zachary. Zachary had disappeared during the fighting, and it seemed to Polly that Tav was looking at him with scorn.

But instead of accusing Zachary he demanded, "Where did the snake go?"

"Louise the Larger," the bishop panted.

"Hush, Heron," Cub said, and pressed his palm more strongly against the old man's chest. Cub's own breathing was slow and rhythmic, and the pressure of his hand reinforced the rhythm.

"Where?" Tav repeated.

"Hey," Zachary said. "Translate for me, Polly."

"They're talking about the snake," Polly said. "Tav wants to know where she went."

Zachary said, "I saw her going along the path there, and probably she went three thousand years into the future."

"You—" Now Tav's voice was definitely accusing.

Zachary's fingers were white as he held the sides of the stone chair Karralys had assigned him. "You're talking much too fast for me to understand you, but if you want to know why I wasn't in that beer-parlor brawl with you, I wouldn't have been any help. I have a weak heart and I'd just have been in the way." He spoke with stiff pride.

Quickly Polly translated as best she could for Tav and the others.

Cub withdrew his hand from the bishop's chest. "There. That is better."

"Yes, my son," Bishop Colubra said. "I could feel my heart steadying under your hand. I thank you."

"Is he all right?" Anaral asked anxiously.

Cub nodded. "His heart is beating calmly and regularly now."

"I am fine," the bishop said. His breathing had steadied with his heart, and he spoke normally. "Now we must think what to do next."

"Please," Zachary said. "I saw that kid"—he indicated Cub—"steady the old man's heart. I saw it. Please. I want him to help my heart."

Polly spoke in Ogam to Cub.

"Yes. I will try. Not now. Later, when we are back at the tents," Cub assured her.

"He will try to help you," Polly translated for Zachary, "later."

"The snake," Tav insisted. "The snake who came for Poll-ee—"

"No—" Polly started to deny again.

But the bishop held up his hand. "Yes, Tav. We must not forget Polly's snake."

"But she's not—"

Karralys addressed the bishop. "Can you explain?"

"I'm not sure. You said that for you the snake is sacred?"

"We revere the snake," Karralys agreed.

"And the People Across the Lake? They ran from the snake."

"True." Karralys leaned on his elbow, his chin on his hand. "They did not retreat just because we fought well."

Tav said, "They thought that if Poll-ee could call the snake, then she could cause the snake to do them great harm. That is how I would feel." He looked at Polly and she remembered his first reaction to Louise.

She spoke directly to him, then turned to the others. "Louise—that is what we call her—is the first harmless snake I've ever met. Where I came from before I went to live with my grandparents, the snakes were mostly very poisonous."

The bishop said, "The Anula tribe of northern Australia associates a bird and a snake with rain."

Karralys shook his head. "The People Across the Lake have different traditions from ours, but as far as I know, they do not believe that snakes can bring rain. But neither they nor we would kill a snake."

Eagle Woman said, "The kindred of the snake would come and cause harm in vengeance. If we kill a snake because otherwise it would kill us, or by accident, we beg pardon of the snake's spirit."

Tav pointed his spear at Zachary, and all eyes turned in his direction.

"This is Zachary Gray," Polly said.

"He is from your time spiral?" Cub asked.

"He is the one who saw Anaral," Karralys explained, "because he is near death."

"What's he saying?" Zachary asked.

Polly was grateful that Zachary could not easily understand Ogam. No matter what he said about his heart and his brief life expectancy, she was certain he was not ready to hear anyone talking about his imminent death. She tried to make her face expressionless as she turned to him. "Karralys wants to know where you're from."

"California," Zachary said.

Tav stood. "Karralys, you fought well."

"I did not want to fight," Karralys said. "What I wanted to do was stop the fighting."

"They would have taken Anaral and Poll-ee, and the Heron, too."

"And so I fought. Yes, we fought well. But they were more than we, many more, and if the snake had not come—"

"Bless Louise the Larger," the bishop said.

Karralys's blue eyes brightened. "Is that not enough for you, Tav? That Polly was sent to us by the goddess for this?"

"I was so certain," Tav murmured. "But perhaps he—" He looked at Zachary.

"Hey!" Zachary's voice was urgent. "Slow down! I'm

not quick with languages like Polly. What are they talking about?"

"Well—" Polly prevaricated. "We were outnumbered by the raiders—"

"We? Are you part of this 'we'?"

She looked around the circle of stone chairs protected by the great standing stones. "Yes." She was one with Anaral and Karralys and Tav and Cub and the others. And so was the bishop. He had proven that.

Tav looked at her hopefully, and the paleness of his eyes was not hard or metallic, like a sky whitened and glaring from too much sun, but tender and cool, like the lake. "You were right when you told me the snake was your friend. Perhaps I have been wrong about the Mother's needs."

"You are wrong, indeed." Karralys stood. "Bishop Heron. Polly, Zak. You must go. Now, while there is still time."

The bishop looked around. "I don't think we can."

"Why not?" Cub asked.

"I may be wrong, but I do not think the time gate is open."

Karralys looked startled. He went to the central flat altar stone and climbed up on it, then lay down on his back, arms outstretched, eyes closed. Motionless. Time seemed to hang suspended. No one spoke. The People of the Wind seemed to have moved into another dimension where it was possible for them to wait infinitely. The bishop sighed. Zachary restlessly shifted position. Polly tried not to move, but began to be afraid that her legs would cramp.

At last Karralys sat up, slowly shaking his head. "The threshold is closed."

Chapter Nine

It was getting dark. The sun slid down behind the standing stones. A northwest wind blew cuttingly.

"Perhaps we should go someplace warm and make our plans?" the bishop suggested.

Karralys raised a hand for attention. "There is a fire and a feast being prepared. We need to celebrate our victory—and then be sure that we have people keeping watch all through the night."

"And collect all our weapons." Tav moved away from his chair. "The feast, and our thanks to Poll-ee."

"It was only Louise the Larger," Polly insisted. "It had nothing to do with me."

"We will talk later about the time gate." Karralys started toward the lake and the tents.

Zachary shouted after him, "Wait!"

Karralys paused.

"I don't understand your time gates," Zachary said,

"or how I could possibly be here, but I saw that kid in the wolf skin—"

"Cub. Our young Grey Wolf."

"I saw him calm the old man's heart."

"The bishop," Polly amended.

"Please. I don't want him to forget me."

Karralys looked at Zachary compassionately. "He will not forget you. Now. Come with me."

At the lake a great bonfire was blazing, so bright it almost dimmed the stars, which were coming out as night deepened. The wounded men and women were attended by other members of the tribe so that they would not be left out of the celebration, and the two raiders were there, too. The man with the concussion had regained consciousness, and Eagle Woman had been placed next to him. Despite her arm and shoulder held in the sling, and the fact that her lips were white with pain, she was watching him with care.

"The dark of his eyes is back to normal," she said. "He will be all right."

Polly, the bishop, and Zachary were given seats on skins piled near the star-watching rock. Near them was the young raider with the broken femur, and Anaral sat by him, helping him to eat and drink. Behind them, the oaks rose darkly and majestically, their great branches spreading across the sky, with stars twinkling through the branches as an occasional bronze leaf drifted down.

Across the lake, the mountains loomed darkly, their snow-covered peaks just beginning to gleam as the moon prepared to rise. The shore where the People of the Wind had their tents was invisible in the distance.

Karralys stood at the water's edge and raised his arms to the sky. "Bless the sky that holds the light and life of the sun and the promise of rain," he chanted, and one by one the other council members joined him, echoing his song.

"Bless the moon with her calm and her dreams. Bless the waters of the lake, and the earth that is strong under our feet. Bless those who have come to us from a far-off time. Bless the one who summoned the snake, and bless the snake who came to our aid. Bless the east where the sun rises and the west where it goes to rest. Bless the north from where the snows come, and the south that brings the spring. Bless the wind who gives us our name. O Blesser of all blessings, we thank you."

He turned from the lake and smiled at the people gathered around skins spread out on the ground. A deer was being roasted on a spit, and a group of young warriors danced around it, chanting.

"What're they singing about?" Zachary asked Polly.

"I think they're thanking it for giving them—us—its life."

"It didn't have much choice," Zachary pointed out.

Perhaps it didn't, but Polly felt a graciousness in the dance and in the singing.

"When's that kid going to feel my heart?"

"Soon," Polly assured him. "At the right time, Zachary, please trust him."

Bowls of vegetables were spread out, with fragrant breads, wooden and clay dishes of butter and cheese. Half a dozen girls and boys, long of limb and slim of body, nearing puberty, began passing food around. Two young warriors carved the deer, and an old woman, wearing a crown of feathers with an owl's head, poured some kind of pale liquid into small wooden bowls; she had been one of those in the stone circle.

Anaral brought bowls to Polly, Zachary, and Bishop Colubra. As he accepted his, Zachary tentatively touched Anaral's fingers, looking at her with eyes which seemed unusually dark in his pale face. Anaral withdrew her hand and returned to the young raider, holding his head so that he could drink. Polly noticed that on the stone altar there was a great bouquet of autumn flowers, set amidst squash, zucchini, eggplant, all the autumn colors arranged so that each seemed to brighten the others.

"It's crazy," Zachary muttered to Polly. "Here we're sitting and stuffing our faces as though we'd won some kind of great battle, and those goons who rowed off across the lake could come back any minute and slaughter us all."

The bishop replied, "I think Karralys is aware of their intentions, but he also knows that the human creature needs special celebrations. The rites themselves cannot give life. Indeed, they can be hollow and meaningless. The heart of the people is what gives them life or death."

"Is this all in honor of some god?" Zachary asked.

"It is a form of thanks to the Presence."

"What presence?"

The bishop spoke softly. "The Maker of the Universe."

"Oh, zug," Zachary grunted.

"Not necessarily." The bishop smiled slightly. "Sacred rites become zug, as you so graphically put it, only when they become ends in themselves, or divisive, or self-aggrandizing."

Polly saw a young man with a spear standing at the head of the star-watching rock, looking across the lake. A woman with a bow and arrow stood at the path which led to the standing stones. There were probably others on guard where they were not visible to her. Karralys was not leaving his people unprotected. He moved about, from group to group, greeting, praising, and wherever he went, Og went with him.

After the young people had cleared the food away, there was singing and dancing, and the moon rose high and clear, casting a path of light across the lake.

Karralys and Anaral led the dancing, at first moving in a stately and gracious circle, then dancing more and more swiftly.

"You know, that girl is beautiful," Zachary remarked. "Things haven't improved in three thousand years. By the way, I think that Neanderthal is interested in you."

"Who?" Polly asked blankly.

"That tow-headed guy with bow legs and monkey arms."

He meant Tav. Perhaps Tav's legs were not quite straight. Perhaps his strong arms were long. But he was no Neanderthal. Polly prickled with indignation but held her tongue. She was uncomfortable both with Zachary's obvious fascination with Anaral and with his jealousy of Tav's interest in her. She kept her voice quiet. "I don't think it's a very good idea for either of us to get involved with someone who's been dead for three thousand years."

"They're not dead tonight," Zachary said, "and neither are we. And if I can lengthen my life expectancy by staying here, then I'll stay. Anyhow, didn't the bishop say the time gate was closed? We're stuck here, so we might as well make the best of it."

Cub approached them, spoke to Zachary. "I would feel your heart. There is, I think, trouble there."

Zachary turned toward Polly. She explained. Zachary looked at her with anxious eyes. "Please, tell him to go ahead."

Cub slid his hand under Zachary's shirt, closed his eyes, breathed slowly, slowly.

"Well?" Zachary asked impatiently.

Cub raised his hand for silence. He kept his hand on Zachary's chest for a long time, feeling, listening. Then he raised his eyes to Polly's. "There is bad damage there. The Ancient Wolf might have been able to repair the hurt. I will do what I can, but it will not be enough."

"But the bishop's heart—"

"Bishop's heart is only old, and he is not used to being in the middle of a battle. But this—" Slowly he removed his hand from Zachary's chest. "This demands skills I do not yet have. But perhaps we should not take hope away from him."

"What's he saying?" Zachary demanded. "I wish he'd slow down."

Polly replied carefully, "He says that your heart has damage, as you know, and that it will not be easy to fix."

"Can he fix it?"

"He will do his best."

Zachary moaned. Put his face in his hands. When he looked at Polly, his eyes were wet. "I want him to be able to fix—"

"He will do his best." Polly tried to sound reassuring, but she was getting impatient.

Cub said, "Each day I will work on the strangeness I feel within his heart. The rhythms are playing against each other. There is no harmony."

"What?" Zachary demanded.

"He will work with you every day," Polly said. "He really is a healer, Zachary. He will do everything he can."

Cub frowned with worry. "Perhaps if Karralys—" He looked at his hands, flexing the fingers. "Now I must go see to the others who have been hurt."

"What do you think?" There was renewed eagerness in Zachary's voice. "I'd be glad to stay in this place even with no showers or TV or sports cars or all the stuff I thought I was hooked on. I guess I'm more hooked on life."

"He's a healer," Polly repeated.

The drums were increasing their rhythms, and the dancers followed the beat. Tav came and took Polly's hands and drew her into the circle of dancers, and the touch of his strong hands did something to her that Zachary's did not, and she did not understand her reaction to this strange young man who thought she had been sent by the goddess as a sacrifice to the Mother.

Dr. Louise's words about sacrifice flicked across her mind and were wiped away as Tav took her hands and swept her into the circle of the dance.

When she was panting and almost out of breath, he took her to the edge of the lake, his arm tightly about her. "I cannot let you go."

Still caught up in the exhilaration of the dance, she asked, "What?"

"It is very strange, Poll-ee. The Mother is usually clear in her demands. But now I am confused. The drought across the lake is bad. If they do not get rain, not just a little rain, but much rain for those who have taken our cattle—if there is no rain, they will come again, and they are many, and we are few, and we will not be able to defend ourselves."

"But you were marvelous," Polly exclaimed. "You dashed in single-handed and you fought like—" If she likened him to one of the heroes of King Arthur's court, it would have no meaning for him. So she just repeated, "You were marvelous. Brave."

He shrugged. "I am a warrior. At least I was, at home. There had to be warriors. Here we have been so away from other tribes that only the drought has brought back an understanding that land must be protected. Land, and those we love." He reached out his hand and gently touched hers, then withdrew.

Polly sighed. "I wish people could live together in peace. There's so much land here. Why do they want yours?"

"Our land is green and beautiful. We have had more rain than across the lake. We use the water of our river to—" As he tried to explain, she understood that the People of the Wind used some form of irrigation which the People Across the Lake did not. Even so, there had not been enough rainfall. If the winter snows did not come, everybody would suffer. "When you came, it seemed clear to me that the goddess had sent you. But now there is not only the old Heron who came before you but this strange young man who is as white of skin as I am white of hair."

"Do you pray for rain?" Polly asked.

Tav laughed. "What else have we been dancing and singing about?"

Of course, she realized. All ritual for the People of the Wind was religious.

"To dance and sing is not enough," Tav continued. "We must give."

"Isn't your love enough?" The question sounded sentimental as she asked it, but as she looked at the moon sparkling off the lake, she understood dimly that the love she was thinking about was not sentimental at all but firm and hard as the star-watching rock.

Tav shook his head. His voice dropped so low that she could scarcely hear. "I do not know. I do not know anymore what is required." As his words fell into silence, the soft wind gently stirred the moonlit waters of the lake. He spoke again. "There are many women of the People of the Wind who are beautiful, who would like to please me, to be mine. But none has brought me that gift without which everything else is flat. That gift! Now I look at you and the mountains are higher, and the snow whiter on the peaks, the lake bluer and deeper, the stars more brilliant than I have ever seen them before."

Polly tried to put what she wanted to say into Ogam.

Tav reached out his hand and smoothed out her frown. "Tav, it is very strange. I don't understand anything that is happening. When you touch me, I feel—"

"As I feel?"

"I don't know. What I feel has nothing to do with—" She touched her forehead, trying to explain that her reaction had nothing to do with reason. "But"—she looked at his eyes, which were silver in the moonlight— "you still think the Mother wants blood, my blood?"

Tav moaned. "Oh, my Poll-ee, I do not know."

"I don't think the Mother—" She stopped, unable to think of a word for "demand" or "coerce."—Nearer our time, she thought,—one name for the goddess was Sophia, Wisdom. A divine mother who looks out for creation with intelligence and purpose.

She shook her head, realizing that even if she could put what she was thinking into Ogam, it was not within Tav's frame of reference.

Tav took both her hands. "We must go back to the others, or they will wonder—"

She had hardly realized that the singing had changed. No longer were the drums sounding the beat of a dance. The song was similar to the one Polly had heard that first morning when she crossed the threshold to the People of the Wind, but now it was gentler, quieter, almost a lullaby.

"We sing good night." His arm about her, Tav

returned her to where Bishop Colubra and Zachary were sitting. Anaral was behind them, with the young raider. The singing drifted off as, one by one or in pairs, people went to their tents.

Karralys came to the bishop, his long white robe pure as snow in the moonlight, the topaz in his torque gleaming. "It will be my honor if you will share my tent. And, Zak—"

"Zachary."

"And you, too, Zachary."

Anaral left her tending of the raider and took Polly's hand. "And you will come with me."

Anaral's tent was a lean-to of young saplings covered with cured skins. It backed against a thick green wall of fir and pine and smelled fresh and fragrant. There were two pallets of ferns covered with soft skins. Anaral handed Polly a rolled-up blanket of delicate fur. Polly took off her red anorak and sat down on one of the fern beds.

Anaral squatted beside her. "Tav is, well, Poll-ee, you must know he is drawn to you."

Polly wrapped the fur blanket around her. "And I to him, and I don't understand how I could be."

Anaral smiled. "Such things are not understood. They happen. Later, if two people are to be together for always, then understanding comes."

"Is there going to be a later?" Polly asked. "I know the

threshold is not open now, but I—I do need to get home to my own time. Before"—she could hardly bring herself to articulate it—"before I have to be sacrificed to the Mother."

"That will not happen," Anaral protested. "There will be rain."

"Across the lake?"

"Across the lake."

Polly said, "If it hadn't been for Tav this afternoon when the raiders came—"

"And the others."

"But Tav leapt in and fought when he didn't know if the others were coming. And it was, oh, in a strange way it was exciting."

"You were a warrior, too," Anaral said.

"I just wasn't going to let those strange men carry you off."

Anaral sighed. "And I am grateful. To Tav. To you. And Karralys."

"He tried to stop the fighting," Polly said. "But when he couldn't, he fought as well as Tav did."

"We People of the Wind"—Anaral sighed again—"we have always been what the bishop calls paci—paci—"

"Pacifists," Polly supplied.

Anaral nodded. "It is the drought that has changed things. If it would only rain! The Old Grey Wolf told us that there was drought many years ago and that we—my people—came here to this fertile place because our own grounds were parched, the grasses brown instead of green, the cattle with their bones showing, the corn not even making its tassels. We have been in this place since the Old Wolf was a baby. We cannot just leave and let the People Across the Lake take our home. Where would we go? Beyond the forest there are now other tribes. If only the goddess would send rain!"

"Do you think the goddess is withholding rain?" Polly asked.

Anaral shook her head. "It is not in the goddess's nature to destroy. She sends blessings. It is us, it is people who are destructive." She left the tent abruptly.

In a few minutes she returned with a wooden bowl full of water, and a soft piece of leather for a washcloth. She wet the leather and gently washed Polly's face, and then her hands, and it was as much a ritual as the banquet and the singing and dancing had been. She handed the bowl to Polly, who understood that she in her turn was to wash Anaral. When Anaral took the bowl out to empty it, Polly felt as clean as though she had just taken a long bath. She lay down on the fern bed, wrapped in the soft fur blanket, and slid into sleep.

When she woke up, she thought at first that she was at home with her grandparents. But there was no Hadron sleeping beside her. She reached out her hand and touched hair, not the fur of the blanket, but living hair, and Og's moist nose nuzzled into her hand, his warm tongue licked her fingers. She was comforted and lay listening to the night. The quiet was different from the quiet of her own time, where the soughing of the wind in the trees was sometimes broken by the distant roar of a plane going by overhead, by a truck on the road a mile downhill from the house. Here the lake covered the place where the road was, and she could hear small splashings as an occasional fish surfaced. There was also a sense of many presences, that the People of the Wind surrounded her. Her eyes adjusted to the dark and she could see Anaral's curled-up form on the other pallet, hear her soft breathing.

Polly sat up carefully. It was cold, so she put on the red anorak and crept out into the first faint light of dawn, Og following her. Stars still shone overhead, but the moon had long since gone to rest, and there was a faint lemon-colored streak of light on the horizon far across the lake. She saw someone sitting on a tree trunk, facing the lake, and she recognized Bishop Colubra by his plaid shirt. Quietly she walked to him.

"Bishop—"

He turned and saw her, and invited her with a motion to sit beside him.

"The time gate—"

He shook his head. "It is still closed."

"Yesterday, when Dr. Louise came over, she said you'd gone off in hiking boots—"

He looked down at his feet in laced-up leather boots. "I thought I'd better be prepared."

"You mean you knew—"

"No. I didn't know. I just suspected that something might happen, and if you came to this time and place and couldn't get back, I wanted to be here with you."

"Are we going to be able to get home? To our own time?"

"Oh, I think it's highly likely," the bishop said.

"But you aren't sure?"

"My dear, I'm seldom sure of anything. Life at best is a precarious business, and we aren't told that difficult or painful things won't happen, just that it matters. It matters not just to us but to the entire universe."

Polly thought of the bishop's wife, of Dr. Louise's family. She did not know that Karralys was there with them at the lakeside until he said, "Zachary is not in the tent."

Karralys stood with his back to the lake, looking down at Polly and Bishop Colubra. "I do not wish to raise an alarm. You have not seen him? He has not spoken to you?"

"No," both the bishop and Polly replied.

"I had hoped he might be with you. Wait here, please.

I will check the other tents. If Zachary should come to you, please keep him here till I return." He turned away from them, walking rapidly. Og looked at Polly, licked her hand, then took off after Karralys.

"Bishop," Polly said softly, "Zachary is terrified of dying."

"Yes." The bishop nodded.

"And he thinks his best hope is here, in this time. So I don't think he'd go off anywhere. He tries to be so glib about everything, but he's frightened."

The bishop's voice was compassionate. "Poor young man, with his house slipping and sliding on sand."

Polly said, "If it was my heart, and I was told I had only a year or so to live, I'd be afraid, too."

"Of course, my dear. The unknown is always frightening, no matter how much we trust in the purposes of love. And I do not think that Zachary has that trust. So the dark must seem very dark to him indeed."

"It can seem pretty dark to me, too," Polly admitted.

"To all of us. But to you, and to me, there is the blessing of hope. Isn't there?"

"Yes. Though I'm not exactly sure what my hope is."

"That's all right. You've lived well in your short life."

"Not always. I've been judgmental and unforgiving."

"But on the whole you've lived life lovingly and fully. And I suspect that much of Zachary's life has been an avoidance of life. Now I'm sounding judgmental, aren't I?"

Polly laughed. "Yes, well. Being judgmental has always been a problem for me. And Zachary's the kind of person who just seems to get judged. If he weren't so sort of spectacular, people probably wouldn't care."

They looked up as Karralys returned, his face grave. "I cannot find him. And the raider is gone, too, the one whose head was nearly broken. Brown Earth, he is called. His pallet was by Eagle Woman's, but Cub gave her a potion to ease her pain and she is still asleep."

The bishop asked, "You think Zachary and the raider went off together?"

"It is possible the raider took him as hostage," Karralys suggested.

"But how would they get away? You had watches posted at all points."

Karralys sat down beside Polly on the fallen log. "Those across the lake move as silently as we do. Brown Earth could have gone into the forest and come out to the lake from another direction. There are many miles of shoreline."

"But the raider couldn't have taken Zachary if he was unwilling," Polly objected. "Wouldn't he have yelled and made a noise?"

Karralys appeared to be studying a bird who was flying low over the lake. "We went through the raider's clothes. We took away his knife. He had no arrow, no poison to make Zachary helpless." Suddenly the bird swooped down and flew off into the sky with a fish.

"But why would Zachary have gone with him?" Polly was incredulous. "Karralys, he thought his hope for life was here, that Cub could help his heart. He wouldn't just have gone off."

"No one knows what that young man would or would not do," Karralys said. "Is he not—"

"Unpredictable," the bishop supplied.

"Well, yes," Polly agreed, "but this doesn't seem reasonable."

"Many things that people do are unreasonable," the bishop pointed out. "Now what should we do?"

The lake was bathed in a radiant light as the sun rose, and with the sun the rich singing of the morning song. "I will ask the others," Karralys said. "Then we shall see."

Karralys went around the compound asking people singly, in pairs, in small groups, Og at his heels, whining a little, anxiously. There was consternation over the disappearance of the raider, more than over Zachary.

Eagle Woman berated herself. "I should have heard him. Normally, my ears are tuned—"

"Normally, you do not have a shoulder that has been pierced by an arrow," Karralys said.

"And the young man—where can he be? Cub told me his heart sounded like a dry leaf in the wind."

"We will call council at the great stones," Karralys said. "Meanwhile, we must get on with the day's work. We will continue to keep watchers posted to look out for canoes, or perhaps an attack from the forest."

Polly and the bishop were asked to join the group in the circle within the ring of standing stones.

"If they think they can use this Zak—" Tav started.

"Zachary."

"—as a hostage, they are wrong. He is worth nothing to us."

"He is our guest," Karralys said quietly. "Under our hospitality."

"I do not understand why he came," Tav said. "I fear that he will bring us grief."

"We are still responsible for him."

Cub turned to Karralys anxiously. "If they treat him roughly, I do not think his heart will stand it."

"That bad?" Eagle Woman asked.

Cub looked at her soberly.

"Then," Tav deliberated, "it was just as well he did not fight yesterday?"

"It might have killed him," Cub said.

"He is young for his heart to be so feeble," a man wearing a red-fox skin protested.

"Perhaps he had the child fever with the swollen joints that weakens the heart," Cub suggested.

—Rheumatic fever, Polly thought.—Yes, that sounded likely.

"Enough," Tav said. "What are we going to do? Why did the raider take him? Of what use can he be—except as a hostage?"

"If it is as a hostage," Karralys said, "we will hear from them, and soon."

There seemed nothing more to discuss. Karralys dismissed the council, doubled the watch. Polly helped Anaral make bread in an oven made of hot stones. She looked around for Og but did not see him. He must be with Karralys, she thought.

"This goddess," Polly mused, "and the Mother. Are they one and the same?"

Anaral punched down the risen dough. "To me, and to Karralys, yes. To those who are not druids—Tav, for instance—the goddess is the moon, and the Mother is the earth. For some, it is easier to think of separate gods and goddesses in the wind, in the oaks, in the water. But for me, it is all One Presence, with many aspects, even as you and I have many aspects, but we are one." She placed the bread in the stone oven. "It will be ready when we return."

"Where are we going?" Polly asked.

"To the standing stones. In that place is the strongest energy. That is why council is always held there."

The standing stones. Where, three thousand years in the future, Polly's grandparents' house would be, and the pool which could not be dug as deeply as planned because there was an underground river.

"Below the place of the standing stones"—Polly followed Anaral away from the tents and the lake—"there is water?"

"A river. It runs underground and then comes up out of the earth where it flows into the lake. But its source is beneath the standing stones."

"How do you know?"

"It is the old knowledge."

"Whose old knowledge?"

"The knowledge of the People of the Wind. But Tav would not take my word for it, so I gave him a wand of green wood and told him to hold it straight in front of him, and not to let it touch the ground, and then I asked him to follow me. He thought I was—what does Bishop call it? Oh, yes, primitive. But he followed me, laughing, and holding the wand. And when we got to the standing stones, he could not keep it still, he could not keep it off the ground. It leaped in his hands like a live thing. Then he knew I told true."

When they got to the standing stones there was

someone lying on the altar. With a low cry, Anaral hurried forward, then drew back. "It is Bishop talking with the Presence."

While Polly watched, the bishop slowly pushed himself into a sitting position and smiled at her and Anaral. Then he returned his stare to some far distance. "*But, Lord, I make my prayer to you in an acceptable time,*" he whispered. "The words of the psalmist. How did he know that the time was acceptable? How do we know? An acceptable time, now, for God's now is equally three thousand years in the future and three thousand years in the past."

"We are sorry," Anaral apologized. "We did not mean to disturb your prayers."

The bishop held out his hands, palms up. "I have tried to listen, to understand."

"Who are you trying to listen to?" Polly asked.

"Christ," the bishop said simply.

"But, Bishop, this is a thousand years before—"

The bishop smiled gently. "There's an ancient Christmas hymn I particularly love. Do you know it? *Of the Father's love begotten*—"

"*E'er the worlds began to be.*" Polly said the second line.

"*He is alpha and omega, He the source, the ending*—" the bishop continued. "The Second Person of the Trinity always was, always is, always will be, and I can listen to Christ now, three thousand years ago, as well as in my own time, though in my own time I have the added blessing of knowing that Christ, the alpha and omega, the source, visited this little planet. We are that much loved. But nowhere, at any time or in any place, are we deprived of the source. Oh, dear, I'm preaching again."

"That's okay," Polly said. "It helps."

"You've had good training," the bishop said. "I can see that you understand."

"At least a little."

He slid down from the great altar stone. "Zachary," he said.

"Do you think he's all right?"

"That I have no way of knowing. But whatever all this is about, our moving across the threshold of time in this extraordinary way has something to do with Zachary."

"How could it?" Polly was incredulous.

"I don't know. I have been lying here contemplating, and suddenly I saw Zachary, not here, but in my spirit's eye, and I knew, at least for a flash I knew, that the true reason I had gone through the time gate was for Zachary."

Anaral dropped to the ground, sitting cross-legged. Polly leaned against one of the stone chairs. "For his heart?"

The bishop shook his head. "No, I think not. I can't explain it. Why go to all the trouble to bring us three thousand years in the past for the sake of Zachary? I don't find him particularly endearing."

"Well, he can be——"

The bishop continued, "But then I think of the people Jesus died for and they weren't particularly endearing, either. Yet He brought back to life a dead young man because his mother was wild with grief. He raised a little girl from the dead and told her parents to give her something to eat. He drove seven demons out of Mary of Magdala. Why those particular people? There were others probably more deserving. So, I ask myself, what is there that makes me think I have crossed three thousand years because of Zachary?"

Polly plunged her hands into the pocket of the red anorak. None of this made any sense. Zachary was peripheral to her world, not central. If she never saw Zachary again, her life basically would not be changed. Her fingers moved restlessly in the anorak pockets. She felt something hard under her left hand. Zachary's icon. She pulled the small rectangle out, looked at it. "I guess Zachary could use a guardian angel."

"A great angel and a small child." The bishop, too, looked at the icon. "The bright angels and the dark angels are fighting, and the earth is caught in the battle."

"Do you believe that?" Polly asked.

"Oh, yes."

"What does a dark angel look like?"

"Probably exactly like a bright angel. The darkness is

inner, not outer. Well, my children, go on about whatever it is you need to do. I will stay here and wait."

"You are all right, Bishop?" Anaral asked.

"I am fine. My heart is beating steadily and quietly. But I probably should not fight in any more battles." He glanced at the sun, which was high in the sky, then clambered up onto the altar again and lay back down. The shadow of one of the great stones protected his eyes from the glare.

Polly followed Anaral back to the compound.

There was an unease to the day. The normal routines were carried on. Fish were caught. Herbs were hung out to dry. Several women, each wearing the bright feathers of her bird—a finch, a lark, a cardinal—were making a cloak of bird feathers.

Cub called to Polly, "I may need your help."

Polly had forgotten the second raider, the very young man with the compound fracture, whom Anaral had tended so gently the night before. Now he was lying under the shade of a lean-to. His cheeks were flushed and it was apparent that he had some fever. Cub squatted down beside him. "Here," he said, "I have some of Eagle Woman's medicine to help take away the fever. It is made from the mold of bread and it will not taste pleasant, but you must take it."

"You are kind," the young raider said gratefully. "If you had been wounded and taken prisoner by my tribe, we would not have cared for you in this way."

"Could you have cared for me?" Cub asked.

"Oh, yes, our healer is very great. But we do not waste his power on our prisoners."

"Is it a waste?" Cub held out an earthen bowl to the raider's lips and the lad swallowed obediently. "Now I must look at the leg. Please, Poll-ee, hold his hands."

Polly knelt by the raider. Anaral had followed her and knelt on his other side. Polly found it hard to understand him, but she got the gist of what he was saying in a language that was more primitive than Ogam. "What is your name?" She took his hands in hers.

"Klep," he said. At least, that is what it sounded like. "I was born at the time of the darkening of the sun, of night coming in the morning as my mother labored to bring me forth. Then, as I burst into the world, the light returned, slowly at first, and then, as I shouted, the sun was back and brilliant. It was a very great omen. I will, one day, be chief of my tribe, and I will do things differently. I, too, will take care of the wounded and not let them die." He gasped with pain, and Polly saw Cub bathing the broken and raw skin with some kind of solution. Anaral turned away while Polly held Klep's hands tight, and he grasped her so hard that it hurt. He grimaced against the pain, clenching his teeth to keep from crying out. Then he relaxed. Turned and looked at Anaral. "I'm sorry."

She smiled at him gently. "You are very brave."

"And you are doing well," Cub said. "I will not need to hurt you any more today."

Klep let out a long breath. "I hear that Brown Earth, my companion, is gone from you, and also one of yours. Or is he one of yours, with the pale skin and dark hair?"

"He is not one of ours," Cub said. "He comes from a far place."

Anaral asked eagerly, "Do you know where they are?"

Klep shook his head. "Not where they are, or how they left. Your medicine made me sleep like a child and I heard nothing."

Cub asked, "Do you think Brown Earth took Zak with him?"

"I do not know. Would this Zak want to go?"

"We don't know," Anaral said. "It is very strange."

"We don't understand," Polly said.

"If I knew anything," Klep assured them, "I would tell you. I am grateful. Brown Earth has a big mouth. It may be that he has made promises."

"Promises he can keep?" Cub asked.

"Who knows?"

"Rest now," Cub ordered. "Anaral will bring you food and help you to eat. I will be back this afternoon to put fresh compresses on your leg."

They reported their conversation to Karralys.

"It solves nothing," he said, "but you have been help-ful. And Klep may yet be helpful, who knows? Thank you. Eagle Woman sends her thanks to you, Polly. Cub will need you again when he dresses her shoulder. Anaral"—he smiled gently at the girl—"is a nourisher, but she cannot take the sight of blood."

"It is true," Anaral agreed. "When I cut my finger, I screamed. Poor Bishop. But I will be glad to help Klep eat."

"We are glad you are here, Polly," Karralys said. "And we wish you could return to your own time. You must wish that, too."

Polly shook her head. "Not until we find Zachary. And not until there is rain."

The attack came during the night. Og woke Polly, bark-ing loudly. Anaral was up in a flash, spear in hand. Polly followed her. Torches cast a bloody glow over the fight-ing people, and at first Polly could not tell which were the People of the Wind and which were the raiders. Then she saw Og rushing to Karralys's aid, jumping on a raider who had a spear at Karralys's ribs. Og clamped the man's wrist in his jaws, and the spear fell.

Then Polly felt something dark flung over her, and she was picked up like a sack of potatoes. Her screaming mingled with the general shouting. She tried to kick, to wriggle free, but her captor held her tight as he ran with her. She could not tell in which direction they were going. She heard the snapping of twigs underfoot. Felt branches brushing by. Then at last she was put down and the covering removed from her head. They were on the beach, out of sight of the village. Trees reached almost to the lake's edge. The moon was high, and she gasped as she saw Zachary standing by a shallow canoe.

"Zach!"

"You brought her," Zachary said to her captor. "Good."

"Get in the canoe," Zachary said. His face was white and pinched in the moonlight, but his voice was sharp.

"What is this?" Polly demanded.

"It's all right, sweet Pol, really it is," Zachary reassured her. "I need you."

She drew back. "I'm not going anywhere."

Her captor's hands were around her elbows and she was propelled toward the canoe. He was not Brown Earth, the raider who had had the concussion, but an older man, muscled, heavy.

"He won't hurt you, as long as you don't make a fuss. I promise," Zachary said. "Please, Polly." He was cajoling. "Just come with me."

"Where?"

"Across the lake."

"To the people who are trying to take our land?" Her voice rose with incredulity.

"Our land?" Zachary asked. "What do you care about it? It's three thousand years ago. You don't know anything about the People Across the Lake. They aren't enemies."

"They attacked us."

He overrode her, speaking eagerly. "They have a healer, Polly, an old man, wise, and full of experience. Brown Earth saw Cub."

"Cub will help you."

Zachary shook his head. "He's too young. He doesn't know enough. The healer across the lake has power. He can make me better."

"Fine," Polly said. "Go to him. But leave me out of it."

"I can't, Polly love. I would if I could. But they want to see you."

"Me? Why?"

"Because you called the snake and it came. They think you're some kind of goddess."

"That's nonsense. Anyhow, how can you understand what they're saying?"

"If I can get them to speak slowly enough, I get the gist of things. I'm not good at Ogam like you, but I get enough. And sign language can be very effective," Zachary said. "How else do you think Brown Earth got me to go with him? Please, Polly, please. I don't want him to have to hurt you."

"You'd let him? I thought you cared about not hurting—ouch!" Her captor's hands tightened about her arms like a vise.

"Please, Polly, just come, and everything will be all right."

"Take your hands off me," Polly snapped. She opened her mouth to scream for help, but her captor silenced her with a rough hand. From the village she could hear sounds of shouting, so probably her cry would not be heard. Her captor shoved her toward the canoe. He was taller than she was, and full of brawn. To try to fight him was folly. At the moment it seemed the simplest thing to get into the canoe, to go with Zachary and the raider, to see what all this was about.

The raider pushed the bark off the narrow beach, grating it over the pebbles, then leapt in lightly, barely causing it to sway.

Zachary reached out to touch Polly's knee. "I'm sorry, Polly. You know I don't want to hurt you. You know that." His face was drawn and anxious. "They sent this goon with me because they were afraid I mightn't bring you. I'm the one they don't trust, not you. You'll be treated well, I promise you, just like a goddess. And that's what you are to me, even if I think of you as a goddess differently from the way they do."

She sighed gustily. "Zachary, when the fighting's over and I'm missing, they'll be frantic."

"Who will?"

"Karralys, and Anaral. The bishop, Tav. Cub. Everybody."

Her captor made two guttural sounds, which Polly interpreted as "Let's go." He pointed, and they could see several longer canoes moving swiftly across the lake.

The battle, then, was over, though Polly had no idea who had won, who had been hurt, or even killed. Swiftly she leapt into the water and sloshed toward shore, but her captor was after her and grabbed her before she could reach land.

"You have no right to take me against my will," she struggled to say.

He did not reply. He picked her up and carried her back to the canoe.

"Polly! Don't do that again!" Zachary sounded frantic.

Polly struggled to catch her breath, which had been nearly squeezed out of her by the strong arms of the raider.

"Polly, don't deny me my chance. Please. I know their healer can help me."

"But there's a price on it?"

"They just want me to bring you to them because they think you're a goddess."

Polly shook her head. "I'm no goddess. I didn't call Louise. She just happened to come. I don't have any magic powers." She held on to the side of the canoe as the raider paddled swiftly. "Does he have a name?"

Zachary laughed. "It sounds something like Onion, I think, but their language isn't pure Ogam. Lots of grunts and noises and arm waving. Polly, I'm sorry I had to get you this way, truly I am, but I didn't know how else. I need you. If you come with me, then their old healer will fix my heart."

—Fix it, she thought wearily.—He's used to having money fix everything. And not everything can be fixed.

Suddenly they were surrounded by other canoes, and paddles were held aloft triumphantly, and those without paddles raised their hands above their heads, clapping.

"See?" Zachary gave her his most charming smile. "See how happy they are to see you?"

Once ashore, she was greeted by an old man with a face full of fine wrinkles, like the lines of an etching. He held out his hands to Polly and helped her out of the canoe. "Poll-ee."

She nodded.

"Tynak," he said. "Tynak greets Poll-ee." He led her across the narrow beach and then over grass that crunched dryly under her feet. He took her to a lean-to, where there was a couch of ferns, similar to Anaral's fern beds. Tynak indicated that Polly was to sit, and he himself squatted back on his heels.

Speaking with Tynak, who had an authority that de-clared him to be the leader of the People Across the

Lake, was not easy, but Polly managed to learn that the battle had been no more than a cover-up for her abduction. No one had been seriously wounded, no prisoners taken, other than Polly.

Zachary stood just outside the lean-to, and the old man summoned him in with a smile so faint that there was no joy in it, but rather a sense of solemnity.

"See, I've brought her, Tynak," Zachary said. "Now will the healer fix my heart?" He put his hand to his chest and looked eagerly at the chief.

Tynak embarked on a long, vehement speech which Polly could not follow. His language was mostly short, sharp syllables, and he was speaking quickly. She understood only isolated words: goddess, rain, anger. But nothing coherent fitted together.

She looked out at a land far drier and browner than that of the People of the Wind. What grass there was between beach and lean-to was brittle. The leaves of the trees drooped dryly, drifting listlessly to the ground. Over the lake the sky had a mustardy-yellow tinge at the horizon, staining the night. The air was so humid that the farther shore was not even visible. Only the mountains rose out of the murk. They were higher, looked at from this side of the lake, and their peaks held more snow. The melting of the additional snow might be what would help keep the land of the People of the

Wind fertile and green. The moon shone hazily through drifting clouds.

Tynak rose and turned to Polly, indicating that she was to follow him. He was much shorter than she had realized when he met the canoe. His legs were short sticks under a skin tunic. But he moved with authority and dignity. She followed him across a compound of tents, many more than on her side of the lake. There were people moving about. Tynak spoke and what she understood was that in the daytime the sun was no longer gentle, but was hot and burning. He took her toward what should have been a cornfield of stalks that had been harvested and cut down but which, in the moonlight, were dark midgets, barely tasseled. Tynak spoke again, more slowly, and she thought he was telling her that his people were kind to the land, treated it with respect, but it had turned on them. He looked at her with small, very dark eyes, and told her that without rain they would starve.

He led her back to the lean-to and showed her a rolled-up fur covering in the corner. Then he bowed to her and left, signaling to Zachary to come with him.

A few minutes later one of the young women of the tribe brought Polly a bowl of some kind of stew, put it down by her, then looked at her shyly.

Polly thanked her, adding, "I am Polly. You are—"

The girl smiled. "Doe." Then she hurried away.

Polly saw that the tribe was gathered around a fire, sharing a meal together from which she was excluded. Why? The raiders had been included in the feast of the People of the Wind. But Klep had said that the People Across the Lake treated their prisoners differently from the way the People of the Wind did.

She ate the stew, which was passable, because she knew she needed to keep up her strength. Probably the meat from which the stew was made came from one of the beasts stolen from the People of the Wind. Then she sat, knees drawn up to her chin, thinking. She realized that the People Across the Lake might have had no feast, no meal, without what they had taken during the raids made on the more fortunate people whose land was still fruitful. She had seen poor or primitive people before, but never those who were starving.

She lay down, knowing that she needed to rest, but every muscle was tense, and the singing and shouting of the tribe kept her awake. It was not the happy singing of the People of the Wind; rather, it was a plaintive chant. Were they worried about Klep, who had been taken prisoner—Klep, who was to be their next leader?

She lay with her eyes closed, trying to rest so that she would be ready for whatever was in store, feeling within herself a desperate quietness. It was inconceivable that she should be trapped three thousand years in the past, that she might never get home. And yet here she was, a prisoner.

Because of Zachary.

But Zachary had not closed the time gate.

No, but he had brought her here, across the lake. Zachary was too terrified of dying to think of anything or anybody else. In his case, what would she have done? She did not know. She closed her eyes and drifted off into a state between waking and sleeping. In her half dream she felt a strange security, that she was surrounded by love that came to her from across the lake, from the People of the Wind, from the bishop and Anaral, Karralys, Tav, even from Klep, who knew where she was and who she was with far better than the others. She turned on her side, relaxing into the protection of their love.

In her half sleep she saw Tav, and looked into his silver eyes, saw his fair, thick lashes, his mop of pale hair. He was questioning her, affirming that she was a goddess to the People Across the Lake, and wanting to know how they captured her. Longing for the reality of his presence, she slid more deeply into sleep.

"Zachary and one of the men kidnapped me."

She saw Tav's outraged scowl. "Why would anyone, even that Zak, do such a thing?"

Polly murmured, "Klep was right when he said that maybe Brown Earth promised something to Zachary."

"Promised what?" Tav demanded.

"Zachary was promised that their healer would fix his heart if he brought me to them."

"But Zachary should never have done that!" Now it was Anaral who was angry.

"I guess if you think you're going to die, and you're told someone can keep you alive, that becomes the only thing you can think of. Anyhow, I'm sure he doesn't believe that there's any kind of threat to me. I mean, they wouldn't hurt someone they think is a goddess, would they?"

"They will not do anything until the moon is full," Tav said. "And oh, Poll-ee, we will not let them do anything to you. Klep is grateful to you for having helped set his leg, for having held his hands against the pain."

"He is nice," Anaral said softly. "He is good."

"He says that his honor is bound to you, to help you, and to help us free you." Polly shifted position, holding on to the dream, not wanting to wake up. In the dream Tav leaned toward her and placed his fingers gently over her ears. Then he touched her eyes, her mouth. "We give you the gift of hearing," he said. "Klep sends you the hearing of the trees."

"We give you the gift of hearing," Anaral said softly. "I give you the gift of hearing the lake, for I know that you have much love of water."

"And I"—Tav's voice was soft—"I give you the gift of understanding the voice of the wind, for we are the People of the Wind, and the Wind is the voice of the goddess. Listen, and do not be afraid."

"Do not be afraid," Anaral repeated.

"Do not be afraid." Their words echoed in her ears as she turned again on the hard earth and slid out of the dream into wakefulness. She tried holding on to Tav's promise that nothing would happen to her, but despite her own affirmation that the People Across the Lake would not do anything to harm someone they thought to be a goddess, an inner voice told her that to these people, whose land was devastated by drought, the sacrifice of a goddess would be a sacrifice of great power.

She lay on the fern pallet, pulling the fur rug over her. She wanted to recover the comfort of the dream but she could not. Her mind began searching for ways of escape. She was a strong swimmer. She had swum all her life, and her stamina and endurance were far greater than ordinary. There had even been a suggestion that she try for the Olympics, a realistic suggestion, considering her capabilities, but she agreed with her parents that it was a competitiveness she did not want. She thought about the lake and realized that the distance was too great, especially in cold water. Her grandparents' pool was heated and was barely seventy-two or -three degrees. The lake would be much colder. Unless it was her last hope, she would not attempt the lake.

Where was Zachary while she was isolated in this small lean-to? The sound of people singing and shouting was fainter. She knelt on the rug and could see several groups leaving the fires and going to their tents. The feast, if, indeed, it had been a feast—for what? the coming of the goddess?—was over.

The darkness was tangible. She felt it as a heavy pressure on her chest.—But this is fear, she thought.—If I can only stop being afraid.

She shuddered. How were sacrificial victims killed? With a knife? That would be the quickest, the kindest way . . .

She breathed slowly, deliberately. There was no sound from any of the tents. The water of the lake lapped gently against the shore. She listened. Tried to remember the gifts Tav and Anaral had given her in her dream. There was the gift of listening to the water. Hush, the water said. Hush. Hush. Peace. Sleep.

The wind lifted, stirred in the trees, rattling dry leaves. The lean-to was attached at the back to the trunk of a great oak. The branches overarched the skin roof, adding their protection. In the summer when the tree was fully leafed, the lean-to would be protected from the sun. Klep had sent her the gift of hearing the trees.

She listened, with a certainty that indeed gifts had been sent to her, blowing in the wind across the dark waters of the lake. She heard a steady throb, like a great heart beating. The rhythm never faltered. It was an affirmation of steadfastness. The oak was older than any trees in her own time. Hundreds of years old. It *was*, and its being was a strange comfort.

Last she turned to Tav's gift, cherishing it, the gift of hearing the voice of the wind, and she listened as the wind stirred gently among the dry leaves above her. Touched the waters of the lake, ruffling its surface. Reached into the lean-to and brushed against her cheeks. She heard no words, but she felt a deepening of comfort and assurance.

She slept.

When she opened her eyes, it was daylight. Tynak was squatting by her, looking at her. Behind him, the dawn light was rosy on the water. The sun was rising behind the snow-capped mountains that shielded the People of the Wind. But now, as Polly looked at the mountains from the far side of the lake, they seemed wild and menacing. Around the compound, people were stirring, and she could smell smoke from the cook fires.

Long rays of light reached into the lean-to, touched Polly. Tynak held up one hand, pointing. At first she had no idea what he was indicating with his ancient finger.

Then she realized that it was her hair. Tynak had never seen red hair before. At night it would not have shone as it did in the long rays of sunlight. She did not know how to explain that red hair was not particularly unusual in her time, so she smiled politely. "Good morning."

"Klep—" There was urgency in Tynak's voice.

She spoke slowly. "Klep has a broken leg. Our healer is taking care of it. He will be all right."

"He will return?"

"I don't know about that. I don't know what happens with prisoners."

"He must return! You are goddess, we need help."

"I'm not a goddess. I'm an ordinary human being."

"You called snake. It came."

"I'm sorry. It didn't have anything to do with me. I don't have that kind of power. I don't know why she came. It was just coincidence." She hoped he could understand enough of her faltering Ogam to get the gist of what she was saying.

"Snake. Who is?"

"Louise is just an ordinary black snake. They're harmless."

"Her name?"

"Louise the Larger."

Tynak grunted, gave her an incomprehending look, then turned and without speaking further left the lean-to. In a few minutes he returned with a wooden bowl full of some kind of gruel.

She took it. "Thank you."

"Can you call rain?" he demanded.

"I wish I could."

"You must try." His wrinkled face was kind, sad, in no way sinister or threatening.

—Even in my own time, she thought,—where we think we have so much control over so many things, we haven't succeeded in forecasting the weather, much less controlling it. We, too, have droughts and floods and earthquakes. We live on a planet that is still unstable.

"You will try?" Tynak prodded.

"I will try."

"Where you come from, you have gods, goddesses?"

She nodded. Because of her isolated island living, she had had little institutional training in religion. There had been no available Sunday schools. But family dinner-table conversation included philosophy and theology as well as science. Her godfather was an English canon who had taught her about a God of love and compassion, a God who was mysterious and tremendous, but not to be understood as "two atoms of hydrogen plus one atom of oxygen make water" could be understood. A God who cared about all that had been created in love. And that included all these people who had lived three thousand years ago. Bishop Colubra, too, believed in a God of total love. And so, despite her pragmatism, did Dr. Louise.

Anaral had talked of the Presence. That was as good a name as any. "We believe in the Presence," Polly said firmly to Tynak. "The One who made us all and cares about us."

"This Presence wants sacrifice?"

"Only love," she said. But perhaps that was the greatest sacrifice of all.

"This Presence sends rain?"

"Not always. We have droughts, too."

"Where you come from?"

—When, she thought, but nodded. It was impossible to explain.

Did she have anything from her own time which would be impressive to Tynak? She felt in the pockets of the red anorak. Yes, she had several things, artifacts, that might seem to Tynak to have power. Her fingers touched Zachary's icon. She pulled it out. Held it in front of Tynak. Zachary had bought the icon for her because he cared about her.

Tynak stared at the icon intently, almost fearfully, then looked at her questioningly.

She pointed to the child in the icon, then to herself. Then she pointed to the angel, and stretched out her arms as though embracing all of Tynak's compound, the tents, the lake, the great snow-capped mountains on the far side.

Tynak took the icon from her and again stared at it, then at Polly, then back to the icon. He pointed to the angel, his fingers touching the great wings. "Can fly?"

"Yes."

"Goddess?"

Polly shook her head. "Angel."

He sounded the word out after her. "An-gel. An-gel will help you?"

She nodded.

"Angel will let no harm come to you?"

"Angel loves me," she replied carefully.

He nodded several times. Turned the icon over, looked at the plain wood of the back, turned it so that he was looking at the angel and the child again. "Where you get?"

"Zachary gave it to me."

"Zak. Zak. You speak now to the Zak."

She held out her hand for the icon. "Please give it back to me."

He pulled his hand away, still holding the icon.

"Please give it back," Polly repeated, and reached for it.

"No! Tynak keep an-gel power."

Why did she care so much about keeping the icon? If she tried to grab it away from him, others would come to his rescue immediately. She stared into his dark eyes. "Angel has good power for me. Bad power for you."

"Not so. I take an-gel. I take your power."

It was absurd to feel so threatened by Tynak's taking the icon. It was nothing more than a painting on wood. Zachary had said that it had no value. But it was affirmation that he cared about her, that he meant it when he promised that he never wanted to hurt her. Her voice shook. "Bad power for you." She could only repeat herself.

She stopped as she heard a low growl. Wet and dripping, Og bounded toward her.

"Og!" She was almost as glad to see him as she had been to see Tav.

He was at her side, baring his teeth at Tynak.

"Give." She reached for the icon again. "See? Good power for me. Bad power for you."

Tynak put the icon into her hand and walked away, very quickly.

Og licked her hand gently and she burst into tears.

Chapter Ten

Og's frantic efforts to lick her tears away made Polly laugh, and she wiped her hands across her eyes. "Oh, Og, am I ever glad to see you! How did you get here?" Perhaps Anaral or Tav or Karralys had brought Og most of the way in a canoe. There was no way of guessing. She was just warmly grateful that the dog was with her.

She looked at the icon of the angel and the child. Undoubtedly, Tynak had never seen a painted picture before. If she had a camera with her, one of those instant ones, and took his picture, that would surely convince him of her power. But she didn't have a camera.

Og growled slightly and she looked up to see Zachary in his elegant hiking outfit, incongruous in this ancient village devastated by drought.

"Polly, sweet, are you okay?"

She looked at Zachary, at his pale face, his darkly shadowed eyes. "You kidnapped me."

He put his hand against one of the poles that supported the lean-to. "Polly, don't you understand? I needed you. I needed you terribly."

"Why didn't you just ask me?"

He dropped down to sit beside her on the fern pallet. "I didn't think you'd come."

"But you didn't even try. You let that man kidnap me."

"Oh, sweet Pol, don't call it that. They made it very clear to me that the healer wouldn't come near me if I didn't bring the goddess to them."

"You know I'm no goddess."

"They don't."

"Zachary." She looked straight at him. "You do understand that Tynak is planning to sacrifice me in order to get rain?"

"No, no, he'd never go that far." But suddenly Zachary looked very uncomfortable. "You're a goddess. He just wanted to have you here because you have power." He looked at Og. "And you do, don't you? The dog has come to you, and Tynak would think that was terrific power, wouldn't he?" He was talking too much, too fast.

"Zachary, would you let Tynak sacrifice me?"

"Never, never, Polly." He looked at her pleadingly. "Polly, I want their healer to help me."

"At this price?"

"There isn't any price."

"Isn't there? My life for yours?"

"No, no. Tynak thinks you're a goddess." Zachary ran his fingers through his dark hair. "Listen, Polly, this Tynak made it clear to me that the healer wouldn't touch me unless you—okay, that's the problem. I couldn't understand what he wanted. Can you understand him?"

"A little."

"You're angry with me."

"Why wouldn't I be?"

"Polly, you have my icon. You do care about me. Tynak said the healer would help me if you came here. You're a goddess, don't you understand?"

She shook her head. Looked at him. He was tragic and handsome, but she had a sinking feeling that he would do anything to get what he wanted. A big thing, this time: life.

"Don't you want me to live?" He was pleading.

"At my expense?"

"Polly, stop exaggerating."

"Am I?"

Zachary stood up. "Polly, I wanted to talk to you, but I can see there's no point while you're being unreasonable. I'm going back to Tynak. I'm staying in his tent. And in case you're interested, there are skulls on poles in his tent." His voice was tight and defensive. "You've brought me back in time to this place where the people are hardly more than savages. I think you should feel a certain sense of responsibility."

"If they're savages, why do you have so much faith that their healer can help your heart?" she asked.

"Ah, Polly, I can't stand to have you mad at me! I thought we were friends."

Friends? She was not sure what a friend was. She thought of her conversation with Anaral about friendship, about how friends cared for and tried to protect one another. Friendship was a two-way street. She wished Zachary would go away and leave her alone. She put the icon back in her pocket, the icon Zachary had given her because his grandmother believed in angels. Bishop Colubra, too, believed in angels. If the bishop could believe in angels, so could she. Not in the angel painted on the icon, but in real powers of love and care. The icon was not a thing in itself, but an affirmation.

For Tynak it was a thing in itself.

"Have you seen the healer today?" she asked Zachary.

"Seen him and spoken—if you can call it that—with him. He's very old. Older than Tynak. He has long, skinny arms, and enormous, strong-looking hands. Listen, Polly, you will help me, won't you? You will?"

He was frantic, out of his mind with terror, she knew that. But she also knew that his denials that Tynak was going to use her as a sacrifice were hollow. She felt a deep pain in her chest.

"See you." Zachary tried to sound casual. Turned away from her and left.

The sun was well above the horizon and slanted warmly against the lean-to. It was going to be a warm autumn day. Indian summer? She slid out of the anorak. Tav had said that nothing would happen until the full moon. Day after tomorrow, she thought. Many things could change between now and then.

She left the lean-to and walked across the compound, Og by her side. People looked at her curiously, cautiously, even fearfully, but no one spoke to her. She felt as though her red hair were on fire. There were many surreptitious glances at Og. These people were not used to dogs, at least not to domestic dogs. Perhaps they thought Og was part of her magic. Perhaps that was why Og had been sent across the lake to her. Og was protection, the bishop had said. She needed his protection.

The sun beat down with a sulfurous glare. It was hot, actually hot, but a strange heat. The sky was yellowish, rather than blue, and her one hope at this moment was that this odd weather meant a storm was coming, and rain.

Whenever she approached a group of people, conversation stopped. Og nudged her, pushing her gently in the direction of the lean-to, so she went back.

At noon, when the sun was high, Doe brought her a bowl of broth and some heavy bread, but did not stay. Polly ate and lay down on the pallet, hands behind her head, staring up at the skins of the roof, trying to think, but her thoughts would not focus. She rolled up the anorak to make a pillow and raise her head so she could see out of the lean-to, across the compound, and to the lake.

Zachary had said that there were skulls in Tynak's tent, that these Stone Age people were savages. But were the people of her own time any less savage? Within her grandparents' memories, Jews and gypsies and anyone who was thought to be a danger to Aryan supremacy were put in concentration camps, gassed, made into soap, used for medical experimentation. At more or less the same time in her own country Japanese people who were American citizens were rounded up and put into America's own version of concentration camps. Surely they were not as brutal as the German ones, but they were as savage as anything on either side of the lake.

She thought then of Bishop Colubra lying on the great capstone and praying, and she closed her eyes and tried to let her mind go empty so that she could be part of his prayer. He and Karralys knew that she and Zachary were here. They had sent Og to her. She hoped that they were praying for her. She knew that they cared, that they would never abandon her. Tav would rescue her.

But there was still an aching hurt in her heart.

* * *

In the late afternoon, thunder rumbled from the mountains across the lake, and lightning flashed. The clouds came down in a curtain, but across the lake, not on Tynak's side. It looked to Polly as though the People of the Wind were getting a good shower. The smell of rain was in the air, and it was a summer smell. The air continued to be hot and heavy.

Tynak came to her again.

She sat on the anorak, to protect the icon. Og sat beside her. Tynak pointed to the dog and looked at her questioningly. "Animal?"

"He's a dog. Dog."

"Where comes from?"

"He belongs across the lake. We think he came across the ocean with Karralys—the druid. The leader."

Tynak pointed to the storm that still played across the lake. "Power. You have power. Make rain."

Polly shook her head.

"Earth must have rain. Blood, then rain."

"A lamb?" Polly suggested.

"Not strong enough blood. Not enough power."

Only Polly had enough power for a successful sacrifice. A sacrifice must be unblemished. Tynak was afraid of Polly's power. He had considered the possibility of sacrificing Zachary, he told Polly, but Zachary might not provide enough power to appease the anger of the gods and bring rain to this side of the lake, and return Klep to his people.

"You promised to help Zachary's heart," Polly tried to remind him, pressing her hand against her heart.

Tynak shrugged.

"You promised Zak that if he brought me to you, your healer would help his heart," she persisted. "Do you not have honor? Do you not keep your word?"

"Honor." Tynak nodded thoughtfully. "Try." He left her.

She stared after him, wondering if the healer indeed had enough of the gift of healing to give new life to a badly damaged heart.

Doe brought her another bowl of stew in the early evening. Polly ate it and sat listening. The wind moved in the branches of the oak behind her. Sultry. Too hot for this time of year. The village was quiet. Tynak had left her unguarded, probably because there was no place for her to go. The forest menaced behind her. The lake was in front of her.

The water rippled softly. The wind seemed to call her, to beckon. She was not sure what the wind was trying to tell her. The moon rose. Close to full, so close to full. The village settled down for the night. Fires were extinguished or banked. There was no sound except for the stirring of the wind in the trees, ruffling the surface of the lake. The village was asleep.

Og rose, nudged her. Went to the edge of the lean-to,

looked at Polly, tail barely moving, waiting. Then he went to the edge of the lake, put one paw in, looked back at her, put his paw in the water again, looked back, wagging his tail. Finally she understood that he wanted her to go into the lake. To swim. She slipped out of her shoes and socks, jeans, sweatshirt, and left the lean-to in cotton bra and underpants. Og then led her along the lake side, farther and farther away from the tents.

There was no sound from the village. Sleep lay heavy over the compound. The snow on the mountains across the lake was luminous with moonlight. Polly followed Og, trying to be quiet. She could not move silently, like Tav and Anaral. Twigs crackled under her feet. Vines caught at her. Now there was no more beach. The forest went right down to the water's edge. She tried not to brush against branches. Tried not to cry out when twigs or stones hurt her bare feet.

Finally Og slid into the water, again looking back at Polly to make sure she was following him. She walked into the lake, trying not to splash. She slipped into the water when she was knee-deep. Og swam steadily. The water was cold. Bitter cold. On the surface it had been warmed by the unusual heat of the day, but underneath it was cold, far colder than her grandparents' pool. The brazen sun had warmed it just enough so that it was bearable. She followed Og, swimming strongly but not frantically. She had to swim steadily enough so she would not get hypothermia, but not so hurriedly that she would tire before she got across the lake.

The water was quiet. Cold. Cold. She swam, following Og, who moved at an even pace so she could keep up with him without straining. But as they swam, her body felt colder and colder, and her skin prickled with goose bumps. She trusted Og. He would not have led her into the lake if they weren't going to be able to make it to the other side. She had swum all her life. She could swim forever if she had to.

They swam. Swam. Polly's arms and legs moved almost automatically. How long? How far was it? Now, even in the light of the moon, she could not see Tynak's village, which she had left behind her, nor could she see across the lake, except for the snow-capped mountains.

She felt her breath coming in gasps, rasping in her throat. She was not going to make it. She tried to look for land ahead of her, but her eyes were dazzled with exhaustion and all she saw was a flickering darkness. She went under, gulped water, pushed back up. Og looked over his shoulder, but swam on. Her breathing was like razor blades in her chest. She tried to call, "Og!" but no sound came out of her throat. Her legs dropped. She could not go on.

And her feet touched the rocky bottom.

Og was scrambling onto the shore, barking.

And Tav was rushing across the beach to greet her. He

splashed into the water, followed by Karralys and Anaral. The bishop hurried to meet them, bearing a fur robe. Anaral took it from him and wrapped Polly's wet body in warmth.

She was in Tav's strong arms. He carried her into Karralys's tent.

She was safe.

A bright fire was built in a circle of stones in the center of the tent. The smoke hole had been opened and blue tendrils of smoke rose up and out into the night. Anaral brought Polly something hot to drink, and it warmed the cold which had eaten deep into her marrow.

"Did you have rain this afternoon?" she asked.

"Yes. Rain came," Karralys said.

Polly sipped at the warm, comforting drink. She was still shivering with cold and Anaral brought another fur rug to wrap around her legs. Bishop Colubra reached out to touch her wet head. She was so exhausted that she lay down, wrapped in the warm fur, and fell into a deep sleep.

Whether it was strain from the swim, or from something in the warm drink, she moved immediately into dreaming. In her sleep she was the center of a bright web of lines, lines joining the stars and yet reaching to the earth, from her grandparents' home to the star-watching rock to the low hills to the snow-capped mountains, lines of light touching Bishop Colubra and Karralys, Tav and Cub, Anaral and Klep, and all the lines touched her and warmed her. Lines of power . . . Benign power.

Then the dream shifted, became nightmare. The lines were those of a spiderweb, and in the center Zachary was trapped like a fly. He was struggling convulsively and ineffectually, and the spider threw more threads to tie him down. Zachary's screams as the spider approached cut across her dream.

She woke up with a jerk.

"Are you all right?" Anaral asked anxiously.

"You need more sleep," Tav said.

She shook her head. "I'm okay."

"Blessed child"—the bishop's voice was caressing—"we know about Zachary's abducting you. Can you tell us more?"

"Well." She was still chilled to the marrow. "I don't think I can leave Zachary there." It was not at all what she had expected to say.

"Polly." Bishop Colubra spoke gently but commandingly. "Tell us."

Briefly she reviewed her attempted conversations with Tynak, with Zachary.

When she had finished, Tav leaped to his feet in rage. "So this Zak took you to save his own life."

"Heart," she corrected.

"He was willing to have you die so he could live," Anaral said.

Polly shook her head. "It isn't that simple. I don't think he admitted to himself what he was doing."

"Why are you defending him?" Tav shouted.

"I don't know. I just know it isn't that simple." But hadn't she accused Zachary of the same thing? "I think I have to go back."

"No. It will not be allowed," Tav expostulated.

"You are here. Safe. Stay," Anaral urged.

"Why do you have to go back, Polly?" the bishop asked.

Her reasons sounded inadequate, even to herself. But a vision of Zachary trapped in the web kept flicking across her inner eye. "My clothes are there. Zachary's icon is in my anorak pocket, and Tynak thinks it has great power. He tried to take it from me once, but I hope he's afraid of it now. And if I don't go back, I don't know what will happen to Zachary." She shook her head as though to clear it. "I really don't know why I have to go back. I just know I have to."

Tav pounded with the butt of his spear against the hard ground of the tent. "What happens to this Zak does not matter. It is you. You matter. I care about you."

"I can't make rain for them, Tav," she said. "And if there isn't rain they will attack you again. You said that yourself." She wanted to stretch out her arms to him, to have him take her hands, draw her to him, but this was no time for such irrational longings.

"Karralys—" she started, but Karralys was not there.

"He has gone to the standing stones," the bishop told her. "Didn't you see him leave? He gestured for Og to stay here in the tent, and then he went out."

"But he will come back?" Polly asked anxiously.

"He will come back," Anaral assured her. "It is the place of power. He needs to be there."

Polly bit her lip, thinking. "If Tynak believes I have goddess-like powers, he'll hold off. The icon had a terrific effect on him, Bishop. What else have I got?" She thought. "Well, there's a flashlight in the anorak pocket, one of those tiny ones with a very strong light. And a pair of scissors. And a little notebook and a pen. And some other stuff. Tynak will never have seen any of those before."

"Notebook and pen?" Anaral asked. "Like Bishop's? To write with?"

"Yes."

"Karralys is the only one I know who can write, and he writes only on rock or wood. And his real wisdom is not written. It is kept here." She touched first her forehead, then her heart. "What do I have to give you? Oh, look! Bishop gave me this after I cut my finger." She reached into a small pouch at her side and brought out a gold pocketknife. "It would not be much good for skinning a deer, but it is quite sharp. And I have another one of these." And she gave Polly a Band-Aid.

"Stop!" Tav shouted. "No! Poll-ee is not to go back!"

"Tav, I have to."

"You swam. How far you swam! Not many people could swim across the lake, all that way, even in summer. You are here. We will not let you go."

"I have to." She sounded her most stubborn.

"Polly," the bishop said, "you have not yet given us a real reason."

"I can't just leave Zachary there to be slaughtered."

"Why not?" Tav demanded.

"I can't. If Tynak thinks I'm a goddess, maybe I can stop him."

Tav shook his head. "You. They will sacrifice you."

"No," Polly said. "To them, I am a goddess." She wished she was as certain as she sounded.

The bishop's face twisted, as though from pain. "Polly is right. She can't leave Zachary to be a meaningless sacrifice. No matter what he has or has not done, that is not what Polly does."

"No!" Tav cried.

Karralys returned, pushing aside the tent flap. "Bishop Heron is right. Polly is right. We cannot let the young man be sacrificed. It will not bring rain, and we would have sold a life and gained nothing."

"Poll-ee's life," Tav said.

"It is never expedient that one man should die for the sake of the country," the bishop said.

"We will gather all our warriors together—" Tav started.

"They are many more than we are," Karralys pointed out.

"I won't have people fighting over me. People would get hurt or killed. It wouldn't do any good, Tav. You mustn't even think of it. You had rain here today. Maybe there'll be another storm, one across the lake. That's what we need."

Karralys said, "Because of the position of the mountains and the currents of wind, we have rain here far more often than across the lake. But it is possible that rain will come, not just a storm, but a rain all over the lake and shores."

"Yes," Polly agreed. "Rain. Not fighting. Rain."

Karralys looked at her thoughtfully. "I lay on the capstone and listened. The stars are quiet tonight. I hear only that Zachary is to be saved."

"I don't understand." Tav's voice was savage.

"Nor I," Karralys replied. "I know only what I hear."

Polly asked, "You consult with the stars?"

Karralys frowned. "Consult? No. I listen."

"For advice?"

"No, not so much for advice as for—" He paused.

"Direction?" the bishop suggested.

"No. In the stars are lines of pattern, and those lines touch us, as our lines touch each other. The stars do not foretell, because what has not happened must be free to happen, as it will. I look and listen and try to understand the pattern."

The bishop nodded. "The story is not foretold. The future must not be coerced. That is right."

Karralys looked at Polly gravely. "If you are going to return to Zachary, it is time."

Tav turned to the bishop. "You would send Polly back?"

"There is no *would*," the bishop said.

Polly looked at him, nodding. "It is what I am going to do."

Tav said, "Then I will take you in my canoe."

Anaral said, "You will need something warm to wear. I will give you my winter tunic."

"Thanks," Polly said. "I'll need it."

"I go with you, Tav," Anaral continued. "I have talked much with Klep, hoping to find a way to rescue Polly. He has told me of a small island not far from the village, hidden by the curve of the land. From there it is only a short paddle."

"Klep!" Polly had almost forgotten the young man with the broken femur. "Is he better?"

Karralys smiled. "He is better. His fever is gone. The broken flesh is healing cleanly. But it will be weeks before he can walk."

"Perhaps Polly should talk with him," Anaral suggested, "before she goes back to his tribe."

Karralys nodded in approval. "Yes. That would be good. Tav, can you and Cub bring him?"

"Can't I go to him?" Polly asked. "Wouldn't that be easier? Won't it hurt him to be moved?"

"Tav and Cub will be careful. The fewer people know you are here, the better."

Tav was already gone. Anaral detached the leather pouch from her waistband and removed a handful of small stones. Dropped them on the ground at her feet and looked at them where they lay. "If we lose one, we lose all." Her voice was soft. Bent down to touch another stone. "If we save one, all things are possible." Touched another. "The stars will guide. Trust them." And another. "The lines between the stars are reflected in the lines between the sacred places and in the lines that cross time to join people." She looked up, blinking, as though waking from a dream.

Karralys smiled at her. "The stones are well read."

Anaral smiled back. "They read true."

"Annie, dear"—the bishop looked at her searchingly—"these are not fortune-telling stones?"

"No, no," Karralys said quickly. "The stones do not

tell us what is going to happen, or what we are to do, any more than the stars. They speak to us only of our present position in the great pattern. Where we are now; here. Sometimes that helps us to see the pattern more clearly. That is all. This worries you, Heron?"

"No," the bishop said. "I trust you, Karralys. You and Annie."

Polly said, "Some kids in my school got really involved in fortune-telling and the future and stuff, and my parents take a very dim view of that kind of thing."

"I, too," Karralys said. "Only Anaral reads stones, that they may not be misused."

They broke off as Tav and Cub came into the tent, bearing Klep between them, his broken leg stretched motionless between two oaken staves. Gently they set him down before the fire, which still burned brightly, illuminating the interior of the tent. When he saw Polly, he smiled in relief.

"You are all right?" Klep asked.

She smiled back. "Now that I'm thawed, I'm fine."

"You swam the whole way?"

"I grew up on islands," Polly said. "I've swum all my life."

"Even so," Klep said, "it is a long way."

Polly grimaced. "Don't I know. I thought I wasn't going to make it."

"And you are going back?"

She squatted beside him. "Klep. Tell me. If I don't go back, what will happen to Zachary?"

He in turn asked, "We had no rain today, on my side of the lake?"

"No. Not a drop."

He made an unhappy grunt. "There will have to be a sacrifice."

"Zachary?"

"Yes."

"But they will wait till the full moon?"

"Yes."

"Two nights from now," Karralys said. "Polly, Og will go with you. If you need help, send him. Like you, he swims like a fish. However, Polly, know that we are with you. The lines between the stars and between us are like—like—"

"Telegraph lines," Bishop Colubra supplied. "This won't mean anything to you, Karralys. But in our time we can send words across lines."

"Faxes," Polly suggested.

"If you will keep your heart open to us, Polly, the lines, too, will be open."

"Karralys!" The bishop pulled himself up, waving his arms. "I have just had a thought!" He looked around the tent, letting his gaze rest on Klep, then returned to Karralys. "You don't want to keep Klep here as a prisoner of war or a slave, or anything like that, do you?"

"No. He is free to go as soon as he is healed."

"If he is well enough for Tav and Cub to have brought him here, he is well enough to be put in the canoe with Polly. Let us send him back with her. Then she will be the goddess who has rescued Klep."

Klep burst into delighted laughter. "That is splendid! But how strange. I do not want to go." He looked at Anaral, and she returned his gaze steadily, and the line of love between the two of them was almost visible.

"But you will go," Karralys said. "What Bishop Heron has thought of is perfect. And if you, Klep, are to be the next leader of your tribe, the sooner you return, the better."

"I am very young." Klep reminded Polly of her brother, next in age to her, Charles, with his wisdom, unusual for his age, and his lovingness.

"Your Old One still has years to live," Karralys assured him. "We will send two canoes. Polly is too tired to go alone with Klep. Tav, you will paddle Polly and Klep. Cub, you will go with Anaral. When the canoe is near enough shore for Polly to bring it in, you, Tav, will join Anaral and Cub."

"We must hurry," Klep said, "to be there before dawn."

It all happened so quickly that Polly barely had time to think, only to accept that the bishop's plan was the best possible under the circumstances. She was given a warm sheepskin tunic to wear, which she put on gratefully.

Klep was placed in the bottom of one of the canoes. Polly sat in the bow, with Og curled at her feet. Tav took the stern. Anaral and Cub got into a slightly smaller canoe.

They pushed out into the dark water. Polly turned once to wave to the bishop and Karralys. Then she turned her face toward the dark horizon.

Chapter Eleven

The two canoes moved silently across the lake. Tav and Cub paddled in rhythm, making no sound of splashing as the paddles dipped cleanly into the lake, thrusting the canoes forward.

Klep lay silently, looking at the sky, the velvet dark sky untouched by city lights. The stars were there, but dimmed by a faint mist, and a few patches were blotted out by clouds. Polly huddled into Anaral's sheepskin garment. The night air was cold, and she was still chilled from the long swim.

She turned around and looked at Tav, his muscles rippling gently as he paddled. There was no way she could think as Tav thought. She could conceive with her mind a world of gods and goddesses, of Mother Earth, but she could not understand it in her heart, except as part of the glorious whole.

"Tav," she whispered.

"Poll-ee?"

"If Tynak decides that I—that I am to be the sacrifice to the Mother—"

"No." Tav was emphatic. "I will not let that happen."

"But if there is no rain?"

"I will not let Tynak hurt you."

"But if I come back to you and the People of the Wind, and the drought continues, if there isn't any more rain, what would you do then?"

The silence was palpable.

"Tav?"

"I do not know." His voice was heavy, and for a moment his paddle faltered with a slight splash. "My training is that of a warrior. At home, across the great water, there were people we had captured from neighboring tribes. The Mother did not ask us for anyone dear to our hearts."

"But you still believe that the Mother needs blood to be appeased?" Tav would not know what she meant by appeased, which she had substituted for the unknown Ogam word, so she amended, "The Mother needs blood or she will be angry and withhold rain?"

"I do not know," Tav said. "The Mother has been good to us. Karralys with his knowledge of the stars brought us safely across the great water, but the winds were kind. Then we were given a canoe, bigger than this one, and the wind and rain blew us along rivers and into the lake

and to the People of the Wind. The storm ceased and the
rainbow came. I did not die. Karralys is a healer. We
blessed the Mother, and she blessed us, but now the rain
is being held back, and even though our land is still
green, we will not be able to protect it if the drought
continues across the lake. I thought I understood the
Mother and I have tried to be obedient to her ways. But
now I do not know. I do not know."

Polly thought,—I don't know, either, about the Creator I believe made everything.

She glanced at the sky and between wisps of clouds
the stars shone serenely. —But if I knew everything,
there would be no wonder, because what I believe in is
far more than I know.

"Why, my Poll-ee"—Tav interrupted her thoughts—
"does this Zak want so much to see the healer across the
lake when the far greater healer is with us?"

"The greater healer?"

"Karralys," Tav said impatiently. "Did you not know?"

"Cub—"

"Cub has the tribal knowledge of healing. And his
hands are learning the gift, as you saw with Bishop."

"Yes."

"But it is Karralys who has—how do I say it—who
has made Cub's gift to grow."

Now that Tav was telling her this, it became obvious.
Why had she not realized it? Zachary had been so fo-

cused, first on Cub, then on the healer across the lake, that Karralys had been pushed out of her thoughts. "I was stupid," she said.

"There has been much happening," Tav defended her. "Hsh. We are nearly there."

Never before had the Mother asked for anyone dear to his heart, Tav had said. She held those words to her own heart. She wanted him to touch her, to tell her that he could care for and protect her, never let anyone put her on the altar to be sacrificed. Could Tav keep his promise to protect her from Tynak? He was as confused in his own way of thinking as she was in hers, and their ways were so alien that it was impossible to think of them as being connected by one of the lines that patterned the stars and the places of benign power and the love between people.

If she could not understand his belief that the earth demanded blood, would he not be equally horrified by the slums of modern cities, by violence in the streets, drug pushing, nuclear waste? How could the star lines be connected to urban violence and human indifference?

The two canoes drew together. Anaral reached across to hold Polly's hand in a gesture of comfort as well as a way of bringing the two canoes together.

Tav stood, balancing carefully, then transferred to the other canoe. Both canoes rolled slightly, but no more. When Tav was seated, he handed a paddle to Polly.

"You can turn the canoe?" he asked.

"Yes."

"If you will paddle equally to the right and toward shore, you will reach Tynak's village."

"Right."

"Klep." Anaral's voice was soft. "Give your leg time to heal. Do not use it too soon."

"I will be careful," Klep promised. "Do you be careful, too. Oh, be careful, be careful." There was a world of meaning in his repetition.

"I will," Anaral assured him. "I will."

"Hold out your paddle," Tav told Polly.

Not understanding, she did as he asked. He used her paddle to pull the two canoes so that she and Tav were side by side. With one finger he gently touched her lips and it was the most marvelous kiss she had ever been given. She reached out and touched his lips in return.

"Ah, my Poll-ee. Go." He gave her paddle a quick shove.

Polly waited, watching, while the canoe with Tav, Anaral, and Cub headed back across the lake.

Klep's voice was warm and soft. "Tav would draw a line between the two of you."

Polly turned the canoe around, facing in the direction Tav had told her Tynak's village would be. "You think he loves me?"

"Loves? What is loves?" Klep asked.

Was it in Bishop Colubra's notebook? "When two people really want to be together, they love each other."

"Love," he repeated. "To join together?"

"Yes. When you love someone, you would do anything to help. It is like being friends, but much more."

"The lines between you," he said, "they grow short, the way the line between Anaral and me came close, close, and now it is being pulled." He looked longingly in the direction of the canoe with Anaral in it.

"Yes. That is love."

"You love?"

"Yes. Lots of people."

"Love who?"

"Oh, my parents and my grandparents and my brothers and sisters."

"But you do not join together with them as one."

"No. That is different. My mother and father, they are one, that way. And my grandparents."

"You and Tav?"

She shook her head. "You have to know someone for more than a few days. If things were different—"—If three thousand years didn't separate us. If totally alien views of the universe didn't separate us, if, if . . . "If we had a lot of time together, then maybe."

"Anaral and I have not a lot of time, but the line is strong."

Yes. Klep and Anaral reached out for each other as Polly would reach out for Tav, but Klep and Anaral were not separated by thousands of years, and if Anaral was a druid, Klep would one day lead his tribe, having been born under a great omen.

"If rain comes, if my people no longer steal cattle and sheep from your people . . ."

Romeo and Juliet all over again—or presaging—the People Across the Lake versus the People of the Wind? "I hope it will work out for you," Polly said. "It would be"—she had no word for suitable, or appropriate—"right."

"I would make short the line between Anaral and me in a way I have never known before."

There was no word for love in Klep's vocabulary, but Anaral would teach him.

They were nearing the shore. Polly could see a shadow, someone standing there, waiting. She drove the paddle deep into the water and sent the canoe sliding up onto the pebbly sand. She jumped out and pulled the canoe far enough onto the shore so that it would not slide back into the lake. Og was at her side.

The shadow came toward her. It was Tynak.

"I have brought Klep to you," she said.

She was a goddess.

She simply smiled at Tynak when he questioned her.

"I have brought him to you. Isn't that enough?" She was surprised at the haughtiness in her voice.

As for Klep, he, too, smiled and said nothing. Pushing himself up with his arms, he looked about his village, and Polly recognized anew how much larger it was than the village of the People of the Wind. Tynak summoned four young men, who carried Klep to his tent, and it was one of the largest tents on the compound. Tynak and Polly followed, Polly making sure that Klep's leg was not jolted. Og trotted by her side, occasionally reaching out to nudge her hand. He was not going to leave her.

Klep was placed on his pallet, over which hung a great rack of antlers, even larger than the one in Dr. Louise's kitchen.

"When daylight comes," Tynak said, "the healer will look at your leg."

Klep replied, "My leg is good. She"—he indicated Polly—"has the healing powers of the goddess."

Polly had stopped feeling goddess-like.

Klep asked, "You are cold?"

Even in Anaral's sheepskin garment, she still felt the cold from the lake. Drawing herself up again, she ordered Tynak, "Have someone bring me my coat." Not only would it feel comforting and familiar, but she wanted to know whether or not Tynak had taken Zachary's icon.

He spoke to one of the men who had carried Klep. "Quick!" And the man ran off swiftly.

Klep spoke to Tynak. "Across the lake, I was well treated."

Tynak nodded. "Brown Earth told us the same."

"I was not treated as a prisoner or an enemy. I was treated as a friend."

Tynak shrugged. "Trust easily come by can vanish as easily."

Klep asked, "Where is the young man, Zak?"

"In my tent. See, I am treating him with kindness."

"He is well?"

Again Tynak shrugged. "The healer will tell."

The man came back with Polly's red anorak, and she put it on over Anaral's tunic, feeling in the pockets. The icon was gone. That was not surprising. She pulled out the flashlight and shone it directly in Tynak's eyes. "Give me my angel," she demanded.

Tynak put his hands to his eyes in terror.

She turned the flashlight off, then on again. "Give me my angel."

Tynak shook his head, though the flashlight had shaken him badly.

Polly kept it shining into his eyes and he turned away. "The icon of the angel has no power in itself. The power of the angel is for me." She touched her chest. "If you try to keep it, it will turn against you."

"Tomorrow," he promised. "Tomorrow."

Where had he hidden it?

She flicked off the flashlight. "Light that does not burn," she said.

She turned the flashlight on again, not to blind Tynak with its beam, but to give more light to the tent, and she could see that there were beads of sweat on Klep's forehead and upper lip. The trip across the lake and then to his tent had been hard on him. Polly pointed to him with the light. "He needs rest. Someone should be near in case he calls."

Tynak understood. "Doe will stay."

"I want to go now," Polly said. "I am tired and wish to rest." She moved toward the tent flap, Og beside her.

Tynak bowed and escorted her back to the lean-to, taking care not to get too close to Og. They were followed by two of the men who had carried Klep, not Brown Earth, but Onion and another man, squat and strong. Tynak spoke to them rapidly and sharply. Then he bowed and turned back toward Klep's tent. The two men stationed themselves on either side of the lean-to. She was being guarded. She had proven that she could escape, and Tynak was going to see that this would not happen again.

Polly went into the lean-to and pulled on her jeans under the sheepskin tunic. She was shivering with exhaustion as well as cold. She zipped up the anorak, then wrapped herself in the fur. She was so tired that she almost fell down on the pallet. Og lay beside her, warming her.

* * *

When she woke to daylight, Tynak was again squatting at the entrance to the lean-to, watching her, eyeing Og, who was sitting up beside Polly, his ears alert. Her two guards had drawn respectfully away a few yards, but they were still there. It was one day off full moon.

She sat up, regarded Tynak in silence for a moment, then demanded in a tone she hoped befitted a goddess, "Bring me my angel. Now."

He looked at her and his eyes were crafty.

She felt in the anorak pockets and pulled out the notebook and pen. She opened the notebook, which must have been used by her grandfather, for the first pages were filled with incomprehensible equations in his scratchy writing. She held them up to Tynak. Then she turned to an empty page, and took the cap off the pen. She was no artist, but she managed a recognizable likeness of the old man. She held it out to him. Snatched it back as he reached for it.

"Power," she said. "It has great power. Bring me angel icon. Bring me Zachary. Bring me healer."

He stood. Held out his hand again. "I-con?"

"Picture of you is not icon. You bring me angel icon, I give you picture. Pic-ture."

His hand reached for it.

"Not now. When you come back with angel."

He left, walking with what dignity he could. The two

guards drew in closer to the lean-to. After a few minutes Polly was brought a bowl of gruel by Doe, who looked fearfully at the dog. Polly took the bowl, said, "Thank you," and put her hand on Og's neck. "He won't hurt you."

Og's tail swished gently back and forth. Doe smiled, not coming closer, but standing and watching Polly. It was obvious that she would have liked to talk if she could. Polly thought that it was not only Og or the language difficulty. She suspected that Tynak had forbidden conversation.

"Klep says careful," Doe warned. "Careful."

One of the guards peered at them.

"Thanks," Polly said softly as the girl hurried away.

She ate the gruel, which was dull but nourishing. It made her appreciate her grandmother's oatmeal. Would she ever have that again? She put the bowl down at the entrance of the lean-to and waited. Waited. The great oak trunk behind the lean-to rose up high into the sky, much higher than the Grandfather Oak. Polly listened, and seemed to hear the heartthrob of the huge tree, the sap within the veins running slowly as it drew in for the winter. Patience. Do not fear. A star-line touches my roots and my roots are under you.

The wind stirred the branches. Ruffled the waters of the lake. It was a warm wind, unseasonably warm. Listen to the heart of the oak. We are with you. Last night the water carried you safely. Trust us.

Yes, she would trust. The universe is a universe. Everything is connected by the love of the Creator. It was as Anaral had said: it was people who caused problems. And the dark angels who were separators added to the damage.

She waited. Og lay beside her, his tail across her legs. Suddenly he jumped to his feet, tail down, hair bristling.

Tynak.

He handed Polly the icon. She took it and put it back in her anorak pocket, then drew out the notebook and tore out the page on which she had sketched Tynak, and gave it to him.

He held it up, looked at it, turned the page over, saw only the blank page, and turned back to the sketch. Touched himself, touched the piece of paper, then put it carefully in his tunic. Satisfied, he gestured that she was to follow him. "Leave—" He gestured toward Og.

"No. Og goes with me."

Tynak shook his head, but set off across the compound, looking back to see that Polly was following him. Several paces behind Polly, the two guards moved silently. Og walked slightly in front of her, putting himself between Polly and Tynak.

The chief of the People Across the Lake led her to a tent considerably larger than the others. The flap was pegged open, and she could see inside. Zachary had been right: on poles stuck deep in the earth of the tent were skulls. Zachary was there, and an old man, far older than Tynak, thin and brittle as a winter leaf. But his face had a child's openness, and his eyes were kind. He looked at Og questioningly, and Polly gestured to the dog that he was to lie down.

"Where have you been?" Zachary's voice shook with anxiety. "We were frantic. Where were you?" He rose from his pallet, his hair slightly damp, his eyes dark with fear. When she did not answer, he gestured to the old man. "This is their healer. He won't touch me without you."

Polly looked at the old man and bowed slightly. He smiled at her, and it was a child's smile, radiant and without fear. He pointed at her hair, nodding, nodding, as though both surprised and satisfied. Then he looked at Tynak, pointed again at Polly's hair.

Zachary said, "They think your red hair is another sign that you are a goddess. They go in for a lot of signs, these people. Now will you get the old man to take care of me?"

"You may examine Zachary's heart," she said, and the role of goddess was not comfortable. She pressed her hand against her own chest, then pointed to Zachary's.

The old healer indicated that Zachary was to lie down. Then he knelt beside him. He took Zachary's wrist in both his hands, touching it very lightly, just above the palm, listening intently, his eyes closed. Occasionally he lifted his fingers from Zachary's pulse, lightly, seeming to hover over his wrist like a butterfly, or like a dragonfly over the waters of the lake. Then the fingers would drop again, gently.

After a while he looked up at Polly with a slightly questioning regard. She nodded, and he looked at Zachary again, indicating that he was to remove his jacket and shirt.

Obediently, Zachary complied, fingers shaking, then lay back down. The old healer knelt and bent over him, holding his hands stretched out about an inch above Zachary's chest, moving his fingers delicately, cautiously, in concentric circles. After a long time he touched the tips of his fingers against Zachary's skin. The healer waited, touching again, then hovering. Polly could almost see wings quivering. His palms pressed against Zachary's chest. The old man leaned so that his whole weight was on his hands. After a moment he lifted his hands and sat back on his heels, his body drooping. His whole focus had been intensely on Zachary for at least half an hour.

He looked at Polly and shook his head slightly. "Big hurt in heart."

Zachary cried out, "Can you fix it?"

The healer spoke to Tynak and Polly could not understand him, except that he was saying something about Klep.

Tynak said, "You, goddess, did help Klep. Help this Zak."

Polly gestured. "I only held Klep's hands while Cub set his leg. I would help if I could, but I have no training as a healer." She could not tell whether they understood her or not.

The old healer indicated that he wanted to see her hands. Polly held them out, and he took them in his, looking at them, back, front, nodding, making little sounds of approval. He held out his own hands again, then indicated that he wanted Polly to hold her hands over Zachary's chest as he was doing.

"Stay," she said firmly to Og, and knelt beside the healer. He put his hands over hers, and together they explored the air over Zachary's chest, and she felt a strange tingling in her palms, and her hands were no longer ordinary hands, and they were not functioning in ordinary time. She did not know how long their four hands explored, moved, touched Zachary's heart without ever touching his skin. Slowly, discomfort moved into her hands, and a feeling of dissonance.

The old healer raised his hands, and suddenly Polly's fingers were icy. She looked at the healer. "Power," he said. "Good power. Not enough."

"What's he saying?" Zachary demanded.

"He's saying that together we have good power."

"You're not a doctor," Zachary said. "Does he know what he's doing?"

"Yes. I think he does." She wondered what Dr. Louise would feel.

"You really do?"

"Zachary, these people don't think in the same way that we do. They look at healing in a completely different way."

"So am I healed?"

She looked at the old man. "Is he better?"

"Better. Not—"

"His heart?"

The old healer shook his head. "Better, but not—"

"What's he saying?" Zachary demanded anxiously.

"He says your heart is somewhat better, but it is not cured."

"Why not?"

"He says there is not enough power."

Zachary seemed to shrink. "Why not?" His voice was thin, a child's wail.

The healer rose and beckoned to Polly. She followed him, calling over her shoulder to Zachary, "I'll be back." Og was at her heels like a shadow as she and the healer went to Klep's tent.

He greeted them, smiling. "The healer says I am—am a marvel."

"You're healing well," Polly agreed. "You're young and healthy. You'll be fine in a few weeks, as long as you do what Anaral says, and take care of yourself."

The healer spoke to Klep, then bent to look at his leg, nodding in approval.

Klep said, "He wants you to know that you helped. But Zak's heart is bad."

"I know," Polly said. "Oh, Klep, he is so frightened."

"Healer has helped. If he had more power, he could help more. Why is Zak so afraid? Life is good, but where we go next, that is good, too."

"Zachary doesn't believe that," she said.

"He thinks it is bad?"

"No. He thinks it's nothing. That he'll be gone."

Klep shook his head. "Poor Zak. Healer will try again. Try to help."

Could he, Polly wondered, when doctors with all their modern tools of surgery could not? But that the old man was truly a healer in some way she did not yet understand was certain.

There was nothing specific for her to do. Wherever she went, the two guards were in the background, not approaching her, but keeping her in sight all the time. She walked around the village with Og, but the villagers were nervous about the dog and shot fearful glances at

Polly. She did not understand why the fear was also angry, but there was no mistaking their antagonism.

She did not know what was on Tynak's mind. He spent a long time in his tent with Zachary, and came out, looking at the sky as though seeking a sign.

Doe brought Polly her lunch. She drew away, but did not leave. Polly asked, "Why must I eat alone?"

Doe shook her head, glanced at the guards. "Tynak."

"Why are people afraid of me?"

"Goddess." Doe's eyes were troubled. "Where rain?"

Shortly after lunch Tynak came to the lean-to. "Angel?" he asked.

Polly brought the icon out of her anorak pocket and held it up so he could see it, but did not give it to him.

"An-gel has power?"

"Yes. For me. Good power."

Tynak pulled the sketch out from under his tunic. "Power."

"Power is mine," Polly said firmly.

"Mine." Tynak put the sketch away. It was crumpled, as though he had shown it to many people. "Come." He beckoned, and she followed him, Og at her heels. Tynak led her past the village, along a narrow path through the forest of great and ancient trees, until they came to a clearing. All the trees that surrounded the clearing were completely defoliated. Not a single leaf was left clinging to the branches. The trunks and limbs were dark and bare and somehow sinister. The trees farthest from the clearing held a few fading yellow leaves, so pale as to be almost white, and one by one they were drifting list-lessly to the ground. In the center of the clearing was a large rock with a flat top, slightly concave. Tynak went up to it, and Polly followed him. There was a foreign chill to the air. Polly felt an oppressiveness on her chest, so that she gasped for breath. On the rock were rusty stains.

Polly pointed. "What?"

"Blood," Tynak said.

Blood. Dried blood. So this was where sacrifices had been made, and where Tynak was considering a new sacrifice.

Og growled, low and deep in his throat. Polly put her hand on his head and tried to still the apprehension which prickled her skin.

"An-gel protect?"

She tried to look haughty. "Yes." Quickly she pulled out the notebook and pen and made another sketch of Tynak, not as good as the first, because her hands were shaking in her hurry, but still recognizable. She reached in her pocket for the scissors, and cut the picture in half. Then she looked at Tynak. "Power."

Tynak clutched his chest as though she had actually hurt him.

Polly put the pieces together, shut the notebook, and put it back in her pocket.

Tynak was visibly shaken. "An-gel give knife with two blades?"

"Angel guards me. Og guards me. Why are you bringing me here?"

"Place of power."

"Bad place," Polly said.

"Good power. Makes rain. Makes Zak's heart good."

"I want to talk to Zak," Polly said sharply.

Tynak gave her a sly, slantwise look. "Goddess's blood has much power. Tomorrow full moon. Power."

She had to ask directly. "Does Zachary know?"

"Know what?"

"About this place? About—" She swallowed painfully. "About my blood giving the healer more power."

"Zak knows. Zak wants."

"Suppose," Polly said, "I am not here tomorrow? Suppose the angel takes me away?"

Tynak glanced at the two guards standing uneasily at the outside of the circle. "No. Angel not take you away."

"And if it rains before tomorrow?"

Tynak clapped his hands. "Good. More power."

"And the healer will help Zachary?"

Tynak shrugged. "If healer has enough power, will help."

Og's growl was low and deep and menacing.

"Stop," Tynak said.

She pressed her hand against Og's head. Tynak would not hesitate to kill Og. If it would make it easier for himself, or for whomever he would order to capture Polly, to drag her to this clearing with the terrible stone, to add her blood to the blood that had been shed there through the years—yes, Tynak would kill Og if he thought that would lessen her power. Og, if he was not killed first, would not let Polly be taken without a fight. But Og could not hold out against an entire tribe. She looked at Tynak and decided that the only reason he had not already killed the dog was a superstitious fear that Polly's and the angel's powers would wreak vengeance.

What was there to do? Her heart was thumping painfully, heavy as a stone. Was that how Zachary's heart felt all the time?

Tynak turned away from the dreadful rock and led her back to the lean-to. The two guards drew near again. One had a bow and arrow, the other a spear. She might be a goddess. She was also a prisoner.

After Tynak left, she walked out of the lean-to, passing between the guards, and they followed her, silently, as she went to the lake. "Go, Og!" she cried, and the dog ran into the lake and swam rapidly. She swung round on the two young men, stopping the one who was fitting an arrow to his bow. "No!" she ordered.

The two men looked at each other, not knowing what to do. When one hefted his spear, she hit his arm sharply. She was sure that they had been told not to hurt her. Her blood was too valuable to be spilled other than ritually. She watched until Og was barely visible, certainly out of range of arrow or spear, swimming strongly away from them. Then she went back to the lean-to, and the young man with the bow and arrows hurried away, no doubt to report to Tynak.

She had sent Og off and that was all she could do.

She sat on the pallet. Did Zachary know what he was doing? Had Tynak somehow promised him that the healer could cure him if he had just a little more power and Polly's blood would give him that power? She did not know him well enough to guess whether or not in his extremity he would willingly, knowingly let her be killed in the hope that his heart could be mended.

She thought of the healer holding his hands over Zachary with the delicacy of a butterfly, of her own experience of the healer holding his hands over hers, as warmth flowed through them. There had been incredible power and beauty in the old man's hands. Could he be a healer and yet with his healing hands take her blood to enhance his power? Could benign power and malign power work together? Mana power and taboo power were each an aspect of power itself.

Well, she, Polly, meant nothing to the healer. He operated from a completely different view of the universe from hers. And she could not superimpose her mores on him.

There were skulls in Tynak's tent.

She was three thousand years from home.

She tried to breathe slowly, calmly. Tried to pray. Bishop Colubra had made it quite clear that although Jesus of Nazareth was not to be born for another thousand years, Christ always was. She turned to the words of a hymn that had long been a favorite of the O'Keefe family:

> Christ be with me,
> Christ within me,
> Christ behind me,
> Christ before me,
> Christ beside me,
> Christ to win me,
> Christ to comfort
> and restore me.

She lay back on the pallet, her hands behind her head, looking up at the leather roof of the lean-to. In the bright sunlight, patterns of oak branches moved across it in gentle rhythm. Hsh. Breathe softly, Polly. Do not panic. The sap moving like blood in the veins of the oak followed the rhythm of the words.

> Christ beneath me,
> Christ above me,
> Christ in quiet,
> Christ in danger,
> Christ in hearts of
> all that love me,
> Christ in mouth of
> friend and stranger.

Would Bishop Colubra call it a rune? A rune used for succor, for help, and she was calling on Christ for help.

Danger. She knew that she was in danger. From all sides. The healer needed more power for Zachary's heart. Tynak needed power for rain.

Christ in hearts of all that love me.

Right now she was more aware of her grandparents, of the bishop and Dr. Louise, than she was of her parents and brothers and sisters, who knew nothing of what was going on. The bishop, Karralys, Annie, Cub, Tav. They were across the lake, waiting. They loved her. They held her in their hearts. What would they think when Og came? They would know that she had sent him. What would they do?

Christ in mouth of friend and stranger.

Karralys and Anaral were no longer strangers. They were friends. Cub was like a little brother. Tav. She was in Tav's heart. Klep had talked of the lines between himself and Anaral, between Tav and Polly. Love.

Stranger.

Tynak was still a stranger. There was no line between Polly and Tynak. But there was between Polly and the healer. Surely the loving power of Christ had been in those delicate hands as they explored Zachary's pulse, breath, heartbeat.

And was there a line between Polly and Zachary? Did one choose where the lines were going to go? If Zachary was truly willing to attempt to save his own life by urging that Polly be sacrificed, what happened to the line? Where was Christ?

She was sure that the bishop would say that there was no place where Christ could not be.

Where was Christ in her own heart? She felt nothing but rebellion, and rejection of the clearing in the woods with the terrible stone.

She thought of Dr. Louise's words about a blood transfusion. If she could save one of her brothers or sisters by offering all of her blood, would she do it? She did not know. A thousand years away, that blood had been freely given. That was enough. She did not have to understand.

A light breeze, warm, not cold, slipped under the lean-to and touched her cheeks. Little waves lapped quietly against the shore. The oak tree spread its powerful branches above her. Beneath the ground where she lay, the tree's roots were spread from the trunk in all directions. Lines of power. Tree roots reaching down to the center of the earth, to the deep fires that kept the heart of the planet alive. The branches reached toward the lake, pointed across the lake to where people who loved her were waiting. The highest branches stretched up to the stars, completing the pattern of lines of love.

The breeze moved in the oak tree. A leaf drifted down to the roof of the lean-to and she could see its shadow. She listened, and a calm strength slowly began to move through her.

Her peace was broken by the two guards summoning her. The one with the spear banged it on the ground. The one with the bow and arrow reached down to pull her up. She shook him off and stood, putting her anorak on over the sheepskin tunic, though the day was warm. The two men looked in awe as she pulled up the zipper. Here was a showing of power she hadn't even thought about. She reached her hand into the pocket to make sure the icon was there.

If she knew their names, they would have less power over her. "I am Polly." Not goddess: Polly. "You are?" She looked questioningly at the man with the bow and arrow. "Polly. You?"

"Winter Frost," he said reluctantly.

"And you?" She looked at the man with the spear. "Polly. You?"

"Dark Swallow."

"Thank you, Winter Frost, Dark Swallow. You have beautiful names." Even if they did not understand her words, she could convey something with her voice.

Dark Swallow led the way. Polly followed behind him, wishing that Og were trotting along beside her, at the same time that she was visualizing Og swimming ashore, letting the People of the Wind know that she was in trouble. But what could they do? They were a small tribe, less than half the size of the People Across the Lake.

Her steps lagged and Winter Frost prodded her with his bow.

They were taking her to the clearing in the forest, the clearing where the surrounding trees had lost all their leaves, where the great bloodied rock waited. But it was daylight, full daylight. They would do nothing until night and moonrise. Even so, she hung back, and Winter Frost prodded her again.

Tynak and the healer were there. Tynak nodded at the guards, who retreated well out of the open circle, waiting. Tynak and the healer both spoke at once, then Tynak, then the healer, a scrambling of staccato words which Polly found it impossible to understand.

"Slow," she urged them. "Please speak more slowly."

They tried, but still she caught only words and phrases. They kept repeating until she understood that they were asking her if she, a goddess, was immortal. If she was placed on the sacrificial rock, and if her blood was taken so that the healer's power was augmented, would she be dead, really dead, or would she, as a goddess, rise up?

She held out her hands, palms up. "I am mortal, like you. When I die, I am dead, like anybody else." Did he understand? They looked at her, frowning, so she tried again. "This body—it is mortal. If you take my blood from me, this body will die."

The healer took her hands in his, which trembled slightly. When he had held them over Zachary, they had moved like a butterfly, but they had not trembled. He looked carefully at the palms of her hands, then the back, then the palms again.

"Do you really believe," she asked, "that my blood will give you enough strength so that you can cure Zachary's heart? You are a healer. Do you really believe that you need my blood?"

There was no way he could understand her, but she asked anyhow. He shook his head and his eyes were sad.

Suddenly she had an idea. She took Anaral's little gold

knife out of her anorak pocket and opened it. Quickly she made a small cut in her forearm, held it out to the healer so that he could see the blood which welled out of the cut. "Will that do?"

With one finger he touched a drop of blood, held his finger to his nose, to his mouth.

"Not enough!" Tynak shouted. "Not enough!"

Polly continued to hold her arm out, but the healer shook his head. She remembered that Anaral had given her a Band-Aid as well as the little knife. She felt for it in her pockets, opened it, and put it over the small cut. Both the healer and Tynak stared, wide-eyed, at the Band-Aid.

But the Band-Aid was not particularly impressive power. If they cut her throat—was that how they did it? or would they go for her heart itself?—there was no Band-Aid powerful enough to stanch the blood, stop it from draining her life away.

She said, "I want to speak to Zachary."

"Zak wants not," Tynak said. "Not to talk with you."

She spoke with all the hauteur she could summon. "It makes no difference whether Zachary wants to talk to me or not. I wish to talk with him." She turned away from the two men to the path which led away from the clearing.

There were the two guards barring her way.

She turned imperiously. "Tynak."

Tynak looked at the healer.

The healer nodded. "Take to Zak."

Zachary was sitting in the shadows within Tynak's tent. The flap was open, and light hit the whiteness of skulls on poles, emphasized the whiteness of Zachary's face.

"I told you not to bring her here," he said to Tynak.

Tynak and the healer simply squatted at the entrance to the tent. Polly stood in front of Zachary.

"Go away." He looked down at the packed earth.

"Zachary. Why don't you want to see me?"

"What's the point?"

"Tonight is full moon."

"So?"

"Zachary. I need to know. Do you want them to put me on the rock and sacrifice me so that the healer can get the power of my blood?"

"Of course I don't want that! But they won't do it. You're a goddess."

"Zach, you must know they're planning to sacrifice me for my blood."

He shrugged. Looked away.

"Look at me."

He shook his head.

"How do you feel about this?"

He raised dark, terrified eyes. "I don't go in for all that guilt stuff."

"But you'll let them take my blood?"

"How can I stop them?"

"You really think my blood will give the healer power to help your heart?"

"Don't be silly. It's for rain."

"But you think the healer will use the power to make you well?"

"Who knows?"

"Zachary, you're willing to let me die?"

He shouted, "Shut up! I don't have anything to do with it! Go away!"

She turned away from him so abruptly that she faced one of the skulls, almost bumping into it. There had once been flesh on those white bones, eyes in the sockets, lips to smile. But whoever had once fleshed the skull was three thousand years gone, as was Tynak, as was the healer.

If Zachary stayed there at her expense, if she died, and if Zachary lived, he, too, was three thousand years gone.

It did not ease the pain of knowing that he was willing to let her be sacrificed.

Chapter Twelve

The sun burned like a bronze shield. A strange heat reflected from its fires, touching the water with a phosphorescence. It was hotter than it had been when she swam across the lake. The guards kept glancing in her direction. Now that Og had escaped, the guards would be even more careful with Polly.

This was the Indian summer she had been told about, Indian summer that came in November with a last reminder of summer before the long cold of winter. But this was hotter than she had expected Indian summer to be. Hotter than it should be? Perhaps weather patterns were different three thousand years ago. Across the lake, lightning played, and thunder was always in the background, an accompaniment to the steady beating of the drums, Tynak's people drumming for rain, the sound intensified hour by hour. For rain, or for sacrifice?

The pallet of ferns was soggy with heat and humidity.

She pulled it to the entrance of the lean-to, hoping for a breath of air. Lay back with her eyes closed. A warm breeze touched her gently. In her mind's eye she saw her room which had once been Charles Wallace's room. Looked out the window to the view of field and woods and the low, ancient hills that gave her a sense of assurance that the jagged mountains did not. She moved her imaging to her grandmother's lab, where she was always cold; tried to feel her feet on the great stone slabs that formed the floor, chilling her toes. Then in her mind's eye she looked out the kitchen window to see her grandfather on his tractor. Saw Bishop Colubra at the stone wall, Louise the Larger coiled up in the warm sunlight. Saw Dr. Louise in her daffodil-colored sweater walking across the field toward her brother.

In this manner she moved through three thousand years. In eternity, her own time and this time in which she was now held, waiting, were simultaneous. If she died in this strange time, would she be born in her own time? Did the fact that she had been born mean that she might escape death here? No, that didn't work out. Everybody in this time died sooner or later. But if she was to be born in her own time, wouldn't she have to live long enough to have children, so that she would at least be a descendant of herself? Karralys understood riddles such as this one. Polly shook her head to try to clear it.

Energy equals mass times the speed of light squared. What did Einstein's equation really mean? Did her grandfather understand it? Her grandfather, at home in her own time—her grandmother, Dr. Louise, they must all be frantic with anxiety. Dr. Louise would not know what had happened to her brother, who had gone off in hiking shoes.

And on this side of time, across the lake, the bishop, Karralys, Tav, Cub, Anaral, what were they doing? If Og had reached them, they would be asking each other how they could help; they would be trying to make plans.

Leaves drifted down onto the skins of the lean-to. The air was so heavy with humidity that she felt she could reach out and squeeze it.

She looked up as she heard a strange, dragging sound, and coming toward her was Klep, supported on one side by the old healer, on the other by a young warrior; Klep, hopping on his good leg.

"Klep!" she cried out. "You'll hurt your leg!"

The healer and the warrior gently placed him down next to Polly. His face was ashen, and beads of sweat broke out on his forehead.

"Klep! What have you done? You shouldn't have come!" Polly knelt by him.

"I have spoken with Tynak," Klep whispered.

The healer gestured at the warriors, who glanced wonderingly at Klep, then drew back several paces.

Then the healer knelt on Klep's other side and examined the broken leg, lifting the compress of mosses on the wound where the skin was cleanly healing but was still pink and new-looking. He held his hands over it, shaking his head and mumbling. "There is fever again. He should not be upset," Polly understood him to say. "In his tent he did fret, fret . . ." He held his hands over the leg, glanced at Polly, nodded. She held her hands out, too, just over his. The healer withdrew his right hand to place it over Polly's, not touching, hovering delicately. Again she felt the tingling warmth, and then a strange heat, as though they were drawing the fever out of Klep's inflamed skin. Then the heat was gone and there was a sense of color, of gold, gold of sky in early morning, gold of butterfly wings, gold of finch in flight.

The pinched look left Klep's face, and his whole body released its tension. He looked gratefully at the healer and Polly. "Thank you. I am sorry to have caused trouble. I had to come." He looked pleadingly at the healer, who squatted back on his heels. "I have spoken with Tynak," Klep said again. "He has said that you have caused the rain across the lake with the angel you took from him."

"I didn't take the angel from him," Polly pointed out. "He tried to take it from me."

"He is angry and he is fearful. He says that you are withholding rain from us, and the people are angry."

With Klep, Polly could not understand every word, but enough to get the gist of what he was saying.

"I don't control the rain," she said. "I want it to rain here as much as you do."

The healer murmured, but Polly guessed that he was saying that a broken leg was easier to heal than anger.

Briefly Polly closed her eyes. Her voice shook. "I thought when Zach kidnapped me it was for me to be the sacrifice so the healer would fix his heart."

The healer shook his head. "No, no." And from his mumblings she guessed that it was Tynak who had prevented the healer from working with Zachary until Polly came. A healer heals.

Klep said, "That is what Zak thought, what Tynak wanted him to think, maybe what he still thinks. But the people do not care one way or the other about Zak. They are tired of raiding to get food. They want the sacrifice so there will be rain."

Polly thought of Anaral singing her hymn of joy to the Mother after she had placed the flowers on the altar, of the People of the Wind greeting morning and evening with harmony. "Your god demands sacrifice and blood or the rain will be withheld?"

Klep said what she took to mean "For each person the god is different."

"There is a different god?"

"No. Each person sees differently."

"Klep, what do you believe?"

"That you are good. That you have nothing to do with rain or drought. That your blood is your life and, while it is in you, you will use it for good. But the power is when you are alive, not when you are dead and the blood has spilled on the ground." He added, "Anaral says I am a druid," and smiled.

Polly was listening intently, translating Klep's words as he spoke into words she could comprehend.

"The healer has much power," Klep continued. "I have seen him bring back life where I thought there was none. But even he cannot bring your blood back into you if it is spilled out of your body."

The healer spoke. His vocabulary was far more in his hands than in his mumbling and this time she could not understand what he was saying.

Klep translated, "Go back to your own place."

"I wish I could."

Klep turned to the old healer. They spoke together for a long time, and Polly could not understand what they were saying. Finally Klep nodded at the healer and turned to Polly. "Tonight, when the moon rises, there will be much noise, many people. We will help you get to the lake, stop the arrows and spears, so you can swim."

"You can do this?"

Klep was fierce. "There will be no sacrifice. The healer

has great power. No one would dare throw a spear at him, no one would dare try to stop him in any way. He will protect you as you run to the water."

It was a slim hope, but it was a hope. She did not think she could make the swim again, but better to drown than be put on that terrible altar rock. "Thank you. I am grateful."

"You were good to me," Klep said. "Your People of the Wind were good to me. I would become one with Anaral. From you I have learned much. I have learned that I love. Love. That is a good word."

"Yes. It is a good word."

"What I do, I do not do just for you, though I hope I would do what I do even if it were not for Anaral. But if you are sacrificed, do you think the People of the Wind would let me see Anaral, to love? Do I learn love and then let love be sacrificed along with you?" Again his brow beaded with sweat. "You will swim?"

"I will swim." She tried to sound certain, for Klep's sake.

The healer spoke again.

Klep said, "You have the gift. The healer says you must serve it."

"Tell the healer I will try to serve the gift." As surely as Dr. Louise had done, all her life, so would Polly try to do.

Klep nodded. Looked out at the village, where people

talked in small groups, the sound ugly, menacing. "I will stay with you. I cannot do much, but my presence will help."

The healer looked at Polly. "Will stay."

Surely the healer's presence would keep the people from coming to the lean-to and dragging her out, at least until the full moon rose. And the very fact that these two men, the young and the old, were with her, cared enough to stay with her, filled her with warmth.

She asked, "Klep, what about Zachary? I came back across the lake with you because of Zachary."

"Zak? Oh, he is of no importance."

She did not understand. She repeated, "But I thought I was to be sacrificed so that his heart could be mended."

"That is—" Klep searched for words. "That is not in the middle. Not in the center."

Well, yes. She could understand that Zachary was peripheral. But did he know it?

"If rain comes, if the people are quiet, then the healer—" Klep glanced at the ancient man, who remained squatting back on his heels, as comfortable as though he were in a chair. "He will try to help Zak, because he is healer. Where there is brokenness, he must heal. Tynak wanted you to think that Zak was important because he thought the line was drawn close between you. That you—that you *loved* him."

"No, Klep—"

"I know that the line is between you and Tav, not Zak."

Again she shook her head. "Where I came from, it is too soon. I may sense a line between Tav and me, but love—" She could not explain that not only was she not ready to give her heart to Tav or anyone else, that she had much schooling ahead of her, that in her time she was too young, but also that her time was three thousand years in the future. Perhaps in the vast scheme of things three thousand years wasn't much, but set against the span of a single lifetime it was enormous.

Thunder rumbled. She looked across the lake and saw dark sheets of rain.

Klep looked at it. "Ah, Polly, if you could bring rain here!"

"Oh, Klep, would that I could!"

The healer remained squatting on the ground just inside the shadow of the lean-to. The strange light gave a greenish cast to his face and he looked like an incredibly ancient frog. His voice was almost a croak. "Healer will not let healer go." His ancient eyes met Polly's. Not only was he offering her his considerable protection, he was calling her a colleague.

Groups of villagers were muttering, hissing, sounding like a swarm of hornets, looking toward the lean-to but not coming close. Had it not been for Klep and the healer there, with her, for her, she was not sure what would have happened.

The storm across the lake moved away, farther away, and the brazen sun glowed through angry clouds. The heat was wilting the leaves which were left on the trees and they drifted down, sickly and pale.

Polly closed her eyes. Felt a hand touching hers, an old, dry hand. The healer. A cool wind began to blow, touching her cheeks, her eyelids. The waters of the lake rippled gently against the shore. The angry people fell silent.

Slowly the sky cleared. The thunderheads dissipated. But the sound of drums continued.

The day dragged on. Klep slept, lying on his side, breathing like a child, hand pillowing his head. The healer, too, lay down, and his eyes were closed, but Polly thought that he was not asleep, that he was holding her in a still center of quiet. She could feel her blood coursing through her veins, her living blood, keeping her mind, her thoughts, her very being held in life.

Would she give up that blood willingly?

Where was Zachary? Was he still greedily grasping at life, any kind of life, at any expense? There was no willingness in him, no concern, except for himself. Did he really understand what he was demanding?

There was no sunset. The daylight faded, but there was no touching of the clouds with color. It simply grew darker. Darker. Cook fires were lit. The muttering of the people began again. Here the full moon would not lift up above the great trees of the forest as it did for the People of the Wind, but would come from the lake, rising out of the water.

She heard with horror a hissing of expectation. Tynak strode into the center of the clearing, looking first across the lake, then turning around, looking beyond the compound to the heavy darkness of the forest and the clearing with the bloody stone.

A thin scream cut across the air. It was a scream of wild terror, so uncontrolled that it made Polly shudder. It was repeated. Was there already someone at the terrible altar stone, someone facing a sharp knife? She tried to find the source of the scream.

She saw Zachary struggling, screaming, held by two men of the tribe. He was trying to break away from them, but they had him firmly between them, taking him toward Tynak.

A faint light began to show at the far horizon of the lake.

"No!" Zachary screamed. "You can't kill her! I didn't mean it! I didn't! You can't do it, you can't—" He was babbling with terror. "I'll die, kill me, kill me, you can't hurt her—" He saw Polly, and suddenly he was convulsed with sobs. "I didn't mean it! I was wrong! Oh, stop them, somebody, stop them, let me die, don't let them hurt Polly—"

Tynak came up to him and slapped him across the mouth. "Too late."

Zachary was shocked into silence. He tried to pull one hand away to wipe his mouth, but the two men held his arms, and a trickle of blood slid down his chin.

"The sacrifice must be unblemished," Tynak said. "You are not worthy."

Polly was as cold as when she had swum across the lake. Not only her body seemed frozen, but her thoughts, her heart.

The healer stood, helping himself up by pressing one hand against Polly's shoulder. Then he kept it there, in a gesture of protection.

Klep pushed himself up into a sitting position. Polly saw, without really taking it in, that he had a curved knife at his belt, which he now took out and held firmly.

"Tynak, I warn you," he started, but Tynak raised his hand threateningly. With his position of authority as chief of the tribe he did not need a weapon. And Klep, with his broken leg held stiffly between two staves, could not move.

Tynak gestured contemptuously to the two guards who held the struggling Zachary. They dropped him as though he were a dead beast. He fell to the ground, whimpering. The guards came to Polly. They looked at the healer, but he did not take his hand from her shoulder. Polly did not recognize these men, who were not Winter Frost or Dark Swallow. Murmuring what sounded like an apology, one of the guards moved the healer's hand, not roughly, then jerked Polly away.

"Stop!" Klep shouted. "Stop!" But he could only watch in frustration and rage as the men dragged Polly toward Tynak.

"Tynak!" Klep warned. "If you hurt her, it will be disaster for the tribe!"

"Blood!" the people screamed. "Blood for the gods! Blood for the ground, blood for rain, blood for growth, blood for life!" The wind rose, making the flaring torches smoke. The moon began to lift out of the lake, enormous, red as blood. Polly thought her heart would stop beating. The people shouted, stamping their feet rhythmically in time to the drums, in time to their calls for blood. Zachary's thin wails were no more than a wisp of smoke. "Blood!" the people chanted. "Blood! Blood!"

Slowly Polly was being dragged across the compound and toward the path through the forest that led to the terrible stone.

Zachary lurched to his feet and threw himself at Polly. One of the guards struck him and he fell again to the ground, mewling like a sick child.

"Look!" Klep cried, his shout rising above the noise of the mob. "Tynak! People! Look to the lake! Do you not see!"

There were shouts of surprise, of terror.

Polly looked, struggling to stand upright. Silhouetted against the great orb of the moon was a large canoe, with carved and curved ends. As the canoe came closer, she could see two men in it. Holding a great paddle was Karralys, with Og standing proudly by him. Standing in the prow was Bishop Colubra, with Louise the Larger twined about his arm in great shining coils.

"See!" Klep cried triumphantly. "The goddess has called and they come! Do you dare touch the goddess?"

The guards released Polly, recoiling in fear.

"Bishop! Karralys!" Polly raced to the shore.

Tynak was not far behind her.

The bishop and Karralys were dark silhouettes against the sky.

Polly splashed into the water, trying to drag the canoe to the shore. Tynak gestured, and Dark Swallow and Winter Frost pulled the canoe up onto the pebbly beach.

Suddenly the moon was obliterated by a black cloud which spread rapidly across the sky, blotting out the stars. The wind gusted, sending smoke guttering from the torches. Cries of fear and confusion came from the people.

"An omen!" Klep called. "Heed the omen!"

Karralys sprang from the canoe, then helped the bishop out. The old man's legs were wobbly, and he leaned on the druid. Louise the Larger clung to him in tight coils. The healer came up to them, peering first at Karralys, then at the bishop, whose face was suddenly illuminated by a startling flash of lightning. It was followed almost immediately by thunder, rolling wildly between the two chains of mountains, those of the People of the Wind and those of the People Across the Lake.

Then the rain came, at first spattering in heavy drops into the water, onto the beach, the skins of the tents. Then it came in great sheets, almost as though the waters of the lake were rising to meet the rain clouds.

When Karralys and Tav had been blown by the storm to the People of the Wind, the rainbow had arched across the sky and been seen as an omen. Rain had been threatening for days and now it had come, but the People Across the Lake did not accept it as a natural result of clouds and wind patterns, a storm born of a cloud blown by a wind that veered around and came at them from the east, followed by downdrafts producing great charges of static electricity which birthed fierce bolts of lightning and roaring thunder. The storm was seen by the People Across the Lake as a wonder brought by the bishop and the snake, by Karralys and the dog, and by Polly, who had summoned them.

"To the tents!" Tynak cried, and people began to run, women gathering up their children, scurrying across the compound. Tynak held his face up to the rain, his mouth open, swallowing rain in great gulps.

The healer led the bishop to Polly's lean-to, and she and Karralys followed.

"Oh, Bishop," she cried. "Oh, Karralys, thank you. And you, too, Louise, Og. Oh, thank you."

Klep was already soaked by the downpour, and Karralys helped the healer and Polly drag the young man to shelter.

Zachary was still huddled on the ground, the rain pelting down on him. Nobody seemed to notice him.

Polly looked at the bishop. Everybody was dripping rain. Louise the Larger had retired to the farthest corner of the lean-to. The lightning flashed again, hissing as it struck water. When the thunder came, she ran out to Zachary. "Zach. Get up. Come."

"Let me die," he moaned.

"Don't be dramatic. Come on. It's raining. There isn't going to be any sacrifice."

Zachary tried to burrow into the hard ground. "Let me alone."

She pulled at him, but he was a dead weight and she could not move him. "Zach. Get up."

Karralys was at her side. Between them they raised Zachary to his feet.

"Come on, Zach," Polly urged. "Just get away from the lightning." She flinched as it struck again, thunder roaring on top of it.

Karralys helped her drag Zachary to the lean-to. When they let him go, he fell to the ground and curled up in fetal position.

"Leave him be," Bishop Colubra said gently.

The rain continued to sweep from the lake across the village. The lean-to was small protection, but the rain was warm. Lightning arrowed down, striking into the lake, onto the rocks of the shore. There was a horrible cracking sound, and then a crashing, which echoed as loud as the thunder.

"A tree," Klep said. "The lightning has hit a tree."

Slowly the storm moved off. Polly counted five beats between lightning flash and thunder, then ten. Then the lightning was only a general illuminating of the sky at the horizon; the thunder was only a distant rumbling.

Tynak came to them, holding his palms out to show that he was weaponless, and bowed to Karralys. Then to Polly. "You brought rain." His voice was awed.

"No, Tynak. Rain came. I did not bring it."

But there was no way she could make Tynak believe that the rain had not come because of her powers. Polly was a goddess who brought rain.

She did not like the role of goddess. "Bishop," she implored.

The bishop was sitting on the pallet. The clouds had gone with the storm, and a flash of moonlight entered the lean-to and struck the topaz of his ring. "It is enough that the rain has come," he said to Tynak. "We do not need to understand."

"You are healer?" Tynak asked.

"Not as your healer is healer, or as Karralys. But that has been my aim, yes."

Tynak looked at him, looked past him to Louise the Larger coiled in the shadows, then nodded at Karralys. "You will come?"

Karralys nodded. "Polly, too."

"Where?" Polly asked.

"To hold council," Karralys said. "It is meet."

"Zachary—"

"Zachary will wait." There was neither condemnation nor contempt in Karralys's voice.

"Bishop Heron," Karralys said, "it is fitting that you come, too." He held out his hand to help the bishop to his feet.

"I go, too," Klep announced. Klep had authority. Ultimately he would be the leader of the tribe. Winter Frost and Dark Swallow were summoned to help him.

"Klep," Polly demurred, "you promised Anaral you'd be careful. This is going to be terribly hard on your leg."

"I go," Klep insisted.

There was still a tension of electricity in the air. Clouds were building up again, scudding past the brilliance of the moon so that light was followed by shadow, shadow by light, making strange patterns as they walked. When they reached the end of the path that led to the clearing, they were blocked. A great oak, the tree the lightning had struck, lay uprooted across the path. There was no way they could get across it to the clearing with the rock.

Karralys went to the felled tree, putting his hand on the enormous trunk. Og leaped up to stand at his side. Tynak drew back, but only slightly, standing his ground.

"This tree will do for our meeting place," Karralys said.

"The goddess"—Tynak bowed toward Polly—"she has great and mysterious powers."

"I am not—" Polly started, but Karralys raised his hand and she stopped.

Karralys's eyes regarded her calmly, their blue bright as sapphires in the moonlight. "Polly, it is fitting that you tell Tynak the terms of our peace."

She looked at him, totally unprepared. His face was serene. The stone in his torque burned like fire. She swallowed. Breathed. Swallowed.

Then she turned to Tynak. "There will be no more raiding. If you are hungry, if you need food, you will send Klep, when he can walk again, to speak with Karralys. The People of the Wind are people of peace. They will share what they have. They will show you how to irrigate so that your land will yield better crops. And if, at some time, they are in need, you will give to them. The People of the Wind and the People Across the Lake are to live as one people." She paused. Had he understood?

He stood beside Karralys, nodding, nodding.

She continued, "To seal this promise, and with Anaral's consent, she and Klep will be"—there was no word for "marry" or "marriage"—"will be made one, to live together, to guard the peace. Klep?"

"That is my wish." Klep's smile was radiant.

Tynak stood looking at Polly, at Karralys, who was leaning against the fallen body of the great tree, at Klep held upright between Winter Frost and Dark Swallow.

Polly said, "These are our terms. Do you accept?"

"I accept." Tynak suddenly seemed old.

"Klep?"

"I accept. Gladly. Anaral and I will seek to bring peace and healing to both sides of the lake."

Polly felt a small nudge in her ribs. The healer was poking her. "Blood," he said.

She nodded. She did not know why she understood what he meant, but she did, perhaps because of childhood stories about blood brothers and sisters. She took the gold knife the bishop had given Anaral, then opened the notebook to a fresh page. She flipped out the blade, which was bright and clean. Looked at Tynak. "Hold out your hand."

Without question, he held his hand out to her. She

took the knife and nicked the flesh of the ball of his middle finger, then squeezed it till a drop of blood appeared. This she smeared on the clean page of the notebook.

"Karralys?" He, too, without question, held out his hand, and she repeated the procedure, then blended the two drops of blood on the page.

"This is the seal and sign of our terms of peace." She took the page, then reached for the scissors and carefully cut the page in half, so that there was mingled blood on each piece of paper. One piece she handed to Karralys, the other to Tynak. Then she took the cut sketch of Tynak and handed him one half and gave the other to Karralys. "This is the sign that you will never break the peace. If you do, Karralys has your power."

Again Tynak clutched his chest as though in pain.

"Karralys will never hurt you," Polly said. "Only you can hurt yourself." She felt infinitely weary. "I would like to go now. Back across the lake."

The healer nudged her. "Zak."

She was too tired to think of Zachary. "What?"

The bishop reminded her. "There is the matter of Zachary."

She leaned against the fallen tree. She was too tired even to stand any longer.

The bishop continued, "You came back here to the People Across the Lake because of Zachary. However, you can forget about him now if you wish."

"Can I? Oh, Bishop, can I?" She never wanted to think of Zachary again. But she pushed away from the fallen tree. "We'll go back to him. I suppose he's still in the lean-to."

The procession moved back toward the village, Winter Frost and Black Swallow supporting Klep so that he could hop without any strain to his injured leg. People were beginning to emerge from their tents. The air, cleansed by the storm, felt fresh and fragrant. Now they looked at Polly with wondering awe.

Zachary was still huddled under the lean-to. She knelt down beside him, put her hand to his cheek, turning him so that she could look into his eyes.

He squeezed his eyelids tight.

She turned to the bishop. "I think he's decompensated," she said. "I mean, I think he's beyond us."

"No," Bishop Colubra said. "Never say that, Polly."

The healer knelt on Zachary's other side.

Zachary whimpered.

The bishop said, "Often an alcoholic can start to recover only when he's gone all the way to the bottom. When there's no place to go but up. Zachary's self-centeredness was an addiction just as deadly as alcoholism." He bent over the stricken young man. "Open your eyes." It was a stern command.

Zachary's eyelids flickered.

"Sit up," the bishop ordered. "You are not beyond redemption, Zachary."

Zachary moaned, "I was willing to let Polly die."

"But not when it came down to it, Zach!" Polly cried. "You tried to stop them."

"But it was too late." Tears gushed out.

"Look at me! I'm here! There will be no sacrifice!"

Now his terrified gaze met hers. "You're all right?"

"I'm fine."

He sat up. "I'll die if it will help you, I will, I will."

"You don't need to, Zach. There is peace now on both sides of the lake."

"But what I did—I can't be forgiven—" He looked wildly from Polly to Tynak to the bishop.

"Zachary." The bishop spoke softly but compellingly. "William Langland, writing around 1400, said, 'And all the wickedness in the world that man might work or think is no more to the mercy of God than a live coal in the sea.'"

Zachary shook his head. "I went beyond—beyond mercy." He gasped, and the blueness around his lips deepened. The healer reached out and placed his palm on Zachary's chest. As Cub had steadied the bishop's breathing, so the healer steadied Zachary's.

"Help him," Tynak commanded. "It would be a bad omen to have a death now."

Karralys knelt and lifted Zachary so that the young man lay against his chest. With one arm he supported him. His right hand reached under Zachary's wet clothes, and he nodded at the healer. The old man opened Zachary's jacket and shirt, baring his chest. Then his hands joined Karralys's, hovering delicately, as though his ancient fingers were listening. Karralys breathed slowly, steadily, so that Zachary's limp body, held firmly against the druid's strong one, could feel and catch the rhythm. He looked at the bishop. "Please."

The bishop, too, knelt, placing his long, thin hands over Zachary's chest.

The healer nodded at Polly.

She lifted her hands, held them out, and then she was caught in the restoring power of the healer and Karralys and the bishop, their hands not touching, but tenderly moving over Zachary's pale and flaccid chest. Again Polly felt the golden tingling, and then a stab of acute pain went through her body like lightning, eased off, leaving her weak and trembling. Again came the warmth, the gold.

Karralys's hands seemed to have a life of their own. They hovered like bird wings, like a firebird. His eyes changed from their serene blue to the burning gold of the stone in his torque and the faint lines in his face deepened. He was far older than Polly had realized. She felt that her hands, her eyes, her mind, her whole body was caught in the electric power which Karralys and the healer and the bishop were sending through Zachary. They were, she felt, mending his heart, but far more than his heart. The depth of the healing was not merely physical but poured through the core of Zachary himself.

Time shimmered. Stopped. Polly was not sure that she was breathing, or that her heart was beating. Everything was focused on Zachary.

Tynak let out a hissing sound and time began again. Polly could feel the steady beating of her heart. The tingling warmth left her hands, but this time they were not cold but warm, and dry. Karralys sat back on his heels, Zachary still leaning against him.

"It is well," the healer breathed.

Karralys smiled. "It is well."

The bishop rose, looking down at Zachary. "It is well."

Now Polly, too, sat back. "Zachary?"

The blue was gone from his lips. "I—I—" he stammered.

"Hush," the bishop said. "You don't need to say anything." He looked at Karralys. "His heart?"

"It will do," Karralys said. "It is not perfect, but it will do."

"Much power," the healer said. "Great, good power." He looked at Og, who was sitting watching, ears pricked high; at Louise the Larger, who was lying quietly, coiled into a circle. "All work together. Good."

"Am—am—am I all right?" Zachary's voice trembled.

"Not perfect," the bishop said, "but Karralys tells us that your heart will do."

"Yes. Yes." A touch of color came to his cheeks. "I don't know what to say."

"Nothing."

"But I was willing to let Polly die, and you still helped me."

"You will not do Polly, or any of us, any good by holding on to your guilt. You will help by taking proper care of yourself. There is more to be renewed than your heart."

"I know. I know. Oh, this time I know."

"Come." Karralys stood. "The storm is over. Now there is rain." The clouds deepened and rain fell, soft, penetrating rain, quenching the thirst of the parched earth. Now winter wheat could be planted, the ground prepared for spring. "Let us cross the lake," Karralys said. "Anaral, Cub, Tav are all anxiously waiting."

Tynak and the healer escorted them to the canoe. Klep, helped by Winter Frost and Dark Swallow, stood on the shore and waved goodbye.

"To Anaral you will give my love." Now that Klep had learned the word "love," his face glowed with joy each time he said it.

The healer raised his arm in blessing.

"Come," Tynak said to the healer and Klep. "At the

sixth of the moon we will invite them—all the tribe—
for a feast. They will not mind that the food has come
from them."

Karralys laughed, and Winter Frost and Dark Swallow
splashed into the water, pushing the canoe until it
floated free.

Cub and Anaral were waiting eagerly to greet them and
ran into the lake to help pull up the canoe. Once ashore,
Polly found that she was trembling so that she could
hardly walk. Cub put his arm around her and led her
into Karralys's tent. "You have given too much." He
helped her onto one of the fern beds.

Where was Tav, she wondered.

The bishop looked at her lovingly. "The virtue has
been drained from her. It will return."

"I don't want to be a goddess anymore," Polly said.

Anaral brought her a warm drink, and she sipped, letting it slide down her throat and warm her whole body.

"Klep—" Anaral asked.

"He is all right," Polly assured her.

"Truly all right?"

"He has moved his leg more than he should, but he's
all right. He loves you, Annie."

A gentle drifting of color moved over her cheeks. "I
am so glad, so glad." She reached out and pressed
Polly's hand.

Polly returned the pressure, then looked around for Tav, and realized that not only did she not see Tav, she did not see Zachary. "Where's Zachary?" she asked.

"With Karralys." Cub squatted by Polly, taking her wrist in his gentle fingers, letting it fall only after he was satisfied.

"Don't let him come here," Polly implored.

Cub looked at her questioningly.

"I don't want to see him." If she had to do it all over again, she would do the same thing. She would go back across the lake. She would hold her hands with the healer and Karralys and the bishop over Zachary's heart. But now it was done; it was done and there was nothing left except an exhaustion that was far more than physical.

The bishop smiled at Polly. "I have a great question that will never be answered: Did the time gate open for me, and then for Polly, because of Zachary?"

Karralys entered as the bishop spoke. "Who knows for whom the time gate opened." His voice was quiet. "What has happened here, in this time, may have some effect we do not know and cannot even suspect, here in my time, or perhaps in yours. Let us not try to understand the pattern, only rejoice in its beauty."

Was Zachary part of the beauty, Polly wondered. But she was too exhausted to speak.

"Cub." Karralys turned. "Will you go to Zachary, please, and stay with him?"

Cub nodded and left, obediently, just as Tav burst into the tent.

"Poll-ee!" He rushed to her.

"Tav!"

Tav knelt on the packed earth in front of her, raised one hand, and gently touched her lips. "Are you all right?"

"I'm fine."

"Truly?"

"Truly, Tav." There was a deep sadness in her heart. She would not see Tav again, and that was grief.

"And that Zak?" Tav demanded.

"He is all right, too."

Tav scowled. "He would have let you be killed."

"But he didn't."

"He wanted to."

"Not really, Tav."

"He is not worth one hair of your head."

Anaral nodded. "I am still very angry with him."

"Annie," the bishop chided gently. "You do not think that all that Polly went through was for the sake of Zachary's physical heart."

"I don't know." Anaral's voice was low. "It is Poll-ee I care about. Not Zachary."

"Don't care?"

"Bishop! Maybe his heart"—she touched her chest—
"is better. But what about the part of his heart that
would let Poll-ee be sacrificed, her life for his?"

"Change is always possible," the bishop said.

Anaral looked rebellious. "For Zak? Who helped kidnap Poll-ee? Who would have let her be put on the altar
stone? Who would not have stopped the knife? Can he
change? Can he?"

"Can you truly say that change is not possible? Can
you refuse him that chance? Can you say that only his
physical heart was healed?"

Tav growled, "He would have harmed my Poll-ee."

"Zachary hit bottom," the bishop said. "It was an
ugly bottom, yes. But in the pit he saw himself."

Tav pounded his spear angrily on the ground.

The bishop continued, "Now it is up to him."

Anaral scowled.

The bishop smiled. "Your anger won't last, Annie. You
are warm of heart."

"Poll-ee is back." Tav reached out again to touch her.
"Poll-ee is back. That is all that matters. I do not think
about that Zak. I think about Poll-ee, and that the rain
has come."

"Yes."

"And now you will go." He held his hands out to her
with longing.

She sighed deeply. "To my own time, Tav. If the threshold is open."

"And Zachary?" Tav demanded. "Do you have to take him with you?"

At last Polly laughed. "Do you want him here?"

Tav scowled. "He did not want my Poll-ee out of obedience to the Mother, or for any good save his own."

The bishop looked around the tent. "When Zachary saw Annie, he entered the circles of overlapping time. *Behold, I have set before you an open door, and no man can shut it.*"

"Words of power," Karralys said.

"Yes," the bishop agreed. "From John's Revelation."

"And is the door to stay open, Bishop?" Anaral asked.

"No, Annie. No. But it was wide open when Polly made the decision to return across the lake to Zachary, and you must honor that decision." He turned to Polly. "You were very brave, my dear."

"I wasn't brave. I was terrified."

"But you went ahead and did what you had to do."

Og reached out and licked her fingers. Cub opened the tent flap and came in with Zachary. "It is time?"

Polly looked at Zachary and felt nothing. No anger. No fear. No love.

"Yes," Karralys said. "It is time."

Zachary stood between Karralys and Cub, his face pale, but there was no blueness to his lips. "I don't know what to say."

"Then don't speak," Karralys said.

Zachary looked from one to the other. "What I did was beyond apology."

"You were out of your mind with self," Karralys said. "Now you must understand that though your life has been lengthened, ultimately you will die to this life. It is the way of the mortal."

"Yes," Zachary said. "I know that. Now."

"And in you there is still much healing to be accomplished."

"I know." Zachary was as subdued as a small child after a spanking. But he was not a small child. "I will try." He turned to Polly. "May I come see you?"

Her hand stroked Og's head. "No, Zachary. I'm sorry. I don't want to see you again. It wouldn't be a good idea, for either of us." Her voice was level, emotionless. She had had to go back across the lake for Zachary. But what had to be done had been done.

"But—"

"There are things which you have to learn alone," Karralys said. "One is that you have to live with yourself."

"I don't like myself," Zachary said.

"You must learn to." The bishop's words were a command. "From this moment on, your behavior must be such that when you go to bed at night you will be happy with what you have done during the day."

"Can that happen?" Zachary asked. He looked at Polly. "Can it?"

"Yes, Zachary. It can happen, if you will let it."

Louise the Larger slid across the packed earth, out of the tent.

"Follow her," Karralys ordered.

Tav went to Polly, spoke longingly. "I must let you go?"

"From your presence," Karralys said. "Not from your heart."

"Now I know," Tav said softly, "I was wrong about the Mother. The Mother asks the sacrifice of love. You have shown me that." He touched Polly's lips with his finger and turned quickly away.

Anaral stretched her hands out toward Polly but did not touch her. "We will always be friends."

"Always."

"And Klep and I will hold you in our hearts."

"You will be in mine."

"The lines of love cross time and space." But a tear slid down Anaral's cheek.

Karralys turned toward Polly, took both her hands in his. "We will never forget you."

"Nor I you."

"And, Bishop Heron, when you came to us through the time gate you started it all."

The bishop smiled. "I, Karralys? Oh, I think not."

At the entrance to the tent, Og barked impatiently.

Karralys stroked Og's head, then said, "I will send Og with you, Polly. You and your grandparents have need of a good guardian dog, and Og is that."

Again Og barked, imperiously.

"Come." Bishop Colubra led the way out of the tent. Polly followed him, and Og nudged his cold nose into her hand. Behind them, the lake shimmered. The white peaks of the mountains reached sharply into the sky.

When they reached the stone wall, Louise the Larger was lying in a warm splash of sunlight. She raised herself up, then slithered down between the rocks.

Polly looked around. The trees were their own young trees, the Grandfather Oak overshadowing them all. The snow-capped mountains were gone, and the ancient hills lay quietly on the horizon. She was back in her own time.

Someone must have been keeping watch. The Murrys and Dr. Louise came running through the apple orchard, across the field, running to greet them. There was much hugging, tears of relief, joyous barking from Og.

Zachary stood quietly apart.

Then Polly's grandparents urged them all into the kitchen, the warmth, the scent of applewood and geraniums and freshly baked bread. Polly and the bishop started to speak at once, telling their own versions of what had happened. Zachary stood in silence.

Then Dr. Louise had her stethoscope out, listening to Zachary's heart. "There appears to be a slight murmur," she said at last. "I'm not sure how much clinical importance it has. Certainly it is not a perfect heart. You will need to check in with your own doctors as soon as possible."

"I will. But there's a difference. I can breathe without feeling I'm lifting weights. Thanks, Doctor. All of you." He went to Polly and took both her hands. "Polly." He looked at her, but said nothing more. She waited, letting him hold her hands. He opened his mouth as though to speak, closed it, shook his head.

"You will—" she started. Stopped.

"Yes, Polly. I will." He withdrew his hands. "I'd better go now."

Polly said, "I'll go out to the car with you."

The bishop put his hand on Zachary's shoulder. "It will not be easy."

"I know."

"Remember that the lines of love are always there. You may hold on to them."

"I will. Thanks."

"God go with you."

"I don't believe in God."

"That's all right. I do."

"I'm glad."

Polly walked with Zachary through the garage and to

the lane where he had parked his car. He got in. Rolled down the window.

"Polly." She looked at him. He shrugged. "Sorry. Thanks. Words aren't any good."

"That's okay. Just take care." She plunged her hands into the anorak pockets and her fingers touched Zachary's angel icon. She pulled it out.

"You still have my icon."

"Yes. I always will."

She put the icon back. The bishop came out, walking rapidly across the lawn on his heron's legs. "Come, dear one. Let's go into the house."

"Goodbye," Zachary said. "Polly. You have on that sheepskin tunic."

She ran her hands lightly over the warm fleece that hung well below the anorak. "Anaral's tunic. I can't return it, can I?"

The bishop smiled. "She would want you to have it. For herself and Klep. For the good memories."

Zachary looked at Polly. At the bishop. Rolled up the window, started the ignition. Waved one hand. Drove off.

The bishop put his arm around Polly and they started back toward the house, to all these people Polly loved. But there were others she loved, too, and she would never see them again.

"What happens to what's happened?" she asked the bishop.

"It's there. Waiting."

"But the time gate's closed, isn't it?"

"Yes. But that can't take away what we've had. The good and the bad."

Again her fingers touched the angel icon. She looked across the fields to the low shoulders of the ancient hills. It seemed that flickering dimly behind them she could see the jagged snow-topped peaks of mountains.

They went into the house.

GOFISH

What did you want to be when you grew up?
A writer.

When did you realize you wanted to be a writer?
Right away. As soon as I was able to articulate, I knew I wanted to be a writer. And I read. I adored *Emily of New Moon* and some of the other L. M. Montgomery books and they impelled me because I loved them.

When did you start to write?
When I was five, I wrote a story about a little "gurl."

What was the first writing you had published?
When I was a child, a poem in *CHILD LIFE*. It was all about a lonely house and was very sentimental.

370

Where do you write your books?
Anywhere. I write in longhand first, and then type it. My first typewriter was my father's pre–World War One machine. It was the one he took with him to the war. It had certainly been around the world.

What is the best advice you have ever received about writing?
To just write.

What's your first childhood memory?
One early memory I have is going down to Florida for a couple of weeks in the summertime to visit my grandmother. The house was in the middle of a swamp, surrounded by alligators. I don't like alligators, but there they were, and I was afraid of them.

What is your favorite childhood memory?
Being in my room.

As a young person, whom did you look up to most?
My mother. She was a storyteller and I loved her stories. And she loved music and records. We played duets together on the piano.

What was your worst subject in school?
Math and Latin. I didn't like the Latin teacher.

What was your best subject in school?
English.

What activities did you participate in at school?
I was president of the student government in boarding school and editor of a literary magazine, and also belonged to the drama club.

Are you a morning person or a night owl?
Night owl.

What was your first job?
Working for the actress Eva La Gallienne, right after college.

What is your idea of the best meal ever?
Cream of Wheat. I eat it with a spoon. I love it with butter and brown sugar.

Which do you like better: cats or dogs?
I like them both. I once had a wonderful dog named Touche. She was a silver medium-sized poodle, and quite beautiful. I wasn't allowed to take her on the subway, and I couldn't afford to get a taxi, so I put her around my neck, like a stole. And she pretended she was a stole. She was an actor.

What do you value most in your friends?
Love.

What is your favorite song?
"Drink to Me Only with Thine Eyes."

What time of the year do you like best?
I suppose autumn. I love the changing of the leaves. I love the autumn goldenrod, the Queen Anne's lace.

What was the original title of *A Wrinkle in Time*?
"Mrs Whatsit, Mrs Who and Mrs Which."

How did you get the idea for *A Wrinkle in Time*?
We were living in the country with our three kids on this dairy farm. I started reading what Einstein wrote about time. And I used a lot of those principles to make a universe that was creative and yet believable.

How hard was it to get *A Wrinkle in Time* published?
I was kept hanging for two years. Over and over again I received nothing more than the formal, printed rejection slip. Eventually, after twenty-six rejections, I called my agent and said, "Send it back. It's too different. Nobody's going to publish it." He sent it back, but a few days later a friend of my mother's insisted that I meet John Farrar,

the publisher. He liked the manuscript, and eventually decided to publish it. My first editor was Hal Vursell.

Which of your characters is most like you?
None of them. They're all wiser than I am.

SQUARE FISH

THE L'ENGLE CAST

Books featuring the Murry-O'Keefes:

A Wrinkle in Time (WT)

A Wind in the Door (WD)

A Swiftly Tilting Planet (STP)

Many Waters (MW)

The Arm of the Starfish (AS)

Dragons in the Waters (DW)

A House Like a Lotus (HL)

An Acceptable Time (AT)

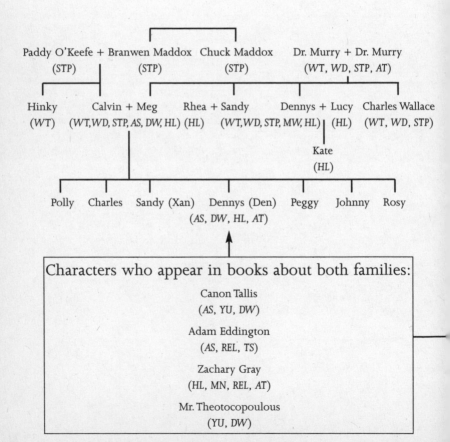

Paddy O'Keefe + Branwen Maddox Chuck Maddox   Dr. Murry + Dr. Murry
      (STP)   (STP)   (STP)   (WT, WD, STP, AT)

Hinky   Calvin + Meg   Rhea + Sandy   Dennys + Lucy   Charles Wallace
(WT)   (WT,WD, STP, AS, DW, HL) (HL) (WT,WD, STP, MW, HL)   (HL)   (WT, WD, STP)

                                                        Kate
                                                        (HL)

Polly   Charles   Sandy (Xan)   Dennys (Den)   Peggy   Johnny   Rosy
                                (AS, DW, HL, AT)

Characters who appear in books about both families:

Canon Tallis
(AS, YU, DW)

Adam Eddington
(AS, REL, TS)

Zachary Gray
(HL, MN, REL, AT)

Mr. Theotocopoulous
(YU, DW)

OF CHARACTERS

Books featuring the Austins:

Meet the Austins (MA)   The Young Unicorns (YU)

The Moon by Night (MN)   A Ring of Endless Light (REL)

The Twenty-four Days Before Christmas (TDC)   Troubling a Star (TS)

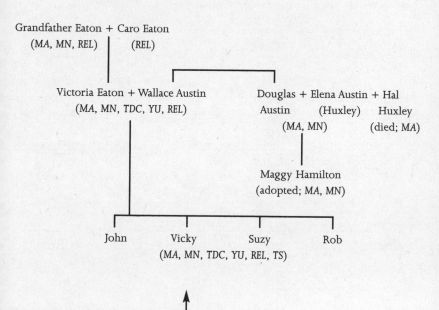

Grandfather Eaton + Caro Eaton
(MA, MN, REL)   (REL)

Victoria Eaton + Wallace Austin
(MA, MN, TDC, YU, REL)

Douglas + Elena Austin + Hal
Austin   (Huxley)   Huxley
        (MA, MN)   (died; MA)

Maggy Hamilton
(adopted; MA, MN)

John   Vicky   Suzy   Rob
(MA, MN, TDC, YU, REL, TS)